DAVIE

For Matthew, Carroll

with Compliments

Donald McDougall

15·10·77

DONALD McDOUGALL

DAVIE

ST. MARTIN'S PRESS   NEW YORK

Library of Congress Cataloging in Publication Data

McDougall, Donald.
    Davie.

    I. Title.
PZ4.M1373Dav3 [PR6063.A1786] 823'.9'14 77-76644
ISBN 0-312-18385-2

American golf will never be able to repay its debt of gratitude to Scotland . . . no matter what it has cost us in coin of the Realm, there will always be a hefty balance due to the land of the Heather and the Gorse, especially to such communities as St Andrews, Carnoustie . . . Prestwick, Musselburgh . . . who shipped us the cream of their golfing talent . . . hard working professionals, clubmakers, greenkeepers . . . laid our game on a sure foundation . . .

(H. B. Martin, *Fifty Years of American Golf*. Quoted by permission of Dodd, Mead & Co., Inc., New York.)

PART ONE

BEGINNINGS

CHAPTER ONE

I.

HE sprawled on the soft, warm sand, his back supported by a board fence. Above and about him was the blue vault of the sky, unmarred save for a few wisps of drifting white cloud.

The scene around him was in character, except for one feature, the golf bag from which he was taking the clubs one by one, and cleaning them. The bag was so large, so colourful, so garnished with pockets, gadgets, straps and fancy buckles that it seemed out of place in its pleasant, but rather austere surroundings.

The blue of open sea showed dark against the sandy knolls to the east. South stretched the wide expanse of beach, dunes and golf course, beyond them, the hills of Fife showed a lilac smirr in the distance. Behind him lay the little town with its clean, straight, wind-swept streets, neat blue-slated, grey stone houses, with the spire of an occasional church thrusting up to the sky.

A hundred yards or so up the narrow street which terminated at the board fence, a local shop had put out a newspaper puff, 'Peace Treaty Signed', it announced, 'Lloyd George says—' But what Lloyd George has said was lost, for the bottom half had been torn away, maybe by a petulant gust of wind, maybe by one of the Welsh Wizard's political opponents, for the breeze was a mere light air from the south-west. It gently riffled the grey-green grass of the bents, and carried with it the scents of early summer – the cool, salt tang of the sea, and the warm, moist smell of fresh cut grass.

But David Forbes Crombie had no eyes for the scenery. He was intent on the job in hand. Now he drew another club from the bag, and squinted down the shaft with a professional air. He was a sturdy, stocky boy. Thick, brown hair, bleached in places by the sun, had been neatly combed earlier in the day, now it fell over his eyes as he worked, but it could not conceal his firm jaw. His eyes were grey and steady.

With knees drawn up, ankles turned in, he put the end of the shaft in the hollow formed by his insteps, wrapped a scrap of worn emery round the socket, and twirled the club-head with his right hand. Alongside him, another boy, taller and older than Davie, was busy at the same task. But the bag was smaller, and strictly functional. The clubs were sound, of good design, but unobtrusive. Now Davie rested the blade of the mashie on his knee and polished vigorously. He held it up to inspect the result, then remarked, 'Thae's braw clubs the yank has.'

'Aye,' Chae's voice was malice. 'Yet the Dominie beat him with only half the tools.'

'Ach – the American didna know the course,' Davie said loyally, 'and forbye, he didna take it so seriously. Look at the fun he was making aw' the time.'

'Showin' off.' Chae's comment was terse. 'The Yanks are the boys for that.' Then, realising that Davie had forced him into the defensive, he returned to the attack. 'He took it serious enough in the tackle he brought – I felt fair sorry for you, humphin' aw' that weight. Fair cruelty to a wee fella like you.'

Davie said nothing. Chae never missed a chance of rubbing in the fact that Davie was short for his age. Chae was fifteen and would have been working now, if he'd been able to find a job. That was the worst of Chae. He could turn from friend to foe in a flash, as soon as he found something to say that was hurtful, something against which the smaller boy could find no comeback. Despite having twice as many clubs to clean as Chae, Davie finished first, but still feeling hurt, he did not offer to help Chae, but picked up the big bag, and went round the end of the fence, then stood waiting at the clubhouse gate, for the notice said, 'Caddies Not Admitted'.

But the big Yank came to the door, and beckoned him, so Davie crunched over the pebble path, to hand over the bag.

'Well, kid – you through?'

'Aye,' Davie told him, 'they're aw' clean now.'

'Well, you sure have prettied them up. Reckon you've done a good job.'

Davie flushed to the praise, loving the smooth warm drawl. Then the Yank said, 'Catch, here's the pay-off.'

The silver coin spun. Davie caught it, and stared – a whole half-crown! 'Is – is this for tomorrow too, sir?'

'Heck no! You help me win tomorrow, and I'll double that.' As he took the bag he said suddenly, 'Whadya think of them?'

The boy was taken by surprise. 'Oh, they're braw clubs, Sir – but – ' he paused, not knowing what to say.

The American laughed, reached out a hand, and punched him in the belly in fun. 'You're dead right, son. I thought they were pretty good myself till I saw some of the ones you make over here. Guess I'll see this Johnston guy tomorrow, and get me some new ones.'

'Och but they're braw clubs,' Davie protested, aghast at the thought of buying a whole lot of new clubs because you'd taken a grue at the ones you had. Imagine having enough money to do a thing like that!

'O.K., sport, see you tomorrow? Around ten, that'll give me time to get some new clubs then you'n me'll take the pants offen the old timer.'

The big silver coin in his pocket, Davie went back round the fence to where Chae was finishing. When he had displayed his half-crown, and told Chae of his engagement for the next day, Chae was scornful. 'Huh, whit did I tell ye! Showin' off, chuckin' money about like that.'

But the words did not hurt Davie, or take away his pleasure, Chae was jealous, for the Dominie would only give him a shilling, or one and threepence at the most, then likely grumble because the clubs weren't cleaned properly.

But that was Chae's own fault, grabbing the Dominie's

bag at the start, because it was light and easy to carry. 'Makin' the best o' a bad job,' he had whispered, leaving Davie to carry for the big Yank.

Now Davie twitched his shoulder, still raw and stiff from the weight. 'Come on,' he said to Chae, 'and I'll stand you treat at Miss Maddens'.'

'Huh you're bad's the Yank, chuckin' yer money aboot,' Chae told him. 'But come on then.'

Miss Maddens' was a house converted into a shop. The front garden was paved, and on fine days like this, the old lady put out all sorts of stuff at each side of the door; sacks of potatoes, bags of carrots and brussels sprouts, wellington boots, tin kettles, fancy printed aprons, spades and pails, and floppy cardboard boxes full of men's cloth caps. But her home-made fruit cakes, the caddies called them fly cemeteries, were wonderful, and only a penny a square, while for another tuppence, you could get a big bottle of sweet, red-coloured gassy water called Kola.

Davie and Chae collected their fruit cakes and bottles, then leaned against the low stone wall to consume them. The fruit cake tasted grand, washed down by a swallow of Kola, and the two-shilling piece he had got as change felt good in his pocket.

The torn newsbill still flapped on the board. The old lady was never quite up to date, but the peace treaty had been signed the week before. There had been a treat, and a picnic for all the bairns in the place, but Davie hadn't bothered. He was finished with the school now.

His father and mother had talked about the war finishing, and the cartoons in the Sunday papers were different. The war cartoon usually showed Little Willie, with a long neck, and a big nose, running away, with a British soldier running after him, to stick a bayonet up his behind. The Kaiser wore a big spiked helmet, and a big turned-up moustache, and he was always encouraging Little Willie to run faster. After the Armistice last November, the drawings had shown Lenin and Trotsky, and other men called Bolsheviks. They wore their shirts outside their trousers, and were always running about with big bombs in their hands.

But the war was over now, and life was going to get better. Chae said the golf would start up again. All the championships would be played, and there would be plenty of folk to caddy for, but Davie knew that would be just for spare time. He'd have to get a job, and learn a trade.

His father had talked about getting him into the foundry, as an apprentice moulder, but Davie wasn't keen on that. He'd looked into the place several times from the road, when the big doors had been open. The noise, the heat and the dust; the wild glow, and the sparks, when they poured the cupolas, were a bit frightening. Maybe he'd get used to it, and anyway, he wasn't going to stick to that job, for this afternoon he had decided what he was going to be.

Chae's voice broke into his thoughts, 'Aye, he's no a bad sort the Yank, even if he does chuck his money aboot.'

Davie's heart lifted. Chae was his friend, even if he did rub you the wrong way sometimes. For a moment he was tempted to tell him of the great decision he had made and then something happened.

Chae had just taken an extra big bite of fruit cake, followed by an equally large swallow of Kola, and then he said suddenly, 'Don't look up now Davie, but here's yer steady bit coming.'

The girl was coming towards them on the far side of the street, and something like panic gripped Davie. Against this sort of attack he had no defence. No matter what he said, Chae would jeer and jibe at him.

'Wee Bethie Johnston, Clubbie Johnston's youngest,' Chae went on. 'You'd be aw' right there, Davie, wi' aw' the money her Da has, and she's just your size and weight.'

And that was true. She couldn't be any more than ten or eleven, but that is practically an infant to a chap of fourteen. Somehow he would have to stop Chae's attack before the girl heard what they were talking about. Her older sister, Mary, now there was the girl Davie had a fancy for, though he'd die before admitting it to anyone. She'd been in his class at school, and was lovely. Just to meet her in the street, and get a bit smile in passing, made his day, though she was always sort of cool and uppish. But even her recognition of him made butterflies flutter in his stomach, and if her young sister went home with the tale that Chae Whitton and Davie Crombie were making fun of her, it wasn't going to help.

Now Beth was almost opposite them. Davie prayed that Chae would shut up, then surprisingly, the girl called out to them across the street. 'What sort of muck is that you two are stuffing into?'

'The cheek of her!' Chae said, quickly, then called back, 'Bairns shouldna ask questions.'

Beth was ready for him, 'I know that Chae's a growing boy, and has to keep up his strength—'

Chae flushed at this, and Davie was pleased, for Chae considered himself a grown man.

Now, what sort of an answer could he give to such impertinence? Beth kept up her skippy walk, giving herself ample margin for escape should they show signs of chasing her, then suddenly she switched her attack. 'There's nothing worse than Kola and fruit cakes for making wee laddies fat.'

Davie growled low in his throat, but took no further action. It was plainly below the dignity of a lad of fourteen to chase and chastise a cheeky bairn of ten or eleven.

Maybe it was his lack of any violent reaction that spurred Beth to her final taunt. 'Never you mind, Davie,' she called, 'Mary doesna mind – I think she likes fat boys.' And with that, she was away like the wind.

A fresh wave of embarrassment gripped Davie when he saw how his friend took in this spicy news. With plainly feigned lack of concern, Chae drank the last of his Kola, and made elaborate pretence of wiping his mouth with the back of his hand, then replaced the stopper in the bottle. Davie wished he could run away, but knew he must wait, appearing quite calm and unconcerned.

At last Chae spoke. 'Oh ho, Master Crombie, so that's the

16

way the wind blows, is it?' He rolled his eyes, and screwed his face up. 'So it's Clubbie Johnston's eldest daughter you're efter! And how do ye think ye'll manage to get off wi' that stuck up bit – wearin a lum hat to the caddyin'?'

'Ach shut up, Chae!' Davie pleaded, but Chae only laughed. 'Aw' right, I'm yer pal. I'll try and stop the bairns from chalkin' up D. Crombie loves M. Johnston on the walls.'

But Davie knew he would tell some of them to chalk it up, then lead Davie to it, and consolingly offer a rag to wipe it off and this after Davie had just stood his hand with fruit cake and Kola.

Maybe Chae's conscience took him a bit then, for he asked, 'Are you watching the club semi-final tonight?'

'I dunno – maybe – I'll see,' Davie said, and turned away. If he stayed with Chae, sooner or later, he'd be teased about Mary Johnston, and besides, he wanted to go off, on his own, to think about the decision he had just made. 'So long,' he called, and turned back toward the links.

2.

Hands deep in the pockets of his shabby shorts, he walked past Hamiltons', the clubmakers, slowly past the last green, then along the burn side. Now, no matter what trade he went to, he knew what he was going to do when he grew up. He was going to America to be a professional golfer. It was the Yank that had decided it. Who wouldn't want to have clubs and a kit like that, or be so free and friendly getting so much fun out of a game? Of course, what he wanted was nothing new. Lots of the top players from the town had gone already, and when a crowd of local men gathered around the last green on a summer's evening, you heard their names being bandied back and forward like camp-fire tales of distant heroes. The Armour brothers and Wilfie Mason, Joe White and Andy Cunningham, Stewart Maiden, McDonald

Smith . . . Davie had never known any of these men. He didn't even know what a professional golfer really did to earn his living, but from the tone of voice the men at home used when speaking of them, it was evident that they were admired and envied. They were big men in America, doing well, getting on in the world.

He turned over the two-shilling piece in his pocket, the promise of five tomorrow if the Yank could put up a show against the Dominie. His mother would be pleased, what with Dad being laid up with a bad chest in the spring.

The Yank was the first American that Davie had met, and now he had to sort out what he knew of America, and try to relate it to him. There was a lot about America in History at school, and the films in the picture house were hardly about anything else. Besides, he'd read one or two books and stories about the U.S.A. But they all presented such contrasted pictures and conditions that it was difficult to understand how the man he'd met that afternoon fitted into any of them. He remembered reading about the Boston Tea Party, and men dressed like Red Indians, but it was difficult to imagine the Yank in that role. Then, right after that, there was the story of a battle fought at Bunker Hill. Had that battle been fought on a golf course? He'd heard about bunkers on ships, but on land, surely it must mean the sand traps on a golf links.

Shooting it out, that was what you saw in the pictures. Cowboys always in and out of saloons, firing at one another with revolvers, then breaking chairs on one another's heads, and falling over bannisters. And the Red Indians . . . peering over rocks at the top of hills, then tearing down the braes on their horses to surround the covered wagons. When the wagons caught fire the Indians rode round and round them, then, in the nick of time, soldiers wearing hats like boy scouts came riding over another hill, trailing a funny wee cannon at their back, and rescued the white folk.

Did the Red Indians play golf or the soldiers? Davie couldn't see how the man he'd met that afternoon fitted into what he knew of America. It was as though stories you were

18

never expected to believe, like fairy tales or Santa Claus were suddenly, beyond any doubt proved to be true, yet in some way, true in a manner quite different from what you had imagined.

And plainly, America wasn't a bit like Scotland, at least the part Davie knew. The big American proved that, for he was very different from any man he had ever met. His mind went back to the flashy bag of clubs. They were American, solid, three-dimensional objects you could feel, see and touch.

Davie had caddied for quite a few men that summer, mostly older ones, swells and head men from the town. The local men carried their own clubs, except when it was a match or a competition, and then one of their pals carried for them. But the men he had caddied for previously had all been much the same in their manner. 'Here, boy,' they said, 'what club shall I use for this shot?' 'Here, boy, tee the ball here.'

Sometimes, when they'd won their match, they might call him 'Sonny', but that was the limit of their intimacy. Whereas the big Yank had been friendly right from the start.

He and Chae had been sitting on the fence when the Dominie and the Yank came out. Chae had left Davie to carry for the American. When the Yank said something that ended up with feeling a heel, Davie understood enough to realise that his ability was in doubt because of his size.

'Ach, its no that heavy,' he'd insisted. 'I can manage fine.' The Yank had patted his back then. 'O.K., son, it's your say-so – you'n me'll get along fine. Let's go!'

There never was a game like it. Even the sour and serious Dominie – he was like that from always having to be stern with the big lads in School – had to relax and smile sour-like once or twice at what the Yank said, and the capers he cut. Davie wasn't sure he approved of the joking and nonsense, for golf was really a serious business; but it was wonderful to go round with him, just for the laugh.

'Yippee!' he'd yell, when he smacked an iron shot up to the flag, or sank a good putt. 'Ain't that a beaut?'

Then, when the Dominie sneaked a hole from him by

sinking a putt the whole length of the green, the Yank would take it out of the hole, and throw it back. 'Just do it again, that's all I ask – do it again.'

It was grand being with him. He didn't seem to mind being beaten. Maybe he knew the Dominie was a top player. America must be a wonderful place, to turn out men like that. The very air he breathed and the grass he walked on seemed a pure delight to him, and he acted friendly to everyone. It would be grand to grow up like him, and have clothes and clubs like his, and if he could get to be a professional in America . . .

But one serious obstacle lay in the way. He might get the clothes and the clubs, maybe have as much money, and be a better golfer . . . but the obstacle was now becoming so clear in his mind that he stopped thinking about it. He could never be as big as the Yank. Already Bob Walker and Cy Gibson were a head taller than him, and just the same age.

A good thing he'd never said a word to Chae about his ambitions. That would only have been another stick for Chae to beat him with when he felt like it. That seemed to be the big difference between the folk here, and the American. Somehow, it seemed all right for him to boast, 'O.K., pardner – now we've got him with his pants down. Here's where we make a killing.' None of the local men would ever talk like that. No, he daren't talk to Chae about his plans, for he'd been teased and bothered enough from that last remark Beth had called back about her sister Mary.

Beth, . . . a queer wee lassie that, but nice. Davie always felt uncomfortable with her, for all that he was so much older and grown-up. His dad called her a dainty wee thing, and made a point of chatting to her when she passed the house. She was always gay and friendly with his father, and had a way of smiling with her eyes. Often she seemed to know what you were thinking before you got the words out. Yet she was quick with her tongue, and just as ready to take a rise out of you as Chae, if she got the chance. But even while he thought that way, Davie knew he could tell her of his plans.

She wouldn't laugh, or say he was boasting. She'd like enough agree it was a fine thing, and be quite sensible about it. Not, of course that he would dream of telling her, she was only a bairn.

Still, he must tell someone, and get advice. Not his mother. He felt sure she wouldn't give him much encouragement. No – his dad would be the one to tell. Maybe tonight, later on, if he went out to put the water spray on the greens. Davie would go with him then, and they could talk.

Suddenly, despite the fruit cake, and the Kola, he was hungry. It must be nearly teatime. If it had been earlier, he would have gone in search of the balls the American had lost. It would be grand to have them, and show them off to the other caddies, for they were all of makes he'd never heard of before. But it wouldn't be honest to keep them, since he knew whom they belonged to. Different when you found a ball in the rough, or the burn. It was yours to keep, or sell, when you didn't know who'd lost it. Maybe the Yank would like to have some of them back. He'd go and look tonight, instead of watching the semi-final.

He walked round to the start of the Burnside course, and scouted to see if the starter had gone home for his tea. He didn't like anyone, even a greenkeeper's son, banging balls about on the course for fun, instead of playing properly.

All clear, so down on his knees among the bushes, he pulled out the mid-iron he'd hidden there earlier on, and taking three balls from his pocket, began to play his way home. Halfway through his first swing, he remembered. He was going to be a professional. Playing must be in earnest now, not just clouting the ball for fun. So he addressed the ball seriously, taking time. His movements had all the free, supple grace of a young animal, as it was with those who take to the game young when their muscles are free, and they play naturally. The first two shots were good ones; nicely hit, with just the right arc of flight, and not too much run on landing. But the third was bad. Struck with the toe of the club, curving left. No good, an American pro must hit straight all the time.

He walked along, twirling the club shaft in his fingers, to strengthen them, like some of the top players did. Just six weeks short of his fourteenth birthday, Davie was beginning to achieve his ambition.

CHAPTER TWO

I.

THE single-storey cottage, with an attendant straggle of tool
sheds and storage barns faced south across the course. The
westerly end was on nodding terms with the tenth green, the
famous 'South America' hole. The fourth fairway of the
Burnside course ran behind the house where the back garden
should have been, and the short fifth diagonally across the
front. A thin screen of willow trees, like despondent sentinels,
stood along the fringe of the burn, as it looped and swirled
about, giving the house some protection from the west and
south.

The cluster of buildings looked exactly what it was, a
douce decent farmsteading; but standing thus, an oasis of
brick, stone, wood and slate, in the rolling expanse of golf
course, it always wore a faintly embarrassed air, like a civic
dignity caught wolfing cream buns at a children's party,
undecided whether to brazen it out, or laugh it off.

Legend had it that it had really been a farmsteading. A
farmer of the county had decided to emigrate to South
America, and his friends gave him a farewell party. At the
end of it he was rather tired and confused when he set out for
home and bed, so tired, indeed, that he lost his way, and lay
down for a nap. Awakening at dawn, to bird song accompanied by the music of the burn, he liked his bedchamber so
much that the ship for South America sailed without him. He
built a croft there, and lived the rest of his days in comfort.
Later the golf course swallowed the land he tilled, but the
name stuck, 'South America' was one of the great holes on a
famous course. Now the only cultivated ground was a strip
in front of the cottage, given over to despairing rows of

cabbages, sprouts, carrots and potatoes. The thin sandy soil gave them little encouragement.

About two hundred yards north ran the railway line, and behind this a thin belt of industry, Andrew Cowans, who made some sort of textile machinery for export. Next to that, a chemical works called the Tannie, the fumes from which were a sore point with houseproud wives. The third factory was a jute mill, an handsome grey stone building. If industry did not add to the amenities, it did not altogether mar the free open beauty of the flat, Angus coastline.

Away to the north rose the rolling Sidlaws, modest handmaidens to the great Grampian range. To David Crombie, this was home, the fairest place in all the world. Every day he was becoming increasingly aware of the world about him, for the teenage years can be the most receptive and impressionable and the scenes and sounds of adolescence remain as yesterday into the fifties and sixties, while things from yesterday are forgotten tomorrow as though they never happened. Davie, if and when he achieved his ambition, would still see this windswept, sandy point on the Angus coastline, which would always be home.

2.

Mary Crombie stood by the front door, peering across the links to see if the boy was coming home for his tea. He was always stravaiging, with one of those stupid golf clubs in his hand, swinging, swiping the whole day long. He was a good laddie right enough, and always brought home the money he earned at the caddying, though that was a daft-like way for a laddie to earn a shilling or two. A pity these men hadn't something better to do than walk about with a laddie trailing after them, carrying their bag of sticks.

Never a sign of him, near-hand teatime, and not a drop of milk in the house. The morning pint had gone sour in the hot day. She sighed, in the weariness of one misused, and turned

24

back into the house. Imagine having to send away into the town for a drop of milk! If James Crombie had stuck to his trade. Why even eggs and vegetables had to be bought at the shop. When he'd been a ploughman, a body took things like that for granted. Maybe this daft job on the golf course was easier on him but the damp and the haar, with the place being so low wasn't doing his chest any good. She longed for the farms high on the Sidlaws, where she'd been born, and spent her childhood.

She was a stocky little woman with a thick topping of dark brown hair, and her face was still comely. Goodhearted, her days were a constant effort to do the best she could for her husband, and her only son, Davie, at the same time convinced in her mind that both of them were on the wrong track, and not inclined to listen when she pointed out things which seemed obvious to her.

Her trouble was really loneliness. Brought up on a farm, she had always enjoyed the close-knit community of the other farm hands, their wives and daughters, and the farm lassies. Here, the cottage stood alone. Over the railway there was plenty of company. Neat streets full of ordinary folk, and, indeed, some of the women had already made friendly overtures. But though the place was hardly more than a large village, the women were urban in their thought and habit patterns.

The country folk she understood had the cycle of the seasons as the unchanging lodestone of their living and thinking, of their toil and leisure. To the human cycle of birth, coupling and death, their outlook was the same, except that to courtship, they brought amused tolerance, well spiced with broad but kindly ribaldry.

But the townsfolk were different, altogether primmer and more genteel. The few women she had tried to make acquaintance with seemed to confine their outlook to the folk next door, or the family across the street. Their envy of a neighbour's new curtains or carping criticism of the woman over the road, whose man had just been made a foreman, and the woman getting so stuck up that there was no living with her, merely bored Mary Crombie, had she understood the meaning of that word.

This, added to her discontent with the job her man liked so much, and her unspoken worries about Davie's future, made her difficult to live with because she was unable to talk fully, and express her doubts and worries. Thus, all her communications were a sort of angry nagging because she loved them both, but she was unable to make any show of affection. There was a streak of self-righteousness in her, she kept her house gleaming, spotless, but because she could not understand the joy her husband found in his work, or the utter enthralment of her son in the game, the rift between them grew ever broader.

When Davie reached the house, he went round the stable end, and put his club in a tool shed. Until a week or so past, his place for it was in the lobby, just behind the front door, but his mother insisted he shift it. 'That stupid thing, forever gettin' in among a body's feet,' she would cry as it clattered to the floor.

Then, as he came back, his mother came out of the front door. 'You'll have to get milk from Cozens',' she greeted him, 'and a wee bunch of carrots and a cabbage. Thae poor things in the yard are no even fit for the hens.' She fumbled in her apron pocket, searching for her purse.

'I have money,' Davie said, and held out the two-shilling piece. Her surprised look at the silver coin pleased him. 'I was caddyin' for an American, and he gave me a tip.'

'Don't take all that with you.' She took the florin and gave him a handful of coppers. 'If you broke it, the rest would just be wasted in rubbishy sweets.'

Davie went willingly on the errand. He would have liked to tell his mother about the big Yank, but she seemed always too busy to listen and always insisted that golf was a waste of time. The only time his mother seemed relaxed and friendly was when they sat together, and talked about the old days on the farm. Davie had liked the farm, especially the horses, but he had no wish to go back to it, especially not now for he was sure his future lay on the golf links.

By the time he returned, his father and mother were seated at the table. Looking at his dad, in his shirt sleeves, always with a brass stud at the neck, but no collar, it seemed to the boy that the man was not nearly so big as he used to seem, but that was because he himself was growing bigger or so he hoped. But his dad's hair was thin and receding now, though his face was lined and healthy-looking, from being constantly out of doors.

Davie put the vegetables under the sink, gave his hands a wash, then carried the can of milk in, and set it down beside his mother. As he handed over the change, he knew it would set her off.

'Sevenpence,' she said, 'sevenpence for a drop of milk and a few carrots, with a bit of cabbage, how can a body live decent and pay prices like that?'

'Och, we're managin' no so bad,' his dad said quietly, but Davie saw he was angry.

Then his mother went off on another tack. 'Its no much of a job, pushin' a lawnmower, and scutterin' away with a rake at a few divots — and forbye — the boy — what's here for him, now he's left the school?'.

'Och, Davie will be all right. We'll find a job for him.' Davie could see his father was holding back anger. 'But, you can make up your mind for this, Mary. I like this job. The committee are gentlemen to work for. They're using this bit of land, takin' their pleasure from it, and tryin' to improve it — to leave it better than they found it — and that's the way all land should be treated.' He paused, then went on, 'And that's better than most o' the fairmers I've worked for do; its them that's gotten this poor auld country into the mess it's in now, takin' every penny they could get outa the land, and stervin' it. Gentlemen farmers, they ca' themselves, and nothin' but pockets for puttin' money in, like old MacKay, the last one I worked for, forever pleadin' poverty, yet he could send his son to college, to be a doctor. Then he gave us the cottage next to the midden, and was so mean he wouldna even mend the roof to keep the rain out. Then, when the young spark comes back as a doctor, he sniffs at oor hovel, and talks about the unhygienic habits of farm servants. No, Mary, you can make up your mind to bide here. I'm no goin' back to the plough.'

His mother got up then, and made a great clatter of clearing away the tea things, as she always did when faced with an argument she couldn't answer.

But there was another factor which Crombie had never confided to his wife and son. After his last bout of chest trouble, the doctor advised him to get a lighter job, preferably one in a district with a mild climate. The little township on the Angus coast, tempered by the river estuary and sea, had just that, with no extreme of heat or cold. Now he turned to Davie, and changed the subject. 'You mind me telling you about that experimental stuff the traveller gave me, to cure the daisies on the twelfth green?'

The new topic pleased and relieved Davie. He always felt rather ashamed when his mother grumbled, and reproached his father about farm work. What would he do for the golf if his dad went back to farming? He was pleased too, that his dad was talking about his job, man-to-man. 'That temporary green's no much,' he said. 'The Yank I caddied for today said it sure was gritty.'

'Did he now?' his dad smiled. 'Well, they'll soon be back on the regular one. That stuff has killed off the daisies, and the new grass that's growin' in is better, a finer strain, just as the traveller said.'

Then his mother called through, 'It dinnae take much to please you, a few blades o' grass.'

But his dad took no notice. 'The committee weren't keen, but I persuaded them to give this stuff a try. Well, son,' his dad knocked the ashes from his pipe and got up, 'I think we'll have a wee turn at the kailyard.'

They began working together, pulling out weeds, loosening the soil round the cabbage roots, firming up the potato

28

drills. Davie was anxious to talk to his father, but before he could say a word, his mother came out, placed her little three-legged stool by the door, in the evening sunshine, and started work on her current task, a rag rug.

She was always making something. Knitting socks for his dad, antimacassars for chair backs and her rag rugs were all over the house, warmly comforting to the feet on a winter night.

Now Davie felt his mother had come out just to emphasise that she had no company. He didn't want to tell his dad whilst she was there, listening, for she was sure to think the whole idea was daft.

His dad didn't really take the garden seriously, it was only an excuse to get the evening air, and have a bit of gossip with the golfers as they played the short fifth hole. When one of them mishit a shot, and it landed in the rough, or in the water of the burn, he would help them look for it, and say he'd have to get the rough cut back, or clear out the banks to make the hole fairer. So Davie worked half-heartedly for a while, then said, 'I think I'll have a bit of a stroll over the links.'

His dad leaned on the hoe. 'Are you for watchin' the semi-final? They say Eck Black's in great form.'

'Maybe – I'll see,' Davie said, then asked, 'Are you for havin' the spray on the greens tonight, Dad?'

His father looked at the blue sky, clear down to the horizon, then he sniffed the wind, it was but the faintest air. 'Maybe I'd better, its no like to rain for a while yet.'

'I'll come and help you,' Davie offered, and warmed to his dad's slow smile. 'That'll be fine, son. We'll go out about half-ten, when maist o' them are makin' for home.'

'Anything so long's he can stay out his bed, and go stravaigin' aboot the links,' his mother called without looking up.

His dad gave him the ghost of a smile, and a wee twitch of his head, telling him without words just to go and pay no heed. So Davie said cheerio, meaning it for both of them, and went round the house to get his club.

29

Once clear, he looked about him. Away to the east, a long dark straggle of people were walking up towards the second hole. Quite a big crowd had turned out to watch the match. Maybe he would watch too, later on, when it grew more exciting.

He turned slowly west, and went idling along, swinging his club at an odd weed or thistle-head by the fairway's edge, on his way to the ninth, to search for the ball the Yank had hooked into the wood that afternoon.

It was cool, crouching under the close-set pine trees and the thick carpet of fallen needles had a lovely clean smell. He found the ball quite easily, and carried his prize out into the open. It was a lovely ball, not a mark on it. He put it in his pocket, and turned south, feeling it in his pocket, turning it over and over. Tomorrow he would give it back to the American, but tonight, it was his.

He took it out, and looked at it again. It had been made in America, and when he was a pro there, he would have dozens and dozens of new balls like this. It was called 'Victor '39', with the name all nice in red and black letters. It would be grand to produce it, casual like, in front of Chae, never letting on about finding it, and enjoying Chae's envy.

Now the crowd were streaming down the long fairway of the sixth. A sudden, delightful thought struck him. Maybe Mary would be in it, along with that stupid brother of hers. He set out to wait at a vantage point beside the seventh tee.

The crowd was ringed about the green, a dark, dull-coloured mass against the light tones of grass and sky. They made no sound or movement, the tense excitement of a big game was something he always liked. The mounting excitement as the player studied his line to the cup, then almost holding your breath as he took his stance, and set the ball rolling over the green carpet towards the hole. Then the disappointed 'Aaaah' from the crowd if it stopped short, or ran past. But he didn't attempt to wriggle through the crowd for a view. Only the sixth hole, it couldn't be very exciting yet. He'd rather get in front here, and have a good view of the

30

driving off.

A scattered ripple of handclaps rose in the air, someone must have holed a long one. Now the ring of crowd melted and broke up, moving towards the tee, with the boys and smaller folk running to get in front and have a good view.

Soon they were all around him, forming a big straggling 'U' shape, packed tight at the base beside the tee, with the two legs thinning out along the fairway, down which the players would drive. Then the two caddies came thrusting through the crowd, followed by the players. Davie learned that it was a grand, tight game, and that Eck Black was now one up.

It was great to watch good players driving off. The crowd going silent, the caddy handing out the driver, then teeing up the ball on the little mound of damp sand from the box. Then the dramatic tension as the player got set and swung. The lovely 'whillipe' as he struck, and sent the shot screaming down the fairway towards the distant flag. Both shots were good ones, and the crowd melted from its 'U' shape into a big loose arc, as it followed the players. Davie walked along with them, wondering if crowds like this would come out at night to watch him play when he grew up, but he'd have to be a good enough player to draw crowds, else how could he be a professional in America?

And then he saw Mary . . .

She was walking along with the crowd, her brother Rodger beside her. He had a club in his hands, swinging it, trying to copy Eck Black. That was always the way with Rodge Johnston. If there was a football match, he would be there watching it, carrying a new ball, or a pair of football boots, telling folk near him that by next year he would be good enough to play for the team. In the winter, the mill dam had frozen and he had been there carrying a braw new pair of skates, bragging he would be a right fancy figure skater by next winter. Chae said his mother fair spoiled him, and that if he wanted the moon, she'd go away up to the town and buy it for him.

Then Rodger saw him, and came over. 'Hullo, Davie – see my new driver?'

Davie hefted the club, and tried a swing. 'It's a braw tool, Rodge.'

'One of my dad's latest, bet you by next year, I'll be able to drive as far as Eck Black, far as anyone,' Rodger said. 'I've been watching how he stands, how he swings, and I've got it now. Bet you in a year or so I'll be in the semi-final, and the final, just you wait.'

'That'll be fine, Rodge,' Davie said, humouring him a bit for the sake of his sister, and maybe a bit because he was a harmless soul, even if he was a pest, with his constant bragging. 'What about me caddying for you, when you get that length?'

'Sure, that'll be fine, Dave. You can caddy for me in all my matches, you'll be able to advise me, and – '

He broke off as the crowd halted, and fell silent. 'Oh, I must watch Bob Crimind play, I'm going to copy his style for irons.' He walked hurriedly along the crowd fringe, but Davie did not follow him. He stood quiet, a few paces behind Mary, just looking without her knowing. She was bonnie! The way her dark brown ringlets fell from behind her wee ears, and lay on her back. The line of her cheek and chin . . . it made him feel soft and warm inside just to see her.

Then she turned and saw him. 'Oh, hullo, David, isn't it a lovely night!'

She seemed so warmly friendly that his throat closed up with pleasure, but he managed to blurt out, 'Aye – its a braw night, right enough.'

She went on talking, and he walked beside her, stopping only when the crowd halted to watch a stroke, and with Mary being so friendly, he hardly saw the golf or wanted to. She was going to attend commercial college in Dundee, she told him, and gave a detailed account of what her mother had said to the principal and what trains she would catch in the morning, and at night. He could hardly believe she was so friendly, making jokes, and laying a hand on his arm to make

32

sure he enjoyed them to the full. He hardly knew what was happening, and they were right round to the twelfth when suddenly the fun and sparkle went out of her. Some of the folk who'd been watching seemed to lose interest in the game, now it was plain Eck Black was going to win.

Davie saw her face change. The smile went away, and she said, cool and curt-like, 'I'm going home now. Coming Rodger?' and left without another word.

Watching her walk away, he felt flat and stupid, not knowing why she had changed so suddenly. Ach, lassies were queer. He'd watch the game for a bit yet, then go home and help his dad.

He perched on a knoll, the crowd still straggling around him, watching the players at the short thirteenth; then Chae sauntered up, chewing a blade of grass, and sat down beside him. 'Aye, she made a bonnie clown outa you, Davie, didn't she?'

Only to be expected that Chae would twit him about Mary – so he just said, 'She's away home now.'

'Aye, so she is.' Chae was sarcastic, and his eyes looked away to where Mary was still visible, Rodger a few paces behind her, swinging his club, trying to copy Eck Black. 'She's fed up tryin', for you were only the bait, Davie, and her fish wouldnae take it.'

'You're just talkin' daft, Chae'.

'Am I? I don't think you're very bright. Aw, her bit tales and laughs and ploys werna for you. They were for the lad aside you. Did you no notice how she aye manoeuvred to be near him? Poor wee Davie – you were fair dazed, its Martin Menzies she was playing for, and him so scared he near hand bursts his collar wi' blushin' when a lassie looks at him.'

'Ach, you're bletherin' nonsense, Chae,' Davie told him but something went cold inside, and the brightness went from the day. He didn't want to believe what Chae said, though he had seen the Menzies lad. His father was the head of Andrew Cowans, and he had a motor car, one of the three in the village; the doctor, and the provost had the other two.

Of course, the Menzies lad was away at a boarding school some place, and it was said he would be allowed to drive his father's car when he was old enough – if what Chae said was true, he could never hope to compete.

The fun had gone out of watching the game now, and to stay with Chae meant he would be ribbed about what happened till he rebelled, or Chae tired. So, trying to sound casual, Davie said 'Well, she's welcome to him. I was only passin' my time.'

'That's the way to talk, Davie. As good fish in the sea as ever came out,' Chae said, but Davie knew he was still being baited, for Chae gave a wink and a sly smile with the words, 'but a blow, just the same, eh?'

Davie turned away, making his steps jaunty, and swinging his club in the manner of a man immune from the wiles of scheming women. He didn't want to believe what Chae said, and anyway, when he was a top golfer in America, things would be different.

3.

He stood beside his dad, hearing the hiss of the falling water as the hose spun round and round, throwing its jet high into the air as it revolved, so that all the velvet expanse of green was covered, and the drops fell like rain, refreshing the thirsty ground.

It was after ten o'clock, now, but the light was still clear in the sky, though even the keenest golfers were now making for home.

And Davie told his father about the big American, of his burning ambition to be a professional golfer in America when he grew up.

'Deed, that would be fine, son, grand, if you could do it, and I suppose a strong mind to a thing is half the battle.'

'And – you wouldnae mind, Da, if I went away out there?'

'Mind?' His father smiled. 'I'd be proud, proud – whit man wouldnae, wi' a son oot in America, doing well.' He fumbled for his pipe, and began to fill it. 'Still and aw', son, you'd be better wi' a trade, something to fall back on.'

Like a black, menacing storm approaching, Davie could visualise the dark moulding shop.

'This golf business in America seems to pay well. Men'll aye pay more for their bit sport than they will for gettin' their bellies filled.' His father put a match to his pipe, his cheeks falling hollow as he puffed to get it going. 'Seems to me the best trade for you would be the clubmaking, for I think the two go together.'

The image of the moulding shop vanished before the glorious prospect of being a golf club maker – Clubbie Johnston – maybe seeing Mary sometimes or maybe working at Hamilton's over the railway.

'Mr Johnston's on the links committee, and he's been very kind to me,' his father went on. 'I'll have a word wi' him the first chance I get, and see if he'll take you on for an apprentice.'

'Oh, Dad!' Davie was glowing. 'That would be great! I could start right away, if he'd have me.'

'Na, na, son. You take yer bit holiday. Once a man starts workin' he's kept at it till he's cairried away feet first – that's my experience. Dae a bit caddyin', when you've a mind to, get some sun and fresh air.' They started for home in the fading day. 'I'll have a word wi' Mr Johnston at the next meeting,' his father went on, 'and see if he can give you a start in the early back-end.'

Passing the pine plantation bordering the fifth, his dad said 'Aye, I'd be proud, if you could make a name for yourself.'

It seemed to the boy that having his dad proud of him would be even better than having clubs and fancy clothes like the big Yank.

'Mind you, son,' his dad said suddenly, 'I'd fair miss you, if you were awa' there in America. I'll just have to get used to the idea.'

Their shoulders touched occasionally, as they walked over the darkening links. A bat flickered out of the trees to pass overhead. Davie's great love for his father grew from that night.

CHAPTER THREE

THE sign had yellow letters on a green ground: 'R. Y. JOHNSTON, CLEEK AND CLUBMAKER'. The shop was a lean-to built against the wall of the house, and the front was so narrow that the sign wasn't above the window, but on the high wooden fence which screened the side of the garden from the people who wanted to look at the window or enter to buy. Not that Clubbie Johnston's customers wasted much time at the window, for there wasn't much to look at. Maybe he felt that dressing up windows was beneath his dignity as a craftsman, like the country tailor, whose sole concession to sales promotion and window dressing consisted of a fifty-year-old fashion plate, a roll of drab tweed draped over an old chair, and a basted jacket with only one sleeve on a coathanger.

There were generally some museum pieces, clubs dating from about 1790, and a new one for contrast, together with a sun-faded invitation to try our latest 'Trubalance' drivers and brassies. These, along with a few gaily coloured but corner-bent cards for 'Challenger', 'Whynot' and 'Colonel' golf balls, completed the display.

Davie thought the inside of the shop the most exciting place in the world. Firstly, there was the glorious smell; a nose-tingling mixture of beeswax, tarry pitch, wood stain, leather varnish and shavings, then there was the Aladdin's cave display of new clubs, all stacked tight along the walls, because the shop was so narrow. Inside the door there was a little counter, and a rubber mat on the floor to let you try a club without scarring the sole, if you didn't buy it; but you could never try a swing, there wasn't room.

But what the shop lacked in breadth, it made up for in length. Only the front part was the shop, the rest of it had a bench right against the wall of the house, customers could watch the men in shirt sleeves and white aprons finishing wooden clubs; staining the heads, trueing up the faces, putting on the grips.

But when you were inside, the most exciting sounds came from the big shed where the majority of the men worked, the forge and the machine shop. But to see that, you had to be a friend of Johnston's or else take the train, for the big shed faced the railway and passengers for Aberdeen had a view of the forge, for often in the summer the double doors were left open.

One side of the shed was also the wall of Clubbie's garden, and the high wooden fence which screened the front started again at the shed door, and went right down to the railway line. The staves at the bottom were always broken and hanging loose, so that a body could squeeze through and walk along the railway embankment till the backyard of the Wallace Hotel was reached. The men called the loose boards the boss's alibi, for he would come into the forge about half-past eleven and looking down the yard, would exclaim, 'Damn me, has the joiner not repaired that fence yet, I'll have to see him about it.' And with that, walk down and inspect it, then nip along to the back door of the Wallace for his morning eye-opener.

After a while he would come back, as he went through he would say, casually, 'He's coming down this afternoon if the weather holds.' And the men said 'Right, Mr Johnston,' and went on with their work, keeping up the pretence. He was not a bad man to work for, and a really good clubmaker, not his fault if his wife was a snob, with her pride and nose-in-the-air manner. It was she who made him buy the house when the Balgowan Club had lost its licence. It boasted big bow-windows and a turret at each gable. The wealthy men of the town had built it, not so much for the golf as a place to get a drink on a Sunday. They even allowed lady members, an exception in those days. Mrs Johnston brought him here from the old smiddy by the Clayholes, where his father had started as a blacksmith. Some said she picked the lesser of two evils, while it was beneath her dignity to have a low common place like a forge and the clubmaking practically in her back garden, at least she could keep her eye on her husband, and keep him out of the bars when he should be working.

And so the two loose staves at the yard foot were always in need of repair, and never a workman would have given him away, for what use to be a boss, if you couldn't go for a drink when the thirst was on you?

2.

Davie started his apprenticeship on a raw September day, with a wet pearly mist drifting over the golf links, and the grass wet underfoot.

He was outside the shop well before starting time at eight o'clock and leaned against the fence as he had often done with Chae, until he remembered that Mr Johnston was his boss now, and might not like an apprentice leaning against his garden fence. So he stood up straight, and tried to get used to the feel of his first long trousers, smart and with a sharp crease because of their newness.

Then he saw Bert Sproggie ambling along, his funny crooked pipe, with the bowl shaped like a skull, in his mouth. Bert always kept his pipe there, he only took it out at meal times, and then replaced it because, he said, his face wasn't the right shape since he was short of so many teeth.

'Aye, laddie, but you are grand and early for a start,' he cried, pulling the key from his pocket. 'Let's hope you are always so sharp in the mornings,' and he opened the door. Davie followed him through the darkened shed through a whitewashed door bearing a big bill headed: 'Regulations and Rules to be observed in the forge and metal-working trades'. It was so grimy with dust and greasy jackets being hung over it, that one could never read it all, it would take most of a day in any case, so how could anyone keep all the rules, but the words at the bottom were plain enough. 'Issued by His Majesty's Stationery Office by order of the Home Secretary'.

It was dark in the big shed, till Bert Sproggie opened the shutters, and told Davie to unlock the doors. Then the pale morning light lit up the dark cold forge, the big power hammer, and the grimy machines with the overhead shafting like branches of a strange steel forest.

'Mr Johnston said,' Davie began, but Bert Sproggie cut him short. 'Aye, aye, laddie, he told me, give me a hand to start the fire and we'll get a brew going. It's a cold-like day.'

As the fire flickered reluctantly, Bert got ready for work. He removed his jacket and vest, and rolled up his sleeves. He put on another vest, it failed to meet by nearly six inches across his chest; tying on a blackened leather apron under his armpits and donning an old greasy cap, he was ready to face the day.

Davie copied him, except that he had no working waistcoat, but he rolled his sleeves up, and Bert gave him a leather apron, it almost touched the floor when he put it on.

'You'll have to grow a bit to fit it, son,' Bert said. 'Or we'll have to cut the tail off it, so you won't trip and fall in the fire.'

Davie wondered if this was the start of the teasing, but now the other men were coming in. A big can of water was placed on the fire, and presently, with a wheeze, the machinery was started up, though the men did not hurry to their tasks, instead they stood in a bunch around the fire, each carrying a soot-blackened tin, with a twist of wire across the top for a handle.

'Give the fire a bit encouragement, son,' Bert told Davie, and showed him how to blow it with the bellows. He knew now that this was to be his job, working the fire draught for Bert. Tam Knox, who had served six months, was now on one of the machines, boring the holes in the sockets.

Suddenly there was a tremendous 'thud, thud', making the

40

very ground tremble, and Davie saw that Tam Knox had started up the power hammer, but it was only hitting the anvil; and the machines were all idling. 'They hear it up at the house, and think we are all working,' Tam whispered to Davie. 'If things were quiet she would chase the boss through before he had his breakfast.'

Now the big can of water was boiling, and Bert, as foreman and master of ceremonies, spooned in generous libations of tea, then added sugar and condensed milk kept handy on a ledge of wall behind the forge. This was allowed to infuse for a few moments, then each man held up his can to be filled.

A can had been found for Davie, but his tin was gleaming silver, and the copper handle shone. His first ambition was to get it fire-blackened like the others. But the hot, strong tea somehow tasted better than any tea drunk before, for he was a man among his mates. Now the fire cast a warm glow over their faces, all standing by their machines in case Mr Johnston came in early.

Then Sproggie put down his can and lit his pipe. 'Aye, we're the lucky lads,' he said. 'Work to see us through the winter, and a bit glass on a Saturday.'

'And odd times a braw lass to take behind a haystack,' Wilf Day, the grinder added.

'Black shame on you,' Bert said angry, but still smiling, 'in front of the lad.'

'He'll get started on the haystack caper soon enough,' Day said. 'Wee lads are usually the worst.'

Davie felt his face go red. But now they were all at work, and he understood how Bert's remark about them being lucky lads was, in some way, like the minister's benediction at the end of a service – a signal to start working and a sort of blessing.

Now he turned all his attention to the job of helping Bert Sproggie. He knew him already by sight, he was a marvellous golfer, and him just a fat butter-ball of a man. Davie's respect for him amounted almost to reverence, for he was the reigning Links Champion, though Chae said that the Dominie and old Sproggie wouldn't have it so easy next summer when the lads got out of the army. The boy soon had fresh cause to admire him, for he was, in his way, an artist with metal. They were forging mashie heads that morning, and Davie found himself forgetting the bellows when he became absorbed watching the man.

Bert picked up a billet of metal, and squinted at it, this way and that. Some he rejected. 'We'll make something of that, but not a mashie.' They all seemed alike to Davie.

Then a suitable one was put on the fire, and the bellows worked to bring it to forging heat. A wink and a sideways jerk of the head were signals Davie soon learned. When it was glowing, Sproggie held it on the anvil, and began beating it into shape. He wasted no energy, his right arm kept the hammer going constantly in a steady rhythm, and when it stopped beating the red hot metal, he still had the hammer going, clinking it on the anvil, using the spring of its rebound to save his own energy.

Satisfied with his first shape, he put it back on the fire, and Davie's job was to lay out the simple cresses and dogs used for the final forming. He grew to love that part of the job as his first morning progressed. Watching the routine, he tried to anticipate the blacksmith's needs, laying out the tools in the order they would be called for, and as he worked the heat up, he watched Sproggie intently, ready at once to respond to his gesture, and hold whatever instrument was needed with the tongs.

Then, at last, heat faded from cherry red to black, Bert would squint at it this way and that. 'Aye, that's not bad,' he said when satisfied. Then the new forged head was placed on the edge of the fire, and left there for the rest of the day. 'Give the metal time to cool and set,' was his dictum. 'If it's cooled too quick, it's only a dead lump, no spring in it at all.'

The morning wore on, and Davie grew more intent as he got into the swing of his task. He was not yet sensitive enough to the atmosphere to feel the change when Mr

Johnston came in. Then he was suddenly aware that the boss was standing at his back, watching him in silence. The discovery flustered him, for his dad had told Mr Johnston that he was a good lad and a steady worker, and now the boss had come in and found him just standing, watching Bert Sproggie, who was more intent than usual in his inspection of the piece he was working on.

Then Sproggie swung the head into the fire for yet another heat, and, Davie, to retrieve his character, began working the bellows like mad. It was his misfortune that Bert took hold of the old fashioned grid damper, and shook it to clear away the clinker and ash, but it jammed.

The fire emitted a great shower of tiny red hot coals, and a thick fog of white ash. 'In the name of God!' Johnston exploded, and stepped back, coughing and half-blinded. The shoulders of his fawn Harris tweed suit were white, and the ash powdered his hair. Davie's stomach went cold, and his heart went to his shoes. Now he would surely be dismissed.

'That wasn't the boy's fault,' Bert said. 'The damper jammed.'

Mr Johnston's face was red and angry; he brushed his shoulders. 'You should be more careful.'

'I didn't see you come in,' Bert said, and added, 'It's only a bit of ash.'

'Tach, I'll feel dirty all day now,' the boss went on. 'I'll get a brush down in the office.'

Davie watched him stalk away, then turned to Bert. The fat blacksmith was not a bit troubled. He smiled and asked, 'What are you so woebegone about? He'll not eat you.'

'Will it be all right,' Davie asked.

'Ach, it could happen to anybody,' Bert stirred the fire and turned the head over with the tongs. 'Our boss is a bit fussy about his clothes, fancies himself as a well-dressed man. We could all do that if we had his money and didn't need to dirty our hands.'

Now the head was glowing, Bert laid it on the anvil, and Davie held the forming dog over the sole. With the tail of his

43

eye, he saw the boss back again, neatly brushed and spruced up. When Bert looked up at him he said: 'Twenty-four deep-faced, Bert, all to the same loft.'

'Aye, aye,' Bert answered. 'They'll all be ready for grinding tonight.'

'That's fine, we'll get them away by Wednesday,' the boss said, and glanced down the yard. 'Dear me, that fence is still hanging loose, I'll away, and get hold of the joiner.'

Bert winked at Davie as he turned away and walked down the yard, and the other men exchanged smiles. 'He'll be in better trim when he comes back,' Day called over, and straightened his shoulders to light a cigarette.

'Will it not take a long time for the shop to sell twenty-four mashies?' Davie asked, as he worked the bellows for a new heat.

'Laddie,' Bert smiled, his pipe dangling, 'the shop trade wouldn't keep the boss's wife in silk stockings. We make heads for other clubmakers all up and down the country, and the big London stores as well, we are even beginning to get orders from America.'

Would that be the big American? Davie wondered, remembering his purchase that day in the summer. Was he now sending over for more clubs.

Twenty minutes later Mr Johnston came back and walked straight over to them. He nodded to Davie: 'You'll remember your first morning, laddie; it's not every apprentice that showers the boss with ash and nearly chokes him, but as long as you stick in at your work, you and I will get on fine, but tell me the next time you mean to do that, and I'll put on an old suit.'

He went off with that, and Bert winked again. 'He's in a good mood now, he's had his morning pick-me-up; right, steady now.'

Before long, Miss Patullo, who was the book-keeper and worked in a small office stuck on the wall of the shed like a pimple, as Bert put it, poked her head out of her little window, and blew the whistle for dinner-time.

Having just one hour, Davie bolted his meal down; gave his father and mother a sketchy account of his first morning, and hurried back. He said nothing of the incident of blowing ash on Mr Johnston. He needn't have hurried, for it wasn't nearly starting time. One or two of the men who didn't go home were sunning themselves in the yard. Bert was with them feeding the crumbs of his sandwiches to the birds, who hopped fearlessly over his fat stumpy legs.

'That's been a gey quick meal you've had,' Bert said as Davie sat down beside him. 'Just a walk round the table, and a kick at the cat?' He crumbled the last crust, and threw it to a sparrow. 'Don't hurry your meals, son, it won't do your stomach any good.'

He lit his pipe, and puffed it in silence, then said, 'They tell me you're a keen golfer.'

'Aye, I play when ever I can,' Davie answered.

'What about giving me a game some Saturday?'

Davie was sure he couldn't be hearing right. 'But you're – you're Links Champion.'

'Ach, maybe it was my turn, maybe it was sympathy for the wee fat man. I doubt it will be a different story next summer, when the young lads are home, but you'll give me a game?'

'Oh, I would like that very much,' Davie said, and felt that this was the last word in wonders.

'Ah, well, I'll have to see you don't give me a beating. We'll say about half-past one on Saturday, eh?'

'Thanks, Mr Sproggie, thanks. I'll put in a ballot.' Already his pride was high as he imagined telling the starters; 'R. SPROGGIE and D. F. CROMBIE at one thirty-two please.' And the comments of Chae when he saw the names on the board.

3.

But Chae was to learn of the high honour before it appeared on the notice board, for he came on Davie that night, snatching a few holes of practice in the shortening evening.

Chae too, had started work as an apprentice builder with Scrappy Lang, who was putting up an extension to the Tannie. Chae was full of his new job, and talked continually, stressing the wonderful technical problems to be faced and overcome, and the great feats of strength he was called on to perform. Much as Davie wanted to describe his first day, and the honour of Bert's invitation, he could not get a word in edgeways with Chae.

'It's a grand job, Davie, but a man's job, if you follow me,' Chae said. 'Both brains and strength needed for it. It would never be the thing for a wee chap like you, so maybe you are just as well at the clubmaking, though mind you if you needed a job, I could have done something for you, for the foreman's a real friend of my dad, and if I just said the word?'

'No, I'll stick to the clubmaking,' Davie said. 'I like it fine.'

'Suit yourself,' said Chae, 'but the building's the trade, we had the architect here this morning, and when he saw the foot course laid he said . . .'

Listening to him, Davie felt that Chae was himself, what he was quick to condemn in other people, a brag. Yet somehow it was right that a chap should be proud of his work, and want to talk about it. Still, even this harmless kind of boasting was condemned. He wanted to tell of his day, of the wonders he had seen Sproggie perform, and of his own determination to do the same, but it was impossible to stem Chae's talk for long enough to get started. He couldn't even tell him about . . . Then his chance came. The light had faded till the flight of the ball could no longer be followed, so they stopped playing and walked home.

'Are you for our usual game on Saturday?' Chae asked, when Davie's house loomed up in the gloaming.

'No, I'll not manage this Saturday,' Davie's voice rang in pride. 'I've fixed up a game with Bert Sproggie.'

This was equivalent to a London housewife announcing that she had been asked to tea at Buckingham Palace. He saw Chae's jaw drop, 'Gees, how have you managed that?'

'It was him that suggested it,' Davie said, adding with great pride, 'I'm meeting him at the forge.'

'Hey, there will be no living with you soon.' Chae was openly envious. 'I suppose you'll expect me to touch my bonnet when I meet you. Are you needing a caddy?'

Was he trying to be sarcastic, half in fun, whole in earnest? 'Och, stop kidding, Chae. Will you be able to fix up a game with someone else?'

'I'll not bother,' Chae said. 'Seeing you are set, I'll go to the match with some of them bricklayers. I would sooner do that seeing as you are playing Sproggie, you're not that keen on football.'

This was the old Chae, making pretence that he only played to please you and that by doing so, he deprived himself of an afternoon at the football match.

'If you are going to the match,' Davie said hesitantly, what he was going to ask was cheeky, but . . . 'Could you lend me your bag, Chae? Mine is a bit . . .'

'Hardly up to laying beside Sproggie's?' Chae put in. 'Sure, Davie, you can have some of my clubs as well, if you like.'

His generosity warmed Davie. 'Thanks, I'll not play them, but they will help to fill out my – your bag.' His clubs were old, nondescript ones his dad had picked up here and there for him, and his bag was the same.

'Well, that's fine, and if you can beat Sproggie, I'll caddy for you for the love of it,' Chae said, and they both laughed at such an impossible thought.

'You're not going in yet surely?' Chae said, as the clubs were stored away. 'Tell your mother you're a working man now. Let's have a walk up the town.'

It was dark now, with the pale gas lamps making pools of wan yellow light on the road and pavement. They strolled along, stopping to peer into darkened shop windows. After-hour lighting of displays was not yet in being. Habbie Jones, the men's outfitters, held them for quite a time. They selected a pair of flannel trousers for purchase when financial circumstances would permit. They progressed to the tweed jackets, thence to the more decorative shirts and ties to complete their ensembles.

Chae was critical of Davie's tastes. 'Tach! You're an old man before your time,' he said. 'You will never get Mary Johnston to look at you in a tie like that.'

Davie ignored the taunt, 'I didn't fancy any of these jackets, except perhaps the one with the brass buttons.'

'Nor wearing a blazer like Martin Menzie's will get her either!' Chae pressed home his attack. 'In fact if I was you, I wouldn't buy my clothes here, for Mary is more likely to take notice if you get yourself rigged out by one of the big shops in town.' Their tour continued. The brightly-lit Italian Ice Cream shop held them for a while. The display of chocolates, boiled sweets and wrapped toffees was such as to make each boy furtively lick his lips and wish . . . what made it worse was the fact that the shop was open.

'See anything you fancy, Davie?'

'No, I'm not much on sweets.'

'Nor me, fair ruin your appetite for real meals, and it's too cold for ice cream, but a bar of that cream chocolate wouldn't go wrong.'

Now Davie felt panic. How could he avoid the humiliation of confessing that he had no money in his pocket if Chae suggested sharing a purchase? For a moment it seemed possible, then Chae turned on his heel. 'Come on along the front.'

So down and along the Station Road and wait for a few minutes because the gates were closed. Presently the express from Aberdeen came thundering past pulled by an engine called 'Dandy Dinmont'. The brightly-lit windows of the coaches flashed past, giving them a brief glimpse of a world of freedom and travels, especially the dining coach with its little pink shaded lamps on the tables and the white-coated waiters hovering about.

'My, it must be grand to get your meals on the train,' Chae said wistfully. 'Imagine sitting down to your dinner, and a lassie like that one we saw, with the yellow hair and the pink dress for company.'

'She must be cold, with her bare arms like that,' Davie said and Chae snorted. 'Not her, these trains are heated up like hot-houses, for these wealthy women don't wear much. Gees, I wonder what it costs for your dinner on the train?'

Something in his voice confirmed Davie's suspicions. Chae had no money either. Instead of being pleased about this, Davie was depressed. Want of money was a terrible thing, when a man couldn't stand his friend even a modest refreshment.

'Come on along the front,' Chae suggested, as the level crossing gates clanged open.

Now the sky was spangled with stars, and the sea quietly murmured; as they walked along alternate pools of dark and light guided their steps. They passed the Wallace Hotel, closed now, for the winter, and only the Bar entrance showing any signs of life.

'And here's your boss's house,' Chae said, and they paused. One of the big front rooms was lit and someone was playing the piano. They stood listening, entranced by the music. 'That's your lass playing,' Chae whispered. 'I'll say that much for her, she's a grand piano player.'

This was an age starved for music. Radio was only stirring in the womb. The gramophone was only in its infancy, and the sounds it produced a wheezy tinny caricature of the music it makes today. True you could hear music at the cinema, but it was just part of the magic, you couldn't watch the screen and listen to the music at the same time.

Sometimes in the summer a brass band had played for an hour or two on the front, generally on a Sunday. This was considered a great concession to the ungodly and consequently was always carefully censored. 'Jerusalem' and 'Ave Maria' were always allowed and the 'Zampa Overture', even sometimes a selection from 'The Bohemian Girl', and inevitably a selection of Scottish folk tunes. But to allow the lilting magic of Gilbert and Sullivan or Lionel Monckton

49

would have been bowing the knee to Satan altogether.

If it was music you wanted, there was the Kirk to attend and the organ to listen to. But to many of the young, music and movement were one, and considered as necessary as food, water and air. But dancing was an instrument of the Devil, and the only covered spaces large enough to dance in were the church halls.

There were dances held in hotels, of course, but only wealthy people could afford to attend them. Maybe it was because the Americans were a young nation that they understood young people better. Now they were sending their music, so compelling in rhythm that it might make a dead man dance. Mary Johnston was playing some of it now. She had dash and attack. Davie liked music but he had never heard anything like this. Every nerve of him quivered to the tune, it was all the good things he had ever known, all rolled up together – like hitting a perfect drive on a fine day or sinking a long putt – or the wonder of watching a mashie head being born from a lump of red-hot metal under Sproggie's hammer, or the feeling when Mary smiled and put her hand on his arm. Davie had never danced but now, of their own accord, his feet began moving to the tune.

Chae was like a daft man, hunching his shoulders and sliding his feet about. 'That's "Swanee", one of the latest,' he said, and began to sing softly.

The music poured over Davie, looking at the lighted window, he saw the shadow of a girl passing over it, just her head and shoulders now and then.It was Beth and she was dancing to her sister's music just as Chae was.

He saw her too, 'Gee, Davie if we were Martin Menzies and his pal we could just knock at the door and have a party with them.'

Now it was the chorus, that happy sad little tune which took Gershwin's name around the world.

'The words, Chae, tell us the words,' Davie pleaded. He wanted to sing them too. But Chae was altogether possessed. He had his left arm stretched out sideways, and his right cuddled an imaginary partner, now he was dancing, cutting capers with his feet, and sticking his behind out in what he considered to be a manner right and proper for an up-to-date dancer.

On and off the pavement, round and round the lamp-post, his shadow growing and shrinking as he moved about the light. 'Gee, I would like to go to the dancing,' he said when the tune finished, and leaned against the wall.

Now other tunes were singing out in the quiet night. 'Whispering', 'Avalon' and 'Dardanella'. Davie loved them all, but 'Swanee' was the best. Never had he heard such a tune which so moved and delighted him. He got Chae to repeat the words of the chorus, and later on, Mary played it again, as though she had sensed his silent wishes. But the concert came to an end, and the light in the room went out. 'Oh well, Dave, nothing for it but home to our beds now,' Chae said. 'See you tomorrow.'

When his friend's footsteps had faded into silence, Davie turned for home. At the end of the road he struck over the golf course in the darkness steering his way from the yellow eye of light from the kitchen window, it blinked now and then as the wind stirred the trees in front. The music he had heard made lovely pictures in his mind. He was sitting at a table with Mary and she was wearing a pink dress of soft silky stuff that left her arms bare. There was a little pink shaded lamp on the table, and a white-coated waiter was hovering around offering them wonderful food. And now the band was playing, softly, but sweet and exciting. They got up to dance, and confident of his privacy on the dark golf course, he took up Chae's attitude, as though holding Mary, and as though they were really dancing. 'Swanee, how I love you,' he began to dance the way Chae had done, but a root caught his foot, and he fell full length.

Serve him right, for capering like a daftie. He brushed himself down, and walked on, still singing his tune. But it would be wonderful if it could all happen.

Now the day's mist was gone and a star shivered in the sky.

51

Making clubs was grand, and on Saturday he was playing a game with Bert Sproggie. Mary was wonderful; maybe she would play that tune for him some day, when his time was out, before he went off to America to become a professional golfer.

CHAPTER FOUR

I.

THE next few years were full for Davie. His aim and ambition grew as news and pictures of the men who had preceded him trickled back.

During these years, he was lucky in the men he liked best, and these were widely contrasting types; his father, Bert Sproggie, and strangely, for neither Davie nor his parents were avid churchgoers, the Reverend Gordon Lawson, M.A., D.D.

It was from Bert and his father, that Davie learned a sense of values, and a love of good sound work for its own sake. Bert Sproggie was a man who had not made the best of his life, and knew it, yet accepted the fact and was happy. Bert was an artist in whatever he did. So lovable was his personality, so great his ability, whether forging a club head, playing a golf match, or singing a bawdy song in the club on harmony night.

The minister was that rare type, a clergyman who was genuinely liked by all manner of men. He was a good golfer, and that was a strong recommendation in a community where the game is a part of life; but he was also a good mixer, yet never in any degree let down his standing and sense of calling. Indeed, when Bert was clowning at any party in the club, the Reverend Lawson was to be found acting as his foil and accompanist. 'Censor it, Bert, you randy, censor it!' he would call out in an interval between verses. 'You'll have me out of my pulpit if word of this gets about.'

One cold day that November, when the winter grass carried a white haar like snow, and it was too cold to sit outside in the meal hour, Davie found Bert sitting on a box beside the fire, his short legs outstretched, and his old pipe, unlit, hanging from his mouth.

'You shouldn't hurry your meat, Davie, it does your stomach no good at all,' was his greeting.

'Ach, what else can I do, there's no sense in hanging around the house,' Davie replied.

'No much better sitting here waiting for the whistle. Why do you not have a kick at the ball like the other lads.'

'I'm not a football player, golf's my game.' Davie gave him a smile, and added, 'But there's not much time to play these days.'

Bert said nothing for a few moments, then quietly, 'I hear you mean to be a pro in the States.'

That Bert knew of his ambition was a shock. Would he tease him about it, maybe tell the other men?

'It was your dad who told me, the day before you started here,' Bert said and added, 'Reach the tobacco tin from my jacket there, like a good lad.'

Now Davie understood why Bert had suggested that first game with him, likely enough at his dad's prompting, to see how good a player he was, if he had any chance at all of becoming a first-class golfer.

'Oh, Bert, do you think I could ever go to America?'

'What's to stop you Davie? Just get on the boat!'

'Now you're kidding me, I mean to be a pro?'

'That's up to you, Dave, it depends on how much you want to. How hard you're prepared to work. I'll tell you this now, you have the makings of a damn good golfer.'

'Honest, Bert? You really think so?'

'I told your dad that after I first played with you. But that's only the start. You have to grow up, and keep getting better at it, practice, practice, practice.'

'One game on a Saturday,' Davie said. 'And dark before we finish work at night.'

'You'll never be much of a player if you wait on light and weather,' Bert said, and Davie looked at him in surprise.

'You live on the course, don't you?' And Davie nodded.

'You walk over it coming to your work in the morning, then back for your dinner, back again when you've had it, then home again at night, what more do you want?'

'You mean play along?'

'Just that,' Bert nodded. 'A pocket full of balls, and one club, and be stern with yourself. Aim at a mark, and try to get your shots within six feet of it, and when you do that consistently, try and get them within three, and your short game, keep at that, for that doesn't need light.'

'You mean pitching and putting in the dark?' Davie was amazed.

'Why not? You have a choice of greens right at your door. Go out on a calm night. Get a candle and put it in the hole. It will cast enough glow to give you a mark. Try and get your chips within a foot or so. Practise putting, down in two, never more; and when you manage that, think of trying to get the first one down.'

'Oh, boy!' The prospect was exciting. 'I'll do that every day now. I should have thought of it myself. But, Bert, why have you not gone to America?'

'Why not indeed, Davie? I had my chance twenty years ago, I have a brother-in-law out there. Doing very well.'

'But why did you not go?'

'Ach, I should have when I got the chance. But I was married with a young family, and the wife wasn't keen. I wish now that I had gone, so I do.'

'It would have been fine for you,' Davie said, wistful for his friend, then with a touch of childish logic, 'but if you had gone – I wouldn't be able to work and play with you.'

'That you wouldn't son, and we'd have both missed something, but I see the Patullo fingering her whistle, we'll have to make a start.' He heaved his squat bulk up from the box. 'I'd like fine to see you making a name for yourself out there.' Then he added, 'I never had a lad, all my family are lassies.'

Davie acted on Bert's advice, and became a local legend. Daily, to and from work, he played his way. Out in the cold and frost of early winter light, full shots played to a mark, and always trying to land them within six feet. With the westerly gales blowing he could hit the ball to tremendous distances down wind, but to keep their flight consistent was difficult, and coming back, punching the ball into the teeth of a gale, was even harder. But he studied this. Down wind now, control was better if he altered his stance just so, and moved his left hand over; not too much, that way, you cut away to the right. And, against the wind, stand so and bring the right hand a little further round. With growing strength and increasing skill, he learned tricks, the tiny bit of fade at the end of flight which aided control when the wind was slightly across, the tiny wrist flick which helped to cut short the long bouncing run when playing downwind. And on fine nights, he practised the short game, with a candle end in the cup, casting its eldritch glow, suggesting witches' gatherings and will-o'-the-wisps on haunted marshes.

And many a local lad and his lass would come on him in the winter darkness, on their romantic strolls over the dark links, and see his small guide light, and hear his movements though they could not see him. And the girl would clutch her companion's arm; if he was backward, and she was shy, it was a good excuse for getting closer, and gasp out, 'Oh, Jock, there's somebody moving there'. And Jock would get a bit startled himself, and maybe a flicker of fear. Then he would remember and slipping a protective arm about his girl, 'Away, you silly thing, it's only wee Davie Crombie at his practising.'

For now the community was watching him. Any departure from the norm of conduct was never missed. No one ever commented on it, for a man is free to do as he likes, though he has no right to complain if his unconventional behaviour provides meat for conversational feasts. At first it was a matter for sly amusement. 'Aye, that's our wee golfing fanatic, he'll soon tire of that game.' Then, as the months slipped into years and Davie still played himself back and forth from home to work, the covert sneers and sly remarks gave way to reluctant admiration. 'Say what you like, he's a sticker that lad, if hard work will get a man some place, he'll get there.'

2.

But before that first winter was finished, Davie went on another quest.

He paused in the dark by the manse gate, and wondered if the minister would laugh at him. Was it a silly thing to want? Yet his dad had said that learning was one thing that stood by a man.

There was a light burning in the hall, shining through the frosted glass door, and a bell jangled as he pulled the polished brass knob. Presently the door opened. It was Meg Ross, the minister's housekeeper. She peered short-sightedly at him: 'If it's about the christening, leave your name for the bairn and see that you have it dressed decent on Sunday. I told you before not to be troubling Mr Lawson.'

Then she seemed to realise that her strictures had been vented on a stranger, for she paused and asked: 'What are you wanting?'

Now Davie was certain that his whole idea was silly and he should turn and run before confessing his purpose. Up to now, the secret was his own, but if he told the woman everybody would know.

'I – I want to see Mr Lawson.'

'What's your business?'

Should he turn and run – no! He wasn't going to tell her, his business was with the minister. 'I just want to see him,' he insisted.

'He has not the time to waste on – ' she began, when a door opened down the hall, and a deep voice called, 'What is it, Meg?'

'Please, Mr Lawson, I wanted to see you for a minute,' called Davie, before she could speak, and the minister came forward.

'Why, it's Davie Crombie, isn't it? The greenkeeper's son.'

'That's right.'

'Come away in, come away in, David.'

He took off his cap and wiped his feet before crossing the threshold. 'That will be all, Meg,' Mr Lawson said, when she hovered near. She had a great reputation for gossiping and her tit-bits of information were always news for the village. She kept the inquisitive well posted when any wedding was arranged, especially the ones in haste.

'Come in and sit down, David.' Mr Lawson ushered him into a warm, comfortable room, with a big fire blazing. 'I'll be with you in a moment.'

It was the biggest house Davie had ever been in, and the nicest room. Big, warm red curtains were pulled right across the bay window, shutting out the cold December night. A bowl of flowers made a splash of colour in front of them, and the table on which the bowl stood was polished like a mirror with the flowers reflected in it. The logs in the fire crackled and hissed, and the big grandfather clock made a deep, tick-tock, tick-tock, like a man content with his job because he knows he is doing it well. His feet sunk into the thick rug, and suddenly Davie knew that this was the sort of home he wanted. Perched on the edge of the deep Chesterfield chair, he would have liked to lean back and revel in the soft comfort.

Then Mr Lawson came back. 'Well, David, this is very pleasant. Last time we had a chat was when you caddied for me against Panmure.'

'I did not bring you much luck that day, Mr Lawson.'

'Not your fault, David, I was up against a better man, but we had a grand time. Now you are a clubmaker with Mr Johnston. Right?'

'Yes,' Davie hesitated, then 'I'm – I'm mindful to be a professional golfer and to go to America.'

'And not a bad ambition, a good many young men have gone and done well, and what can I do to help you?'

Desperately, he raked his mind, trying to find the right words. 'I'd like to learn a lot more. Like the school, but different, things that might help me when – ' But it was no good, words to explain his need just would not come.

'And that's a worthy ambition, David. No man can ever know enough. Let's see now, first thing, I should study and read some American History.'

'Is there a class for that at the night school?'

Mr Lawson smiled. 'I'm afraid not, David. But look, I'll write down a list of books you should read and send it to Miss Smart at the library, she will get them for you.'

'Thanks, Mr Lawson, and anything else?'

'You'd be the better for a course in commercial studies, accounts, book-keeping and so on, if you can face it.'

'I – I wasn't very good at arithmetic at school.'

'Was it because it really beat you, or because you did not try hard enough?'

For a moment, Davie was taken aback. The minister sounded just like the teacher, then he saw the twinkle in the friendly eyes, and relaxed, 'I didn't really try as hard as I should.'

'I like your honest answer, David, and I'll tell you something, even to the day, I'm never very sure what seven times seven amounts to, and that's half laziness to learn and half plain stupidity.' Mr Lawson leaned back in his chair and laughed.

'It was the nine times table that gave me the most trouble,' Davie confessed and laughed with him.

'Still, David,' Mr Lawson sat upright, and put his hands on his knees, 'you will be going to a land of businessmen, and to be able to count and figure would be a necessary thing.'

'If you think I should.' Davie was doubtful, sums and counting were something he had left behind with pleasure, and now to go back to them!

'And most important of all, David,' Mr Lawson went on, 'I think you should make a study of English.'

'English!' Davie was horrified. 'You mean learning to talk

lah-di-dah!'

Now the minister's laugh really rang out. He leaned right back in his chair, then stopped short, and sat up quickly again. 'I'm sorry, Davie I shouldn't have laughed – that was rude – but if you could have seen your expression—'

It was hard to understand what he meant, so Davie just smiled. Then the minister went on more seriously, 'No, David, the last thing I should ever want to hear is you talking with an affected accent. Keep your good Scots tongue. It's the accent of the soil you've sprung from, and a thing to be proud of. By English, I mean the study of language, words, learning to use them properly, you couldn't do better.

'Words, it's through them that man has learned everything he knows. It is in words that we store the wisdom of mankind and communicate new ideas. Learn about words, study them, use them; the man who can talk, express himself properly, no bragging you understand, but able to talk quiet and confident, with the right mixture of assurance and humility, that's the man who can influence other men.'

'If it will help me to be a better – ' Davie began.

'It'll not make you a better golfer, nor yet a better man. But it will help you to make the most of yourself. I'll give you a note for Mr Ness at the night school.'

As Mr Lawson accompanied him to the door, Davie said 'It's kind of you to help me like this, Mr Lawson, I know I should come to the church oftener.'

'So you should. But I don't want you to come because you're made to, or even to please me. I would like to see you there of your own accord – your own free will.'

He stood by the open door in silence, then Davie felt a light touch on his shoulder. 'Just one thing, just one thing, don't tell your father and mother that you're going to church and you're actually sneaking out with a golf club hidden down your trouser leg.'

Guilt made Davie speechless. Sunday play was strictly forbidden, and the club down the trouser leg was the only way of getting a little practice on the Sabbath. That the minister should know of his guilty acts was a shock; would he report it to the links committee?

Lawson saw the stricken look and reassured him, 'We're all backsliders at times, David. Every man has to battle between his duty – and his inclinations. Once or twice on a fine Sunday, I've seen you walking stiff-legged, and knew what you were up to, and I must confess I envied you.'

3.

The following summer, Davie was the first winner of the newly inaugurated junior links championship, open to all boys resident in the burgh, and under sixteen years of age. The local paper, reported the final.

> James Lang and David Crombie were the finalists, and a right good final it was. Quite a gallery followed the boys, and was rewarded by flashes of finished play fit for hardened medallists. David Crombie was the winner by the decisive margin of five and four, and to say the least, this young man is very impressive indeed. He plays with an air of purpose, and a maturity of manner strange in one so young. He is by no means tall, and obviously has still to reach the peak of his power. We will watch this young lad closely. He is a future champion.

That was a wonderful night. Quite a crowd of people were waiting around the starter's box, ready to follow them, his dad and Bert Sproggie among them. His dad had wanted to caddy for him, but Davie thought it wasn't quite the thing, a boy's father carrying his clubs, so Chae Whitton caddied for him.

It was a queer feeling, playing in front of a crowd, and it made him feel self-conscious, though he did try to forget that they were there and concentrated on the game. Of course, he knew how top players behaved in front of their galleries, and acted the part. When you came to play a shot, you just walked through the crowd as if they weren't there, then looked to the hole, then at your lie, exchanged a low word or two with your caddy and took a club from him. After the shot was played, you just walked on, and let the crowd trail after you.

After two or three holes, despite the crowd making him feel nervous, he knew he would win, for Jimmy Lang, though not a bad player, hadn't the power to get ahead. Davie was three up at the turn, then four up and five to play; poor Jimmy knew it was all up for him then, but he was game enough and played his best. But when Davie's fourth shot lipped the hole at the fourteenth, after Jimmy being in a sand trap, and taking five to reach the edge of the green, that was it. Jimmy, too, knew how the good players behaved. He picked up both balls, took off his cap and walked over to Davie and congratulated him, though a tear wasn't far from his eye.

Then the crowd came spilling over the green, patting Davie on the back, shaking hands and cheering, while the grown-ups clapped their hands and applauded.

His dad came over and just touched his shoulder, then went and patted Jimmy on the back. 'Never mind, son, you can try again next year,' he told him. 'Davie will be over the age then.'

They started to walk in. Bert Sproggie was lighting his pipe as Davie came opposite him; he just gave a wink and a twitch of his head. 'That's my boy.'

The crowd gathered round the starter's box, and Provost Rattray made a speech, and said how they wanted to encourage young players, and handed over the cup to be held for one year, then the surprise extra of a voucher giving him two new clubs, and three new balls from Johnston's. Jimmy received a medal and a voucher for a club and ball.

Then it was over, and he walked through the crowd carrying his cup, and everyone clapping. His dad and Bert admired his trophy, then little Beth Johnston came skipping up. She grabbed both his arms, and did a dance, pulling him around with her, cup and all. 'Oh, you won, Davie, you won, I knew you'd win!'

Chae was there with his clubs, and gave an indulgent smile, pleased to see a kiddy happy, so Davie did the same. 'I'll take the clubs now,' he told Chae, and held out his free arm, that way he could get Beth to leave go, but Chae said, 'No, no, champions don't carry their own clubs,' and held on to them.

Bert Sproggie said, 'Your dad and me are off to the Club,' and Davie saw his father's expression. His face was radiant with delight, he was puffed up with pleasure in the cup and the crowd's applause. It was only then that the full wonder of his accomplishment burst on Davie. His dad was happy, because of him. He could hear the glorious sound of 'Swanee'.

Then Mary came forward and held out her hand. 'Congratulations, David, my father said you would win easily.' When her hand touched his, he felt his face go hot, and he choked out his thanks. Then they began to walk away from the crowd, Beth linked her arm in his, still doing her skippy dance; then wonder of wonders, Mary put her hand lightly through his other arm, she did the same to Chae on the far side, but that didn't really matter. He was Junior Links Champion, going home, carrying the cup, arm in arm with Mary. And beside him, carrying his clubs, was his loyal friend, Chae.

4.

Now R. Y. Johnston had a new showcard in his window. 'We are proud to announce that our staff includes R. Sproggie, former Club and Links Champion, W. D. Day, present Links Champion, and D. F. Crombie, Junior Links Champion, they all play and recommend Johnston Thistle

Brand clubs.'

That wasn't really true, for some of Davie's clubs were still the ones that his dad had picked up for him. But now a secret enterprise was in progress.

Bert Sproggie was forging him a completely new set of heads. 'There's no hurry, son, for you still have a good bit to grow. But I want you to play full-length clubs, so we'll make them all flat in the lie, that will keep your swing flat, and give you more power.'

By the time he was sixteen, Davie was working in the front shop on wooden clubs. Now he wore a clean, white apron and stood at a bench.

Mr Johnston served most of the retail customers who called at the shop. Always smart in his hairy tweed suit and highly polished shoes, towards his clients, his air was that of a learned, professional man, giving grave pronouncements on weighty matters, for what could be more important than the choice of a new cleek or putter.

If he happened to be absent, then the counter was attended by Tam Anderson, the leading man in the woods department, a lean fair man, who carved wooden heads with the dedicated passion of an artist, but had little sales talk beyond saying, 'How do you like this one?'

On a wild, blustery day in March, in the second year of Davie's apprenticeship, after his round of the men, Mr Johnston went off on his usual inspection of the fence, which, curiously enough, was still not yet repaired. All the men relaxed, and this morning, even more so, as Anderson, who was inclined to toady to Mr Johnston, was absent from work, suffering from the new scourge of influenza. Then, before the boss could have got his feet on the sawdust of the bar, a customer walked into the shop.

The boss out, and Anderson off ill, the men looked at one another, while the customer waited. Then Tam Knox gave Davie a nudge. 'Away you and talk to him, you're the lad that's studying the fancy talk, away you, and patter to him.'

Not a task Davie fancied at all, but he went forward and

64

said: 'Good morning, I'm sorry that Mr Johnston is out, maybe I can help you.'

Tam Knox muttered, 'Well, I'll be damned, d'you hear the style of him, someone better nip along to the Wallace for the boss, before he gets himself tied in knots.'

One of the lads ran along the railway line, and brought the boss out of the bar, and he wasn't very pleased to have to swallow his whisky quick like a dose of medicine. Still, he hurried along, and came striding through to the front to take over from Davie, but a few paces away, he stopped and listened.

And what he heard amazed him. Davie wasn't exactly an orator, but three sessions at the night school had helped a lot, and he was talking on a subject which was meat and drink to him.

'With your height, sir, I don't think that's the club for you, for one thing, you need a more upright lie, and for another, more weight in the sole, to bring you straight through, and up, for your swing will be steep as you are so tall.'

Mr Johnston was silent, much as he liked to officiate where his customers were concerned, he realised that the apprentice had the situation well in hand. Sure enough, in a few minutes, the man bought two clubs, and thanking Davie profusely for his help, walked out.

It was only when he put the money in the till, and was restacking the clubs brought down for inspection, that Davie saw the men and the boss watching him. Whilst he had been serving the customer, the unaccustomed task, working with words and his mind, instead of tools and his hands, had absorbed him, everything else forgotten, even his shyness. Now he coloured deeply, embarrassed by the knowledge that he had been overheard, and watched.

Mr Johnston said nothing till he finished replacing the clubs, then as he started back to the bench, the boss said, 'Aye, Davie, you're quite a lad.'

From the tone used, Davie found it difficult to decide whether the words were meant as praise, blame or merely an idle remark. It wasn't likely to be the first, for Mr Johnston wasn't lavish with his praise at any time. So Davie said nothing, and picked up the rasp he had been using when the customer came in.

Then, 'Move your tools up to the top vice,' the boss went on, 'and when anyone comes in after this, when I'm not here, you better attend to them. Anderson doesn't like talking to customers.'

A dozen times most mornings, he had to lay down his work, and go forward with a 'Good morning, sir.'

Had he but reallsed it, this was perhaps the best training for his life ahead. It bred self-confidence when meeting strangers, and was the beginning of an easy assurance when talking of golfing matters, since he knew more than most people about it, as he not only made but played clubs.

5.

Due to the minister's choice of books, his earlier impressions of America were now clarified. Whilst the books permitted him to glory, boylike, in the ride of Paul Revere, they had, at the same time, given him to see and understand the impatience and frustrations of the American colonists in their vast treasure house of a country, hemmed in and tied down by the short-sighted stupidity of the British Government. He understood, too, the passions which racked that nation in the middle of the nineteenth century and culminated in the Civil War. Now he began to understand why America offered so much to men of craft and skill, the place was so vast, so rich, so busy.

Happy as his life was, he could still realise the narrowness and shortcomings of it. His dad worked hard, yet all his toil gave him no leisure, and no money to spare for extras, never mind luxuries. It was a grand place to live, there were the links and the seashore, but no money for getting about and seeing other places. The farthest he had been, was over to St

Andrews for a golf match, and that only ten miles as the crow flies. He had, though, crossed the Tay Bridge to get there. And now a letter had come back from Andy Cunningham who'd gone away as a pro in the States. There were photographs in it, of his grand house with a big verandah in front, and the smartly dressed wife he had married out there, and to crown it all, Andy actually had a motor car of his own. No matter how a man worked here, he could never earn enough to buy a motor car, unless he was a head man, like Martin Menzies' father, or the doctor.

So Davie worked and studied toward the day when he could set out to try luck in the New World. He still played himself to and from work, and though he still wasn't as tall for his age as he would have liked, his increasing strength enabled him to hit the ball further and further, and due to constant practice, more accurately.

And the new clubs forged for him by Bert brought more surprises; for now he played often with the veteran, and, indeed, could almost match him stroke for stroke. The hickory shafts he had were all carefully graded for spring, and it was thrilling to discover the wonder of correct timing. Indeed, it seemed to Davie that the slower and easier he swung, the faster and farther went the ball. Now began to emerge that slow, graceful motion that the world was later to call 'The Crombie Swing'.

It was always beautiful to watch. The gentle curving of the clubhead, the easy, almost casual wind up of trunk and shoulders, the nonchalant downswing, as though not caring whether he struck the ball or not, and then the shattering impact as ·he connected, and sent the tiny white sphere hurtling towards its mark with the venomous speed of a rifle bullet.

He worked, he studied, he played, he practised, but now his fun, the hours of relaxation, had dried up, for he and Chae Whitton had drifted apart. They had not quarrelled, it was merely that Chae had developed tastes which Davie could not share. Chae had developed into a dandy with gaudy tastes in socks and ties; he was a frequenter of billiard saloons, and liked to drink. His tastes in companions, too, had changed, rumour had it he was often in the company of Rodger Johnston and Martin Menzies, who, despite his stammering shyness, was said to be a wild devil when off the chain. It did a local girl no good to be seen with either of them. Not that the girls cared much what their elders said, and there was always the temptation of the Menzies car which Martin was now allowed to drive. In these activities, Davie had no part. Not that he lacked the devil, merely that he developed later. But Davie loved the music of this time. Jazz was loud and strident with 'Margie', 'Swanee' and the 'Sheik of Araby'. There were haunting waltzes too, like the Missouri Waltz, 'Bubbles' and 'Wyoming'. But most affecting of all was the memory of Mary Johnston playing 'Swanee'.

CHAPTER FIVE

I.

BERT Sproggie's advice was sound, but not always easy to take, especially in the strain of a tight game like this. 'Play the course, go for par figures, never mind what the other chap's doing,' was his dictum. 'Concentrate on your shots, but in between them think about anything ye like, anything but the game. That way you'll no get aw' tightened up inside worryin'.'

Think about anything. A big crowd tonight, just about the biggest ever to follow me, so far. Can't remember seeing so many before, and more waiting at every green. You read in stories about the sound women's silk frocks make when they walk 'frou, frou, frou, frou'. The crowd following a golf match makes the same sort of sound, but it seems to be in your head, rather than hearing it. Funny – they start off ragged, then seem to fall into step like soldiers. The only ones to break the rhythm are the bairns, always scampering to get in front, and be able to see. Now they've stopped. Queer, how unwilling they are to step back and give you room to swing.

His dad always made way for him through the crowd. Then he looked towards the green. 'Spoon, Davie?' and took it from the bag.

Crowd right round the green. Hope it doesn't hit any of them. Concentrate now. Swing easy.

That's a good one – a wee bit right of the flag. It'll swing in and run forward off the bank. Shouldn't be far away.

Wait until Baxter plays. He's taking an iron, just emphasising he had the length on me from the tee. A good shot too. Wonder if he's nearer than me? This is a tight game. Cut and thrust all the time. The fifteenth now, still all square, and never below par figures.

Stop worrying. Think about anything but the game between shots. Frou, frou, and the bairns scampering. Funny how the dogs always run too, when they see the youngsters.

His dad always insisted on caddying for him now, and seemed to enjoy it. Never thought Miss Patullo would come out and watch tonight. Fair worried about the boss. Now he seems to spend all his time in the bar at the Wallace. Hardly even bothers to serve a customer. Mary Johnston's got a new girl friend out with her tonight. A bonnie bit stuff, but no a patch on Mary.

His dad in front, forcing a way through the crowd. 'Make way for the players, please.' Baxter behind him, not saying a word. Bert Gallet at the flag, doing his referee. 'You to play first, Dave.'

Line it up. Straight road to the hole, maybe about six yards. Now the crowd go dead silent. You can hear and feel them holding their breath. Relax, empty your mind. Let your breath out slow, easy . . . steady now, don't look up after you've struck.

The sudden 'Aaaaah' and the clink of the ball going down, then the great burst of handclapping. Touch the bonnet to acknowledge, and step back. Poor Baxter's got to sweat it out now. Bert Sproggie always said, 'When you sink a long putt, and leave the other man to try for a half, you switch the thing right round, and force him on to the defensive. If you miss, he's always safe for a half, but if you sink it, he tightens up sweating.'

Stand and wait, easy-like. Not fair, hoping that Baxter will miss, but he has! Funny, the sound of the crowd makes when a putt is missed, same sort of 'Aaaaah', yet you can tell the difference. Now the crowd melts and runs in excitement. With the change in the game, the pound of their feet drowns Bert Gallet's cry of 'Crombie, one up!'

Still three holes to go. Anything can happen yet. Don't think about it between shots. Wonder what the papers will

70

say about this game?

It was his dad's idea. At the time, Davie would have hesitated. Now the crowd was really excited, hardly waiting till you'd played before rushing madly on to get into place for the next. The news must have travelled fast. More and more folk were hurrying down, to be in at the finish. Driving off from the last tee, it was practically a lane of people from tee to distant green. The long eighteenth, that heart-breaking two-shotter, where carrying the burn to get home was always a gamble to even the longest hitters.

After two hard halves at the sixteenth and seventeenth, the crowd was running excitedly. The rhythm of their feet had changed now. Clots of people formed at the bridges over the burn, but the youngsters and the keener ones couldn't wait. Squeals and splashes told of those who hadn't jumped far enough.

Empty your mind. Don't think of the game between shots. Dormie one, but anything can happen yet, especially at this hole. Think about other things till it's time for the next shot. Bert Sproggie had said the other day, 'My brother-in-law's comin' home for a few weeks in the winter, Davie. I mentioned you in the last letter I wrote him.'

Davie took his time driving off the last tee. The crowd were still fluid, spreading out, all trying to get a view. Easy now, no strain . . . wait for it . . .

It was the best drive he'd ever struck. Clean as a whistle, with the long boring arc that landed still going forward, and went racing, pounding on. Baxter had a good shot too, but higher in flight, a ball that landed, flopped once or twice, then stopped.

Baxter played first, a whack with a cleek that stopped a few short yards from the water, leaving an easy pitch to the green.

Davie's ball was a good few yards further on. He waited for the crowd to settle, then looked at his father. For a split second, it seemed that time stood still, and the scene burned itself in his mind.

71

The silent crowd about him; the blue evening sky, with its flight of homing gulls overhead. His father carrying the clubs, dressed as always in his rough, drab, clothes, dark against his clean shirt, collarless, with the brass stud at the neck; the trousers always seemed a little on the short side, revealing the tops of his working boots. Two red spots of excitement burned on his cheeks, his voice shook with tension. 'Go for it, Davie', he tugged the brassie from the bag. 'Go for it, son, you can dae it!'

For a moment, Davie doubted the wisdom of this. The obvious thing was to play safe. Then he read his father's mind. You can't always get what you want by playing safe, and if it came off, the crowd would love it. Maybe it was playing to the gallery, but it would give him some satisfaction too. A victory of two holes was more decisive than a narrow, last green win.

The crowd nearest him gasped with excitement when they saw his intention. Steady now, don't tighten up – wait for it but, even as he struck, Davie knew that the daring gamble had come off. His long raking shot dropped in a slow curve beyond the dreaded burn, and went racing on to the green.

Even before the ball landed, the crowd melted into a racing stampede to get a good view of the finish. As he struggled to replace the club, the crowd went surging past, parting to each side as water round a stone. A little boy raced by yelling, 'Hey, you lads, Crombie's gotten his second on the green!' quite unaware that his information was yelled in Davie's ear.

Now carried along, just a unit in the crowd, Davie felt a hand on his shoulder, and looked up to see Baxter smiling down at him. 'You've knocked the nails into my box now,' he said ruefully, 'but we'll have to play the comedy out.'

That week, the local papers said,

. . . After his narrow, but quite decisive win over R. Y. Baxter, young Crombie bids fair to becoming our youngest ever Links Champion. True, he had still to meet

72

the redoubtable Eck Black in the final, but Eck must start carrying a heavy mental handicap, for Davie has already bested him twice this season, in other events. At the tender age of eighteen, we know of no other player in Angus, or Fife, for that matter, whom we could back to match young Crombie. Even lacking inches as he is, Crombie is long hitting and accurate. His future as a golfer, should he ever go over to professional ranks, should be bright indeed.

Then, as if the victory hadn't been sufficiently heady wine to lift his feet from the ground, the Friday evening following, he was playing a game for pleasure with Bert Sproggie, his dad carrying the clubs, 'Jist for the sake o' the walk and the fresh air', as he put it, when approaching the eighteenth hole they met three men, who approached from a knoll and had evidently been waiting for them.

Now the oldest-looking came up to Davie. 'Mr David Crombie?' And Davie, thanks to his studies perfectly at ease said, 'Yes – that's me'.

'My name's Smithers.' He held out a card. The Gothic print swam before Davie's eyes, only the words Royal and Ancient club stood out.

'This is Mr McLaren, and Mr Ross.' He indicated his companions. 'We're looking for new, young blood, to field the strongest possible team against England and Ireland in September. Would you care to take part in a trials game – Saturday week at St Andrews?'

At first the words hardly registered in his mind. Then he saw the radiant delight in Bert Sproggie's face, and the high, burning pride in his dad's. 'Well, thank you all, gentlemen – I'll be pleased to have a try.' He hesitated and said, 'I'm sorry, this is my father, Mr James Crombie and Mr Sproggie – foreman clubmaker.'

'Your son has the makings of a world-class golfer, Mr Crombie,' Smithers said, as they shook hands. 'You must be very proud of him.'

'Oh, Davie's a good steady lad,' his dad said quietly. 'He'll dae his best to make a go of it for you.'

'You'll get confirmation by letter,' the man called Ross told him. 'We asked at your house and your mother directed us here. Naturally, there's nothing in it save honour, but since you're still an apprentice, we'll cover your out-of-pocket expenses.'

As the men walked away, Bert Sproggie threw his arms round Davie. 'That's my boy! The highest honour a laddie can get – to play for his country!'

Now the full extent of it had burst in his mind, 'Oh, Da – isn't it great!'

'Aye, it's just fine, Davie but keep the heid, son. There'll be as good, ay, and even better players than you there. Just you keep the heid.'

Then Bert Sproggie said, 'Ye're richt, Jeemie, dead richt.' And turned to Davie, 'I'm warnin' ye now, Davie – if you get cocky, let Eck Black beat you in the final, and then make a muck o' the trials in St Andrews, I'll kick yer backside right roun' the forge!'

And Davie smiled to both his mentors. 'All right. I'm sure the thought of a sore behind will keep me humble. I'll do my best.'

But after such news, further play was impossible. They walked home together, and despite the warnings he'd had, Davie walked with peals of triumph playing in his mind.

2.

He won the final, beating Eck Black by a narrow margin. He attended the trials at St Andrews, enjoyed the experience of playing over the famous old course, yet considered it not so difficult as the championship circuit at Carnoustie.

On a dull Saturday in September, Davie waited for the train, his clubs on his shoulder, his dad beside him, taking a few days off work, and travelling with him to the course in

England where the International was to be played. His father in a blue suit, and despite all his struggles, his rasping blue tie refused to sit right.

Bert Sproggie came to see them off, regretting he was unable to go with them. 'And if you dinna gie thae English and Irish lads their licks,' he told Davie, 'I'll—'

'I know,' Davie interrupted, 'I'll have a sore behind for weeks.'

Wireless was still far away from the Angus coast, so all the town could do was bite their nails wondering, then make a flying dive for the latest edition of the papers, to find out what was happening. To begin with, it wasn't much then, later in the week, it was better and better, so much so that when the train bringing them home on a golden September evening drew in, Davie was surprised to find nearly all the golf club there, and a crowd of the town's folk.

He and his father alighted to a ragged cheer, and a storm of handclapping. Bert Sproggie greeted them first.

'Well, Auld yin – I'll no need to be standing up to take my tea?' Davie asked.

''Deed no, son. And this damp weather in the week has started my rheumatics again – I doubt if I could lift a leg high enough tae kick you.'

Then the Reverend Mr Lawson. 'Well done, David – well done! The whole town's proud of you.' Then to his father, 'You'll be a proud man tonight, eh, Jimmie?'

And lastly, Mr Johnston. There was a girl with him, and seeing her through the crowd at first, Davie's heart turned over, thinking it might be Mary but it was Beth, growing up certainly, but still a dainty wee thing in a gym slip. 'Oh, Davie – Davie – isn't it great!' she cried, seizing his arm in both hands.

So they set along the front, towards home. Beth walked beside Davie, and with the frankness of a child, took his hand and held it. And Davie listened to her happy prattle, and wished her sister Mary could have come to greet him. Beth was a nice wee soul, right enough. . . .

At the door of the Wallace, Mr Johnston said, 'Well, lads, I think we're aw' due a celebration dram—'

Then Davie's father hesitated. 'It's kind of you, Johnston, and I'll be happy to accept in the club tonight, but the wife's been on her own aw' week and she'll have a meal ready.'

'Say no more Jeemie, say no more. We'll see you later and make a night o' it.'

He and Bert Sproggie went in. Beth left them at her gate.

But after the meal was eaten, his father smiled over the table. 'Ye did well, son – but—'

'Dinna get cocky,' Davie finished for him. 'Don't lose the heid.'

His father nodded, busy lighting his pipe.

'I've learned a lot,' Davie went on. 'It's not easy, playing a course you're strange to – and there was a lot of real grand players there – ' he grinned slightly, 'besides me.'

His father smiled, then grew serious again. 'Jist aye bear this in mind, Davie. You're a grand, strong player today but tomorrow or the next day another lad will come along who's just as good, and maybe even a hair better. So keep trying, son – there's nae perfection.'

'I realise that already, Da, that big Irish lad just about had me on my knees.'

His father nodded. 'Aye, I thought that too, Davie – two down and three to go then you started the fireworks, and took the last three holes.' Davie paused. 'Maybe the luck was with me.'

'No maybe aboot it, Davie. You canna expect the ball to run for you all the time.'

3.

Mary Crombie put her newly emptied ash pan in its place under the fire, and wiped the already gleaming steels on the grate, before picking up a duster to give the kitchen another lick round, for no decent woman would let a new year in with a speck of dirt about the place.

She worked carefully over the big array of trophies displayed on the big, old-fashioned farmhouse dresser; aye, she thought, Davie was a lad for bringing home cups and shields, even if he did have them only for a year.

The big one in the centre was the Links Championship, with his name on the silver plate at the bottom. The shield was the County Trophy, then the Club Cup, and the Calcutta Cup, what a cleaning they made! But he seemed to be a grand player. She had walked round with the crowd one night, watching him, but couldn't make head or tail of what it was all about. Still, she enjoyed the prestige of being his mother, for now folk pointed her out in the street, and strangers came up and asked when Davie's next match was, so they could watch him.

He seemed fair set on going to America, though he never spoke much about it, well, he was a good boy, and if that was what he wanted . . . but now and then she would glance at the array of trophies and think she would have been the proudest woman in the land if they been for ploughing or prize beasts.

Then Davie came out of the bedroom, looking smart in his new suit. 'Do you think the trousers are a wee bit long, Ma?'

'Och, maybe, but they'll come up as you wear them,' she said, and his dad, busy struggling with his hard collar said, 'You're lookin' fine, son,' and got ahead with his task of getting glasses and bottles ready.

Jimmie was the Head Greenkeeper now, with a staff of three, and two of them were due to first-foot them right after twelve. So now the new cloth was set across one edge of the table, all ready with black bun, shortbread and bottles and glasses forming the background.

The last minutes of 1923 ticked away. At the same time, the hooter at Andrew Gowan's blared out its welcome to the New Year, and a train in the station did the same. Its long blast sounded sad and lonely, coming from away down the line. As the sounds died away, Davie took the glass of port wine from his father, and pledged them both. 'Happy New Year, Ma.' He put an arm round her shoulders, and kissed her cheek.

Her eyes softened. She held him by the shoulders for a moment. 'And a Happy New Year to you, Davie – I – I hope things go well for you.'

Moved by the warmth of her words, Davie crossed to his father. 'Happy New Year, Da,' he said, and they shook hands. 'Happy New Year to you, Davie, my son, and I wish you aw' the luck in the world.'

The important thing was never mentioned, yet it was there, in all their minds. In Davie's mind ran the thought, 'Will I be away this spring?' For now the pattern was familiar. A good player won some local competitions, then early in the spring the local paper had half a column saying that so-and-so had accepted the post as Assistant Professional at such and such a place in the States. Then the wise ones, looking very knowing, said they'd known all about it since the New Year. It was all fixed up when that uncle, or brother, or cousin was home . . . And Bert Sproggie had told his brother-in-law and he was due home now.

And he was to meet him soon, and have a game with him. Bert had promised he would arrange it. Davie glanced over the collection of trophies. They were his stepping stones. Now the only obstacle was one he was powerless to correct. His lack of height. Would they say he wasn't tall enough? Always he tried to make the most of himself. His back was ramrod straight, his stride long, so that walking behind or with a taller person, he wouldn't seem to be hurrying.

Steps sounded outside, mingled with cheerful voices. 'That'll be the lads,' his father said, then called out, 'Come away in, boys, dinnae stand chappin' at the door.'

Joe Wallace and Will Gibson came in, their fresh, well-scrubbed faces ruddy from the cold, and gay with New Year drinks and smiles. 'Happy New Year to awbody' they called, and began pulling things from their pockets.

First the ceremonious salute to Davie's mother, 'Happy

78

New Year, Mrs Crombie,' then Joe laid a lump of coal on the hearth, and handed over a red herring all dressed up in fancy paper.

'Come away and have a bit glass,' his father said, and poured out drams for them both.

'Happy New Year, Jimmie.' They pledged him. 'Here's tae a good summer, and enough rain to gie us some growth.'

Then they turned to Davie, 'And here's to the wee daddy o' them aw'.' Will Gibson cried, and maybe a wee thing happy in his dram, 'I'll bet yer Ma and Da's proud of you, wan o' the best golfers this Links has ever had – or likely to!'

Then he saw the empty hands, and grew mock indignant. 'Huh – whit kind of way is this to treat a top player. If yer folk'll no wet yer whistle, I will.' And he began heaving and tugging at the half bottle of whisky stuck in his pocket.

Davie saw the alarm in his dad's eyes, and his mother said quietly, 'Just a wee one, and go easy with it, Davie.'

Easy to see why she was worried. Clubbie Johnston's drinking was the talk of the place now. He only walked through the workshops on his way to the bar, leaving Miss Patullo and Bert Sproggie to run the business.

Davie smiled reassuringly to them both. Joe was happily munching black bun and cheese, while Will was still trying to heave the bottle from his pocket. 'Don't worry, Ma, I'll not be brought home fu'.'

He took the glass offered him, and pledged them, letting a trickle of the rich spirit go down his throat, then, when he saw the chance, poured the rest into Joe's near-empty glass. 'I'll away up the town now,' he told them.

'Aye, sure, have a good time, son,' his dad said. His mother repeated her warning about drink, but this time, only her eyes spoke, and he was grateful for her silence for now both Joe and Will had their eyes on him. 'I'll bet he's got a braw bit lassie dated up,' Will said, then Joe added, 'Gie her an extra cuddle from me, Davie, I'm kinda out the way of it now.'

'I'll leave the door on the latch for you,' his mother called out, 'and dinna be too late, if you're for a game in the morning.'

Outside it was darkly clear, with stars, and the sea murmuring. The haar-covered frosted grass crisped under his feet as he hurried towards the town lights.

The pavement, when he reached it, sparkled with frosty diamonds in the light from the street lamp. Along the front, every house had its room windows lit, and cheerful sounds came from within. Then he saw two figures, and recognised one of them. The other could only be – his stomach tightened up – Andy Cunningham, the pro home from America – if the Scots-American liked him, he might . . . but what if he was considered too small? That was the constant shadow over his dream. He must meet the American now, and judge his reaction.

Lengthening his stride, he was just overtaking them, when Bert looked over his shoulder, and saw him. 'Davie, ma son, and a Happy New Year to you laddie!' his voice maybe warmed by a dram or two.

Then he turned to his companion, 'This is Davie Crombie, our youngest ever Links Champion Davie, this is my brother-in-law.'

'Glad to know you, Davie,' the big man said as they shook hands. 'Bert tells me you're the top man around here. How d'ya make out in a head wind?'

The words were kindly jest, but Davie stiffened and held the tall man's eyes. 'I manage fine. The wind disnae reach far enough down to bother me.'

Sproggie's laugh bellowed out to the stars, and the Scots-American joined in.

Then his hand fell on Davie's shoulder. 'Good boy! Say, what about having a game with me tomorrow – heck this is tomorrow – today?'

This was it. The words he desperately wanted to hear. 'I'll be honoured, any time you like.'

Bert Sproggie stuck his pipe in his mouth, and fumbled for matches. 'I telt you Davie was the boy for you.'

'Say around eleven?' Cunningham asked, and Davie

80

accepted. That would give him some time to get some sleep, and by the progress of these two revellers, neither of them would be quite at their best, even at that hour.

He watched their ambling progress under the gas lamps, and his lips pursed to an almost soundless whistle of 'Swanee'. This was it. He must put on a good show tomorrow. The sensible thing was to get some sleep, but another urge was just as strong as his ambition. Chae Whitton was waiting for him to go first footing and . . .

There he was, under the lamp at the corner, in a tight blue overcoat, with a white scarf at his neck. 'Come on.' His greeting was curt. 'I thought you were bedded.'

Walking beside him, Davie felt excitement rise when he realised where they were going. In all his years of working, he had never been in his employer's house, now he was going to first foot there. Mary would be there.

Mr Johnston, band-box smart in his hairy suit, opened the door. 'Come away in boys, a Happy New Year to you!'

His eyes watered, his walk had a roll, he was carrying a good load, yet still in command of himself.

Then Rodger appeared. 'Throw your coats anywhere chaps, and let's have a song or two.' He had grown very smart in his dress this last year or so, but favoured dark suits with fancy stripes, though he copied his father and wore a bow tie.

Their front room was the brightest Davie had ever seen. It had electric light, from a clear bowl hanging by chains, a coal fire flamed in a grate of dark marble. A thick carpet covered the floors, whilst the big easy chairs and the settee were heaped with gay coloured cushions. The piano stood against the wall opposite the fire. How long ago it seemed since that night he and Chae had stood outside listening.

Mrs Johnston came in, very stiff with a big row of amber beads round her neck. 'A Happy New Year, David.' Her hand was cold and limp, then she turned to Mr Johnston who was presiding behind a side table bearing an array of glasses and bottles and black bun and shortbread. 'I hope you're not giving these young men whisky?'

'Have a heart, mother, it's New Year,' Rodger said, and Mr Johnston, from his corner behind the table, said, 'Dinna fash yerself, woman, just a drop of sherry.'

Handing round the glasses, he asked, 'Whaur's the lassies, what in all the world are they doing?' Then he crossed to the door and called out, 'Come on, lassies, there's some braw lads down here fair gaspin'.'

Mrs Johnston was angry. 'Rodger – what way is that to talk – and your own daughter's guests.'

'Oh, for pity's sake, mum – ' young Rodger, her son, said. Then Mr Johnston laughed again. ' 'Deed. I'm thinkin' they could learn from their mother. You should have seen the way she jumped to it, when she was stalking me.'

Mrs Johnston went white round the mouth, and Rodger laughed shrilly. Suddenly, Davie felt embarrassed for Mrs Johnston – even sympathy for her – still, she rallied, and passed the thing off as a joke, sitting herself down by the fire, smiling. Davie felt his jaws ache in sympathy. Then her smile withered as Mr Johnston poured himself a generous measure of whisky, and downed it at a gulp.

'The girls are poshing themselves up to make an entrance and impress you,' Rodger said to Chae and Davie, and then Beth came in, dressed as Davie had seen her last, in blue gym slip and white blouse. Davie wondered if the girls at school teased her, because she was small; the boys had teased him. But she seemed happy, calling out 'Happy New Year' and then went over to Davie, grasping his arm by the elbows as she'd done the night he won the Junior Championship. 'Davie is my darlin', my darlin', my darlin' ' she sang, doing her wee skippy dance pulling him round with her. 'Davie is my darlin', the Links Champion. The folk all come from far and near, to see our Davie play, oh – and I'd like to sing a whole lot more, but I don't know what to say—'

'I think you've said enough,' Davie told her, and felt his ears burning.

'Och, don't you like my song?'

82

'Of course, I like it, you're a clever wee lass.' He stopped, scared at his boldness, saying that in front of her mother and father.

'Time you were in bed, Miss,' her mother called, and Beth sighed. 'Can I not wait up for a wee while longer, please?'

'Ach, let the bairn have her bit fun.' Mr Johnston half-turned from pouring himself another dram.

And then Mary came into the room, followed by two other girls. One was the girl he remembered seeing with her the night he beat Baxter, and the other was called Vera Duncan. Her father was a lawyer or something in Dundee.

Their greeting had none of the frank happiness of Beth's, they were cool, reserved, young ladies . . . Rodger broke the stiff atmosphere, 'For pity's sake – where's the funeral – let's have a tune or two, sis.'

Shyness gripped Davie. He sat quietly in a hard chair by the piano, there were so many new impressions for him to absorb, so many new things to look at and admire. The three girls were lovely, but none quite so wonderful as Mary. He had never been in such a grand room, in the company of young women before.

It was altogether a different meeting from street ones. They had neither hats or coats on here, but were elegant in fine silky dresses, or smart blouses and skirts.

Now Mary was sitting at the piano, searching for some piece of music. How slim and white her hands were and, watching them fly over the keys, Davie wondered how anyone could learn to make such music with so little effort.

Other things forced themselves on his mind. The creaminess of her neck, the sweep of her hair over her ears. Her white blouse was so thin you could see her arms and shoulders through it, and the narrow ribbons supporting whatever she wore underneath. A faint perfume like musk, came over to him as she moved. He sat quietly, not moving lest he should draw her attention to his gaze.

Now she was playing 'Alabamy Bound' and Chae was making a caper of dancing with the red-haired girl. But

Davie found more pleasure watching Mary's fingers. So quiet was he that Beth came over, and tried to pull him up. 'Come on, Davie, it's New Year – have fun!'

'Och, Davie's just a golfer,' Rodger smirked from the settee, his arm around Vera Duncan. 'But maybe he'll sing a quiet hymn for us when he gets warmed up,'

'I'm enjoying myself fine, Rodger,' Davie said, then Mrs Johnston chimed in. 'I'm sure it's a pleasure to see a young person enjoying things quietly, and not raising the roof with noise.'

'It's a pity it's no business hours, if I had a few customers to bring in, that would get Davie out of his shell,' Mr Johnston said, from his cosy corner by the drinks, and his bottle near empty.

'I'm having a grand time, thanks,' Davie called across the room, then to Mary, 'I like watching you play.'

Now the two other girls came and stood behind her, making sly glances at him. 'I think you have a crush on her,' Vera Duncan said, and the red-haired girl giggled, 'Aren't you flattered – the Links Champion.'

There seemed to be an undercurrent of meaning in the words, a sort of hidden joke. The two girls exploded into laughter. His face reddened, feeling it was at him, yet told himself that was daft.

'Please – ' He broke into their laughter. 'Play "Swanee".'

'There! See how you inspire him?' Vera asked, then to Davie, 'Isn't that the tune you whistle all the time you're playing?'

'Ach, it sorts of keeps running in my mind,' he admitted, then Chae called over, 'He's been like that since the first time he heard it – the pair of us standing outside, listening.'

The full story was told, and Chae, in turn, got a red face when Davie described, not without good-humoured malice, his antics while dancing under the street lamp.

'Go on, show us what he did,' Rodger commanded, but Davie refused. 'You can imagine it fine without me showing you.' Then to Mary, 'Go on, please, play "Swanee".'

'My – you are far behind.' Mary flashed him the only warm smile she'd given to him that evening. 'I've almost forgotten that old thing.'

But she hadn't. Her fingers began to stroke the keys, and the old magic caught at his heart.

Now he was standing behind her, a girl on each side of him. He could never be quite sure of how it happened, whether he brushed the red-haired girl's back with his hand, and she had caught it, and pulled it round her waist, then put her own arm round him, or whether he had boldly initiated the move himself, then put an arm round Vera for balance, but there he was, standing behind Mary, with each arm round a girl, and they clasping him with equal frankness.

But even whilst he enjoyed singing, his senses reeled under the impact of new and delightful sensations. He had never cuddled a girl before, and maybe the tiny amount of alcohol he had taken was getting to work, easing his shyness. He gripped both girls a little tighter, and was at once rewarded by answering pressure from both sides.

'My – would you look at him,' Chae called. 'Thae quiet ones are the devils when they get started.'

'Don't be jealous,' Rodger told him. 'The girls are getting a thrill, not any girl can boast of having been cuddled by the Links Champion.'

'And this is what lassies are for,' Mr Johnston cried from his corner, his voice blurred and thick, and the bottle at low ebb.

Mary looked round from her seat at the piano. 'I thought it was me you were supposed to have a crush on?' It was made to sound in fun, but her eyes weren't smiling.

David smiled to her, but didn't let go, indeed he couldn't for Vera was clasping his hand, pulling it further round her. 'Just a wee bit practice,' he said. 'You'll no grudge me that.'

'By the look of things, you don't need the practice,' she said, and turned to play again. Davie could feel the warmth of the girls through their clothing, and the curve of their waists.

'My – look at the time, past two o'clock,' Mrs Johnston said, not sounding very pleased, and Vera Duncan said, 'I must go, really.'

'We'll see you home,' Rodger said. 'A breath of fresh air will do us all good.'

'You and your fresh air.' Mrs Johnston sounded angry. 'I don't see the need for you trailing away out at this hour.'

'But, mother, we've got to see the girls home.'

'Charlie and Davie can do that.'

'By the way David's behaving, I think I'd better go and protect my friends,' Mary said, the words addressed to Davie, but meant for her mother.

'And I'll go along to bring Sis home,' Rodger added.

There was a tension in the air, a feeling of purposes hidden and unspoken, that Davie couldn't understand, but felt himself to be part of.

'Ach, let them go, if they've a mind to,' Mr Johnston said. 'They'll be all right with Davie.'

'Huh – walking all the road to Barry at this hour of the morning,' Mrs Johnston said, yet it seemed that her anger was more against her husband for not taking her side than against her children. 'Well, they say the young are daft at New Year, but straight back, mind, both of you.' This to Rodger and Mary. 'See that they do, David, please.'

The girls made for upstairs, and Davie thought he saw a meaning glance pass from Mary to Chae and Rodger, then decided it was only imagination. Yet even as he exchanged trivialities with Mrs Johnston the thought flashed through his mind that he was rather the outsider of this group. Local talk always coupled Rodger with Chae and Martin Menzies. Yet Menzies wasn't here tonight, and his name had never been mentioned.

The feeling of being somehow necessary to Chae and the others was heightened at the door of the room when Rodger hung back and said something to Chae in a hurried whisper. Davie pretended not to notice, and crossed the hall to get his coat.

86

As he thrust his arm into the sleeves, Beth tiptoed down the stairs, and pulled at him, turning him round so that he stood between her and the bright light coming from the room. 'Don't go, Davie – please don't go home with them.'

'But I'm only walking them along for company.'

'Please, listen to me. Go home, Davie.'

There was no misreading the earnestness in her voice, yet he couldn't understand. 'But, Beth – ' he was beginning, then the moment was shattered when Mrs Johnston came through. 'Are you not in bed yet?' She glared at Beth. 'Come on, up the stairs with you.'

So Beth said goodnight to him, as though she had only waited for that. She gave him a last, imploring look as she reached the landing, her lips forming the words. 'Please, Davie, don't go.'

But he had no time to puzzle out her warning, for at that moment Rodger and Chae bustled in, ready for the road. 'Heck, these dames not down yet?'

Then, with a flurry of shapely, silk-clad legs, with warm coats, their fur-trimmed collars framing pretty faces, they swept down the stairs in a perfumed cloud. 'All ready, boys.'

As Davie stood aside to let them pass through the dimly lit porch, a whisper in Mary's voice came back. 'Had to or she'd never have let us out.'

Then they were all out in the darkened road together; the street lamps were out, the only light greeting the first morning of the year was the cold stars.

Arms linked, the sextet strung across the road. It wasn't three lads walking three lassies from a party only, because for Davie it was the most glorious adventure ever. For now, he had Mary beside him, her arm linked through his. True, her other was linked to Chae, but that didn't matter, for Chae was his pal. This was glorious, this was 'Swanee', 'Avalon' and 'the Road to Mandalay', all rolled into one.

One street away from home, they sang, 'Margie', 'The Sheik of Araby' then, at his request, 'Swanee'.

Out on the edge of the town, Rodger pulled a bottle from

his pocket and announced that the Band of Hope soirée was now over, and the bar open.

Davie watched the two girls, in turn, tilt their heads back, and take a drink. Then Chae took Vera in his arms, and kissed her, not a quick peck, either, but one like you saw in the pictures when the boys in the front row whistled, and made rasping noises. Vera seemed a very co-operative partner in this, and Rodger was locked in a real clinch with the red-headed girl.

Davie turned to Mary, and even in the darkness, the expression on her face froze his intention. It was coldly hostile. 'Break it up!' Her voice was harsh, 'Here's the car coming.' Even in his hurt, Davie noticed she said 'the car' and not 'a car.'

Two golden scythes of light swung round the bend, then the car accelerated towards them, and stopped at the kerb. 'W-w-where in all the w-w-world have you been?' a voice called from it, and Davie recognised the voice. It was Martin Menzies.

'Just couldn't get away any sooner,' Rodger said. 'Had to do the duty by the family.'

'C-c-come on, d-d-don't waste time, get in,' Menzies called, and swung open front and rear doors.

'Sorry, Davie, we'll have to leave you here – the car only holds six with a squeeze,' Chae said, his foot on the running board.

Mary was already in the car, sitting close to Martin Menzies – she had left his side without a word. 'Hope you don't mind, old chap,' Rodger said,' 'Expect you'll want home, anyway – like enough you'll be playing tomorrow.'

The car snarled away. He watched its red tail-light wink in the distance, standing at the kerb, where they had left him.

Now, at last, he understood the criss-cross tensions and undercurrents of the last hour or so. Old bits of half-forgotten gossip floated to the top of his mind, to clear and explain things. Mrs Johnston was dead against the Menzies lad and wouldn't have him in the house, because of his

88

drinking and ploys with the lassies, yet Rodger, Chae and he had been real pally lately, Mary too. Hadn't Chae warned him about that long ago?

And he'd been made the stalking horse. Davie Crombie was a nice quiet lad, nothing in his head but golf. Davie Crombie was a safe lad. A mother need never fear for her daughter if she was with him, so Chae laid it on, arranged for him to first foot the Johnstons, so that they could all get out together, on the pretext of walking the girls home, and arranged to meet Menzies on the way.

He thrust his hands deeper into the pockets of his coat, then Mrs Johnston's last words came back, 'Straight back here, see that they do, David, please.'

So the responsibility had been thrust on him, though he hadn't realised it at the time. There would be a real stink about this, and she would likely try and blame it on him for not doing as he was told. But that was nothing compared to his own feeling of bleak loss. The precious object he had admired so long, and dreamed one day of possessing had turned suddenly to shoddy dross. Beth must have known. Loyal to her brother and sister she had said nothing to her parents, yet she had warned him.

But he couldn't help feeling the way he did about Mary. He tried to persuade himself that if he got away to America, he would really be free. The Menzies lad and his car were a sort of surgeon's knife, cutting a mental tie. But he could not feel happy in his freedom, even as previous thoughts he had always pushed aside came up again to point the truth about her out to him. She was stuck up, selfish, on the make for herself.

Oh, hell! He turned back for home.

CHAPTER SIX

I.

ABOUT the middle of January, the paper wrote:

> . . . just as we predicted, it is now confirmed that David F.
> Crombie has yielded to the lure of the mighty dollar, and
> accepted the post of Assistant Professional at Cray Creek
> Golf Club, Ohio, U.S.A. By his going, our links will be
> poorer, for not only is Davie a world-class player, but a
> quietly humorous and lovable personality. He is young to
> strike out on his own, but wise in his decision. This paper
> will watch his career with interest, for one thing is certain,
> we shall hear more of this young man.

Only a few people knew about it before it was announced,
for Cunningham was a discreet and careful man. He had
played a few holes with Davie on New Year's morning,
watched him play a dozen or so strokes, then said, 'Not much
for you to learn about this game, Davie, save that it's a
mighty cold morning. Let's get into the warm club and have
a drink.'

Then he'd sought out Mr Johnston and had a talk with
him, then, strangely enough, the Reverend Lawson, and
only after that had he talked to Davie's father and mother.

It gave the local gossips plenty of scope, coming right after
the scandal of the party. The carry-on of the Menzies lad and
Johnston's two was a fair disgrace. Pity to see a decent lad like
Crombie mixed up in it. All very well to say he hadn't been at
the affair, that he left them when the car came and walked
home. Natural enough for his friends to cover up for him,
but there's no smoke without fire, and when the quiet ones
get off the chain . . .

The morning after his future had been settled, Davie had

gone back to work; he was not sailing till mid-March, and idle in winter, wouldn't have known how to pass the time.

He expected the repercussions of the New Year party to be felt immediately; the wonderful promise of a future in America did, to some extent, soften his disappointment about Mary. Since his hours of starting and leaving work did not coincide with her movements, he never saw her, and tried not to think about her.

Menzies' parents had been away, and he had taken them to his home, where what followed, according to local gossip, would make a Babylonian orgy seem like a Sunday School treat. Whatever had happened, the telling and re-telling, with ever greater variety of detail, made tasty meat for the local wives.

Over a week passed before Mr Johnston mentioned it, and then only in passing. At work, the two new apprentices looked at Davie with ever greater respect than before, and Bert Sproggie said it was a damned shame he hadna been there, and had a bit of a fling himself. A man might as well be hanged for a sheep as a lamb, as most folk seemed to think he had been there. 'And believe me, Davie,' he stuffed tobacco into his skull pipe, 'them that talks the loudest aboot the disgrace are just plain jealous, to my way o' thinkin'.'

The day after that, Mr Johnston stopped at Davie's vice. 'Aye, and so you're for away, Davie,' he said. 'Ye're a wise lad – if I was only ten or twelve years younger, damned if I wouldn't come with you.'

'You're kidding, Mr Johnston.'

'In dead earnest, boy, and I'll tell you this. If all I hear is true, you've only got to work away out there, quiet and steady, as you've done for me, and you'll have the States in your pocket. Honest, I envy you.'

For the first time, Davie saw his employer as a man. His appearance was as immaculate as always, but his expression was tired and beaten, like one who knows defeat is inevitable but still fights on. A good craftsman, yet not strong enough a character to rule his own household, or control his family, who had plainly inherited their share of his weaknesses. His clothes were for his own pride, and his drinking, because only in a golden haze of alcohol could he live in fantasy, where his wife did not nag, and his children did not mirror his own futility.

'Aye,' he said before moving on, 'my family has had far too grand a time of it. They've gotten too much without working for it. What happened at New Year was none of your fault.'

Understanding how much it must have hurt his pride having to apologise to an employee for his children's behaviour, Davie felt pity for the man.

A minister's or J.P.'s signature was necessary for obtaining his passport, and with an hour off work, Davie had set out to see Mr Lawson. On the way back, the school was spilling its load of yelling, running, bairns, then following behind, the older ones with, among them, Beth Johnston.

She saw him at once. Davie gave her a wave, and would have passed on, but she ran over the street and caught his arm. 'Oh, Davie, I'm sorry, you should have gone home.'

'Och, it's all right. I went home.' He wished she hadn't spoken, recalling the thing was like an old wound opening afresh. 'It was kind of you to tell me.'

'I never got the chance. It was rotten of them – I know how you must have felt.'

He smiled down at her. 'Now, you're just a wee lassie, you shouldn't be worrying about things like that!'

She pulled away from his grasp, her face reddening in anger, stamping her foot. 'You always keep saying that. I can't help it.'

Suddenly he saw her, not as a schoolgirl, but as she might be in a few years' time – even in her blue sailor coat and school hat she was – why, in a few years' time, she would be even bonnier than her sister. He stopped the thought short. That was something he wanted to forget. His eyes were still on her face, admiring her clear eyes, and soft, childish mouth.

Suddenly she burst into tears, 'Oh, Davie, I wish you weren't going to America!'

He put an arm around her, trying to comfort. 'Och, now, don't cry.'

She wrenched herself away from him. 'I can't help it – you keep saying I'm only wee – ' the rest of her words were lost as she raced away still in tears.

He watched her slim little figure tearing away down the street, then, surprisingly, when she reached the corner, she turned and waved to him. She'd soon got over her tears, just a bairn yet! Would she grow up like her brother and sister? he wondered, making his way back to work.

2.

It was on one of the fabled days that January borrows from June that the beauty of the place struck him afresh. The golf links were green, only the trees showed bare. Away north, on the slopes of the Sidlaws, brown gashes were appearing where ploughing was in progress. Would America be as bonnie as here?

And his impending departure kept his mother busy. She worried a great deal over who would do his washing, and was forever trying to remember the married name of one Meg Purvie, who had married a wise lad, and gone to America with him. 'If I could just mind her married name, you could easy get her address. Meg would do your washing for you, and think nothing of it.'

And socks . . . They shop things are no worth the money, once I get two new pairs done, and the other refooted, you'll have six good pairs to take awa' with you, was her refrain.

As February wore on, Davie felt a secrecy in the atmosphere at work. Returning after a meal, he would find a group, Sproggie among them, in earnest discussion. Immediately he appeared, they broke up, very effusive in their greetings to him, but quite nonchalant about what they were

93

discussing, and Davie, now learning tact, never asked.

For the club, his photograph had been taken, standing beside a little table carrying all the cups and trophies he had won, hands in pockets, a golf club under his arm. Then, from Mr Johnston, in his role of Club Captain for the year, came an invitation. He and his father were to be guests of honour at a party in the clubhouse, a few nights prior to his sailing.

When the night arrived, and they got down to the club, his father said, 'It looks like a big affair, Davie.' Every light was blazing, and Holt the Baker's van was busy unloading trays of pies and cakes. Quiet and proud, he added, 'It might have been better if I'd put the Sabbath suit on.'

'Ach, don't bother about that, Dad,' Davie said, and followed him in. The Reverend Lawson and Mr Johnston were waiting at the door, and gave them a rousing welcome. 'Come away in, gentlemen both,' and Mr Lawson shook hands with his father, 'We'll have a wee bit merriment first, eh? and keep the sad bit to the end.'

As they went into the big club lounge, his dad said, 'This collar'll have the neck sawn off me afore the night's oot.'

The Reverend Lawson overheard this and clapped his back. 'Then, take it off, Jimmie lad, its a stag party, so have your fun in comfort.'

Tables were set all round the room in a big, horse-shoe shape, with the top table opposite the fire. Mr Johnston presided there, with the Reverend Lawson on his left and Davie on his right, his father sitting next to him, with Bert Sproggie on the far side.

What a grand array of knives, forks, tumblers and glasses! Once Mr Johnston had welcomed everybody, and the Reverend Lawson had said a short grace, steaming plates of steak pie were brought in, and attacked with gusto. Dod Watt, the clubkeeper and his two hired lads were working like Trojans serving the drinks. Nips, halfs, pints, bottles of beer and lager, tots of rum and small gins vanished like spring snow down thirsty throats.

The rumble of talk made bass to the clink and tinkle of

eating irons and glasses. Soon, with serious eating done, and the frivolity of cakes and plates of trifle disposed of, tobacco smoke rose like incense, and the serving men were frenetically trying to keep pace with the demand for drinks.

In this symphony of good fellowship sounded a jarring note. But it enhanced the evening rather than marred it. Gave a cue for wits, a trip line for reluctant laughter.

And Wilf Day provided it. Poor Wilf loved a party of this sort. But he had no head for drink. One nip of whisky and a chaser of beer, and Wilf was away, his one-track mind running at full speed for the rest of the evening. Now he seized on the price charged for a small bottle of tonic water, and his opinion and comment formed a running theme for the rest of the evening.

When Johnston saw that serious eating was through – and he made a grand chairman, drinking no more than was necessary to pledge his friends, and always ready with a word at the right time – he stood up and thumped for silence.

The drone of voices expired, and in the silence, the voice of Wilf Day was clearly heard. 'I ken fine he only pays one and thruppence a dozen. True enough, he's entitled to a bit profit, but tuppence – it's a scandal!'

'You're dead right, Wilf, so it is,' Mr Johnston said. 'Tell me what the scandal is later on. Meanwhile Bert Gallet will entertain us with a song. Come away, Bert.'

Bert got up, not needing the handclaps to encourage him, and after one or two false starts, and arguments with the pianist about the key, got into his stride, 'Old Pal, why don't you answer me?' The wings of song soon wafted him away, and before he was half way through the second chorus, the tears were running down his cheeks, and his rendering lugubrious enough to make them all join in, maybe in the hope that his old pal would answer, and put Bert out of his misery.

'He's fair in tears wi' the pathos o't,' Sproggie whispered to Davie. 'And we'll soon be greetin' because we've got to listen!'

But Bert got a good hand for his song, and then the chairman, realising that some comic relief was necessary, called on Mr Sproggie for a song.

Bert Sproggie rose, and waited patiently till the lads down at the far end got Wilf Day back to his place. He had buttonholed one of the serving lads, and was haranguing him on the inquities of his master. Now some of the younger lads were calling on Sproggie to sing 'The Ball of Kirriemuir.'

'Black shame on ye all!' Sproggie called sternly. 'How could I ever haud up my heid in public again, suggestin' that not only do I know the scandalous song, but might sing it in public – in front of the minister, too—'

'Away, you old hypocrite,' the Reverend Lawson said, *sotto voce*, but penetrating enough for the whole company to hear. 'If it wasn't for me restraining you, you'd be bawling out that disgraceful ballad at the top of your lungs.'

Against the company's roars of laughter, Bert called on high heaven to witness his complete ignorance of any such song, then entertained them all with a bothy ballad about the 'Lad who went to Falkirk Fair, lookin' for a fee, and a fairmer he came up to me and said me Lad says he—'

The song went on a great length describing the poor quality of the food, the worn out, spavined old hacks of horses, and the unaccommodating quality of the young women about the farm, suspended forever in a state of perpetual virginity. Bert knew how to make the most of such material, paying off in nods and anticipatory winks the minister's warning to censor the worst lines in advance.

Fuel to the gales of applause the song earned was added by Eck Black, who gained Wilf Day's attention, and asked him what price was charged for a small bottle of tonic water at the Ball of Kirriemuir. 'Three haipence a bottle, no a cent more.' Wilf was insistent, 'And that a fair enough profit.'

Davie sat quietly as song followed song, with Mr Johnston on one side, always with a remark at the right time, and his dad quietly happy, saying little. He took in the rows of flushed faces, glowing among the wreaths of tobacco smoke.

Years might pass before he saw many of them again. He looked round the wood-panelled room, with pictures of former members who had done well, and his own now to be added. He had handed over his trophies to the club for safe-keeping. With so many things to attend to before sailing, he might not even be in the club again.

Then, as the applause for the last song subsided, Mr Johnston rose. 'Well, gentlemen, this is a grand night we're having, but time, mankind's greatest enemy, says we must press on.'

'We are gathered here tonight to do honour and wish God Speed to one of our best young men, Davie Crombie.'

As the cheers died down, Bert Sproggie reached over and patted Davie on the back, 'That's my boy.'

'The golfing fame Davie has won for himself,' Johnston went on, 'is no longer purely local. To be chosen to play for one's country at the age of eighteen is a high honour.

'We, in our little town here, can claim some of the credit this lad has done us, for we nurtured him so far as the game goes. Credit must also go to his parents, for breeding such a fine young man. I'm happy to say his father is with us tonight and we're all in his debt, for quite another reason.'

His dad flushed to the applause, and to the cries of 'Good auld Jimmie, a damned good greenkeeper!' he said, 'Tach, I'm paid for it.'

'Now, alas,' Johnston continued, 'we are losing Davie. He takes his craft and skill to a far country who are prepared to reward him well for it. But we could not let him leave us without some token of our regard.' He turned and gestured to Dod Watt. 'You can bring it in now.'

And Dod came through with an ornate set of gleaming new clubs, set in a bag nearby big enough for a man to sleep in.

'This fearsome-looking bag,' Johnston went on in a lighter tone, 'came from contributions from Davie's club mates; the clubs themselves were made by members of my staff, of whom I'll always be proud to say, Davie was one.'

'And Mr Johnston gave us the materials, and the time we took making them,' Bert Sproggie put in.

'Nothing in that, it was the least I could do.' Johnston laughed as the applause died down. 'We had a fair bit of cloak and dagger stuff to do, measuring Davie's old set, to make sure all the lies and weights were right.' He turned to Davie. 'We now ask you to accept this new set of tools, with all our best wishes.'

He put the clubs into Davie's trembling hands, and through the storm of cheers came the insistent call for 'Speech, speech!'

Davie rose in terrified confusion to face them. Beside him Johnston and the minister quietly encouraging.

'Gentlemen,' he began, in tongue-tripping shyness, 'I'd . . . I'd like to thank you all for this wonderful gift, and for the kind things you said about my dad.'

The applause following this should have encouraged him, but he found tears pricking the back of his eyes, and his throat choking. 'I'll, I'll always be grateful for the things I've learned from Mr Johnston and Bert Sproggie. I've looked forward to – to going to America, and yet I sort of hate leaving here . . .' His voice choked. 'I'm sorry, I cannae say any more – I'm, I'm bunkered.'

Now Johnston rose again. 'Your words came from the heart, Davie. You said all that was necessary, and that's better than fancy speeches.'

'Now,' he spoke out to the company 'in a few moments, I will ask you to be all upstanding with glasses charged, and we will all drink health, good fortune and God Speed to Davie. After this toast you will remain standing, and Mr Lawson, as is right and proper, will offer up a short prayer. Then we will link hands, and sing Auld Lang Syne. This done, each and everyone who wishes to make his personal goodbye to our Links Champion can come forward.'

Then the scraping of feet, and the movement of chairs as they rose, and the lights flickering and flashing from the glasses and tumblers as they were raised, the low bass rumble

98

of the words, 'Here's tae ye, lad, God bless you, Davie.'

Then the glasses were laid down. A few feet moved, a man or two coughed, or cleared his throat, then they bowed their heads for the minister's words.

' . . . Our Father in Heaven, hear this our prayer for our son, David Forbes Crombie, now setting out to build a new life in a far country. Comfort his parents who will miss him so, with his empty chair at their table, and his voice no longer raised in greeting. Guide him always to do the right, as he sees the right. Keep him safe, in the pride of his skill and his beauty. And guard him to be ever as he is to us now, in his gay simplicity of heart. And all this we ask for Jesus Christ's sake.'

There was a brief pause, then like the deep chord of an organ, the company said 'Amen.'

Then the first notes of the old song sounded on the piano, and chairs scraped as the men moved to join hands. 'Should Auld Acquaintance Be Forgot.'

Glancing sideways, Davie saw that both Bert and his dad were openly in tears. When the song ended, the crowd melted from their places and struggled towards him, all wanting to shake hands and pat his back. Bert Sproggie was first. He let out an angry bellow, 'Whit the hell's wrong wi' this country when aw' our best young lads have to go three or four thousand miles away tae make a decent living!'

He flung his arms round Davie. 'I never had a lad – aw' my bairns were lassies.'

Both Johnston and the minister pressed his hand. 'Try and find time to come and see me before you sail, Davie.'

He went down the line, shaking hands with them all. Every one had something for him, the address of a friend or relative in the States. 'If things are no so good, Davie, just knock at that door, they'll see you don't go hungry.'

A little keepsake from this one, a good luck charm from the next. Then he reached Bert Gallet and Wilf Day, both in tears – Bert's, maybe from the emotional hangover of his song, and Wilf, perhaps, from the iniquities of overpricing.

Bert put an uncertain arm round Davie's neck. 'Take – take this wi' you Davie.' He produced a withered-looking root. 'It's a clump o' heather, I took it outa the rough at the twelfth. Plant it next to your place in the States. That way you'll ay have a bit o' Scotland grown' beside you.'

Davie took the tribute, strongly affected by it, and Bert's tears. Wilf Day wrung his hand, and nearly toppled over. 'And I'll tell you this, Davie, the Yanks are straight dealing – hic – honest folk. They'll charge you a fair price for what you buy – no like here – tuppence for a wee bottle – a fair scandal!'

At the door, Davie turned to see if his dad was beside him, and now a new song was started up, ragged and off key at first, then growing in tune and tempo. 'Will ye no come back again, will ye no come back again, better loved ye cannae be—'

He walked home with his father, under the cold stars, with a sliver of moon and the sea murmuring. 'Give's a hold of yer bag, son,' his father said suddenly. Davie was on the point of refusing, for the new kit of clubs was heavy, then he understood. It might be a long long time before his father carried his clubs again, and in this walk home over the darkened links, his dad was reliving the pride he had found in the games won last summer. He handed the kit over in silence. His father slung it over his shoulder.

They walked in silence, their shoulders touching occasionally. Funny, that night long ago, when he had told his father about wanting to go to the States. Davie suddenly knew an intimacy of mind with his father, as if they had changed bodies, maybe the more real because it was unspoken. He saw the kitchen at home after he was away, with only two places set for a meal. His father and mother would not talk much about him, yet they would forever be watching for his letters and not only reading the lines, but trying to read between them in case he might write cheerfully to conceal things not going well with him.

A few days ago, a letter had come from Andy Cunningham, containing all the papers necessary, confirming sponsorship, to get him past the immigration officers when he landed. There were other instructions, even a bundle of dollar notes, in case, as he wrote, 'things get a little snarled up before you get used to counting and using American money, though I hope to meet you at the boat.'

Seeing all these things, together with his passport, his mother had suddenly burst into tears. 'Oh, laddie, it's an awfu' long way, and you just a bairn yet, no nineteen till August month.'

He knew they would pinch and scrape to gather a few pounds, and if things went badly, they would write, 'Here's your fare, come home.'

His mother was in bed when they reached the house. Davie proudly took his new clubs through to show her, and returned to the kitchen to find his father had coaxed the embers of the dying fire into a cheerful flame. Now he brought out the remains of the New Year's whisky, still with an inch or so of spirit left in the glass.

In reply to his gesture, Davie sat opposite, and when he saw his father pour two small drams, he realised this was the last rite in his attainment of manhood. There was little spirit in his glass, but he pledged his father.

'I'll fair miss you, son.'

'And I'll miss you, Dad.'

'Whatever happens, Davie, write to your mother. Never neglect that, write to your mother.'

His father stared into the embers in silence, and seemed rather embarrassed. 'Tell me, Davie, you're no tangled up with any lassie?'

A momentary vision of white fingers flashing over piano keys, then a pair of coldly hostile eyes, and then, oddly enough, of Beth doing her skippy dance . . .

'No, Dad,' he said truthfully, 'no lassie.'

'Aweel, I think it's time we were bedded.'

So Davie lay in his narrow bed, hearing the wimple of the burn, the sound that was always there. A train whistled down the line, and a clang or two from the night shift at the foundry. Then, before he fell asleep, he heard the train whistles as if they were the sirens of ships, calling him over the Atlantic.

PART TWO

AMERICA

CHAPTER SEVEN

I.

THE skyline of New York was familiar from books, and the cinema, but his mind was still not prepared for its gigantic size. His ship seemed dwarfed by the Statue of Liberty, and some of the skyscrapers seemed to have their heads in the trailing grey clouds. But, with customs and immigration to face, and helping the MacKay family to get their gear together, he had little time for looking at the New World.

He had met the Scots family boarding the ship at Liverpool. They had left Skye to try their luck in America, and were on the way to join a relative in California. With few Scots aboard the ship, they were company for Davie, the soft, Highland voice of the Skye man blending with Davie's broad Angus burr. MacKay had heard of golf, but had never seen a golf course. That Davie should be making his living at the game seemed to him nothing short of miraculous. 'To be sure,' he said, 'it is very hard for a man to be knowing how half the world earns its living.'

After mutual promises to write, Davie went through customs and immigration. Then, golf clubs on shoulder, and carrying his suitcase, he stepped down to set foot in the New World.

The crowd assembled to meet the ship were penned behind a crush barrier back from the dock side. The clear space in front of it was a welter of porters, luggage, barrows, trains of silent electric trucks, and bustling dock officials.

He looked for Mr Cunningham, but there was no sign of him. Eagerly he moved along, searching for some sign of recognition among the crowd but now he felt the edge of dismay. Maybe Cunningham didn't recognise him – he had almost forgotten how Cunningham looked. No one claimed him. It was no use going back to the MacKays. They had troubles of their own, and he was a man now, out on his own. Mentally, he counted his dollars. How much would a ticket to Cray Creek cost? Ohio was many hundreds of miles away . . .

Then, through the babble of sound, a voice came through to him, 'Hi – you – you Crombie?'

He turned in the direction of the sound, and saw a slim, flushed young man climbing over the barrier to reach him, brushing aside the efforts to hold him back.

He jumped down, ran across, and caught hold of Davie – 'Sure you're O.K. – you're Crombie? Gee, am I relieved.' He was happily convinced. 'When Al heard your ship had docked, he went plumb haywire. Cummon, let's grab ourselves a cab.'

'But Mr Cunningham was to meet me,' Davie protested.

'Couldn't make it. Got snarled up in a conference around Chi,' the young man explained. ' 'Phoned us yesterday to collect you, show you the town, then ship you out. He'll meet you at Tanooda.'

This information was delivered at top speed, and his accent made it difficult for Davie to follow. All he could grasp was that this man had come in Cunningham's place. It never occurred to him to doubt the *bona fides* of his companion, or ask how he'd managed to recognise him.

The broad roadway outside was a swirling maelstrom of traffic. Alone, Davie would have been terrified to attempt a crossing, but the young man grabbed his suitcase, and stepped out boldly, holding forth in a stream of friendly talk as they dodged the traffic. 'Yessir, the Cunningham guy spent a whole day with us last week and what a stock he bought for you! Are you going to have an opening, I'll say! We shipped the whole consignment out three days back, and I'm telling you there won't be a pro-shop in the whole Mid-West with the range and quality you'll be carrying.'

Davie walked quietly along, expecting every moment to

106

be pulped under a speeding truck. The babble of words made no sense to him. Even in a quiet atmosphere, it was doubtful if he'd have understood. In the crashing impact of New York, his mind seemed numb.

'Hi, hi there, cab!' his companion yelled, and a yellow taxi slid towards them. 'Get in and we'll go on over – guess Al'll be mighty pleased to see you.'

As the cab started, the young man said, 'Gee, I never had any manners – I'm Dick Lawther, and mighty pleased to see you.'

'I was real glad to see you,' Davie said, as they shook hands. 'Where are we going?'

'Over to the warehouse, Algolf Inc. on West Seventy-fourth,' Lawther told him. 'Guess Al'll be tearing his hair out now, if he'd any to tear.'

Still Davie couldn't make it out, but hated to ask questions in case he seemed stupid. Now they were in the city proper. The streets were roaring canyons of traffic, the buildings like great cliffs blotting out the sky.

Their taxi swung into a great avenue, completely blocked by motor cars, trucks and great double-decked buses. At an intersection with another road, a red-faced policeman, swinging a truncheon, was working himself into a frenzy, directing the traffic.

'Guess our little burg seems strange to you,' Lawther smiled.

'Aye, I've seen more restful places,' Davie admitted, his mind on the placid days of home. 'I suppose you get used to it.'

'Greatest lil' old burg in the world,' Lawther said proudly. 'Never lived anywhere else, and never will.'

They swung round into another great street, and among the crowd Davie saw two pig-tailed Chinamen in loose blue robes gazing intently at a huge cinema. Despite it being not yet noon, the fascia was a blaze of coloured lights, and an electric sign carried the boost, '*Douglas Fairbanks in The Black Pirate and Four Great Turns Four.*'

'And you're a top golfer back in Scotland,' Lawther said.

'Och – I wouldnae say that exactly,' Davie countered. 'Do you play, yourself?'

'Me,' Lawther laughed, 'I live in Brooklyn and we ain't got much room for golf in my section. Only golf grounds I ever see is when I go into the sticks for Al.'

Davie's mind flicked back to the big, happy Yank he had once caddied for. The wide sky and open expanse of the golf links at home seemed not only far away, but on some other plane of existence.

The traffic was a little thinner now, but people swarmed everywhere. More long vistas of streets flanked by high, drab buildings, but with something of a raffish air, with gaily bedecked stalls at the kerb, and hanging signs.

They stopped, and on the building, letters three or four feet high announced that this was the headquarters of 'Algolf Inc. Serving American Sportsmen', and there was also a silhouette of a golfer. Following Lawther into the building, Davie decided that the man who had made the silhouette didn't know much about golf. No one could possibly strike the ball from that position.

Inside, the warehouse was dimly lit, save for a bright showcase carrying a display of clubs, balls, bags and gaily patterned shirts and sweaters. Davie sniffed. The smell took him back to Johnston's. That rich aroma of new leather, black pitched whipping and stained woods. Lawther halted in front of the showcase. 'Hey, Al – I gottim – he's here!'

Al was short and stout and completely bald, save for two little black fringes over his ears. 'This is Mr Kurtiz,' Lawther said.

'Al's good enough,' Kurtiz said, and held out a welcoming hand.

'Glad to know you, Davie – yessir! And mighty glad to see you here. Welcome to America, son!'

The handshake was firm and hearty. Why should the man be so pleased, make him so welcome? Fine and reassuring, after his lost feeling at the docks, but some of the things

Lawther had said kept turning over in his mind, like distant rumbles of storm warnings.

But he had no time to puzzle things out. 'See now, Davie, let's send your grip things down to the depot, and get 'em shipped.' Then he called for Zeke who was a tall, stooped, Negro, his crinkly silver hair looking strange against his dark skin. Even Zeke greeted him. 'A fine morning, Mr Davie, and glad to see you here.'

Not without misgivings, he watched his things taken away, both Kurtiz and Lawther telling him not to worry about a thing, they would be on the double century with him tonight. 'Now, cummon'n meet Susie,' Kurtiz went on, and led the way towards a frosted glass door marked 'Invoice Office'.

Then he called 'Susie' and the prettiest girl Davie had ever seen came out.

Her jet black hair was cut short, with a deep fringe over her forehead. Her wide set eyes were grey, and despite the loveliness of her features he couldn't help noticing her clothes. The dark skirt fitted her slim hips like a glove. Her silk stockings were so fine as to be almost invisible.

'Here's the boy we've heard so much of,' Kurtiz cried. 'This is Davie Crombie.'

Under her appraising stare, Davie reddened. 'Oh, ain't he cute, he's just beautiful!' she cried, then giggled, 'Oh why! the lamb's blushing.'

'I'm – I'm pleased to meet you, Miss Susie.' He made an effort at proper behaviour, and held out his hand.

'Listen to the way the lamb talks!' Susie cried in rapture to Kurtiz, then scornfully, 'Shake hands nothing!'

She flung her arms round his neck, and pressed her crimson mouth against his. Her perfume made his head swim, the warm softness of her! And it wasn't just a peck either, but a long hungry kiss, like Vera Duncan and Chae . . . The blood was beating in his ears when she released him. Kurtiz laughed. 'Susie's from Missouri,' he said as though that explained everything. 'Cummon in and I'll show you what Andy bought for you.'

The room he led into was a hotch-potch of everything connected with the game. Clubs, balls, clothing and gadgets of all kinds. Some he was familiar with, some he had never seen before. They littered the room in untidy abundance.

'Shot of hooch, son?' Kurtiz asked, throwing a bundle of gaudy sweaters into a corner, and motioning Davie to sit. Davie shook his head. 'You're dead right, son, and you'll know good stuff when you taste it, comin' from Scotland. This bootleg hooch Volsted's forced on us is the death of hospitality – pure rotgut.'

'Now.' He cocked a fat leg on a corner of his cluttered desk. 'Andy's sure done you proud for a start. Yessir, complete coverage of all the best in clubs, bags, balls and golf wear plus every accessory, and all from Algolf Inc. Thataway, you're not bothered with dozens of small accounts, only one, and every item qualifies against gross take for our bulk discounts.'

The book-keeping class he'd attended at night school made at least the gist of this clear. He had the bewildered feeling of a man falling suddenly into quicksand. 'But, Mr Kurtiz—'

'Al's good enough.' He seemed unaware of the stammered protest. 'And not only our goods, but complete sets of genuine hand-made irons and trubalance woods, all guaranteed hand made in Scotland. They're on a higher price tag, but the customers go for them – yessir! Nothing to beat the real McCoy – nothing – every one hand forged in—'

'I know,' Davie managed to get in, 'I was making them until a fortnight ago.'

Kurtiz's jaw dropped. 'Well, whaddye know – You actually worked in that plant?' He shook his head. 'Small world.'

Rummaging in a drawer, he produced sheafs of papers. 'I got invoices here, the gross is just on three thousand five hundred dollars, but it's all as June, thataway, you've three months before they fall due, and you can kick in with part payment as soon's your shop's open.'

In mounting dismay, Davie took the sheaf of papers and stared at the heading. 'D. F. Crombie, c/o. Neveneck Golf and Country Club, Ohio.'

'But, I'm going to Cray Creek with Mr Cunningham,' he stammered. To find he was in debt for such a gigantic sum was bewildering. 'There must be some mistake. I've never heard of the Neveneck place, and I haven't any money – I owe Mr Cunningham for my fare out here.' His voice choked in distress.

'Oh heck – ' Kurtiz slapped his bald forehead with the heel of his hand. 'Trust me to ball the thing up! Andy left a letter for you.' He reached out and drew an envelope from a pigeon hole. 'And me gassin' on and forgettin' – so pleased about the stuff he bought, I plumb forgot – ' Davie opened it and read—

Dear Davie Crombie, Sorry I couldn't meet you, but friend Kurtiz will look after you, and see you on the train. Now, I've got a better job for you. You're going as full pro to the new club at Neveneck. As you have full merchandising rights, I've bought a good stock for you. This will be a wealthy club, and you should do well. Will explain everything when I meet you at Tanooda. Yours, A. Cunningham.

Still holding the letter, he looked at Kurtiz. 'But, I've never heard of this Neveneck place, and I don't know how I'll ever be able to pay.' All the Scots peasant's dread of debt was in his words.

'Now, just a minute, son.' Kurtiz put a hand on his shoulder. 'I'd never heard of Neveneck either, till Andy told me, but you're gettin' a great chance, son, it's quite a place, and soon you'll be makin' real dough. You got no stake, so what? You Scotties are good boys, you pay soon's you can. Why, I've staked lots of you lads fresh out from the sticks. Dave Mason, Bob Turner, Jim Marr and, anyway, Andy's sponsoring you, and that's good enough for me.'

'I just can't get the hang of things,' Davie said. 'I just hope it'll be all right.'

'Of course, it will!' Kurtiz rose and made for the door. 'Now stop worryin'. You'll be O.K. What you're in the red for is nothing; you'll turn that over in a month or so out there. And I want to keep you for a customer, see? Keep on buying from us. Wire in your orders, and we'll ship 'em out same day. Cummon, now, forget it. I'm sending you out on the town.' He opened the door and called out, 'Hey Dick, come on in here and bring Susie.'

'Now, please, Mr Kurtiz,' Davie began. 'All right then, Al – I expected to be going to Ohio right away, I've very little money.'

'Look son, forget it. Today, it's on the house. You're the most important man in this business – a customer.'

The door opened, and Lawther followed Susie into the room. 'Take Davie out to lunch, and make it a good 'un,' Kurtiz said. 'Then show him around a bit. Suzie had better go too seein' she's fallen for him, maybe make him forget his girl friend back home.'

'Did you have a girl friend?' Susie asked in her throaty whisper, and Davie blushed again. 'No – no really.' And the vision of white hands stroking piano keys faded.

'Well, the girls in your home town must be plain dumb.' Susie was scornful, and took his arm. 'Cummon honeylamb, let's go.'

'Bring him back around five,' Kurtiz said. 'Then we'll all have some eats together before we see him off at Grand Central.'

Now Susie wore a loose, short little jacket, showing off her slim hips to perfection. A wisp of material did service as a hat. Pictures of this journey stayed sharp in his mind for years afterwards, yet it retained a fairytale flavour, like something remembered from the cinema and relived again on the edge of sleep.

Another yellow cab whirled them through the deep canyons of streets. Lawther was the proud host, and the perfect guide. 'Over there is the East River. Now we're gonna go along Central Park, then up Fifth Avenue.'

The teeming opulence of the city, the new vistas at every turn made the ride dreamlike, but Susie kept it firmly anchored to reality. 'Lay off the spieling, Dic,' she said. 'Let Davie enjoy it for himself. He's no hick, the lamb, just that he's never seen anything like Noo York before.'

She sat close to him, her arm linked through his, clasping his hand between both of hers. He judged her to be two or three years older than himself, and whilst at home, her conduct towards him might have been embarrassing, even in his shyness, and the confusion of his impressions, he found her physical touch comforting. Now she was exploring his fingers, touching the hard pads at the base of them. 'Gosh, but your hands feel hard and strong.'

'That's the playing,' he told her. 'A golfer's no use without good strong hands. Mine must be getting soft, I havnae struck a ball for nearly a fortnight.'

'Isn't it cute – the way he talks!' Susie cried. 'Go on, Davie – talk some more, tell us about your home town.'

They ate in an enormous restaurant, decorated with gloomy panels and sham suits of armour. He discovered then that the t-bone steaks and french fries were already known to him by the more homely names of chop and chips. He drank coffee, but longed for a brew of tea, preferably made on the smiddy fire, and served in a blackened syrup tin.

Walking along Fifth Avenue, Susie's arm linked in his, memory took him back to his childhood. At term-time on the farm, the great treat for them was a trip to Dundee, and tea in a little place called Wallace's Pie Shop. It was in a narrow pend, the buildings crowded close about it. After the feeling of space and air on the links, the narrow causeway gave him a twinge of fear, of wanting space and air about him. Looking up at the great skyscrapers he felt the same way. He could never be happy in such crowded surroundings. But Susie's touch allayed his fears. In an elevator, making a fantastic ascent of one of the great buildings, she put

113

a comforting arm around him as the cage shot up at speed. It's O.K. Davie.' She tightened her grip. 'Let's hope we get taken up to heaven as fast when our time comes.'

They landed back at the warehouse on the hour. Kurtiz welcomed them. 'Why, Davie, you must be quite a lad. Van Den Berg's been on the 'phone askin' for you – if you were okay.'

'Who's Van Den Berg?' Davie asked.

'Big Shot, vice president and manager of this Neveneck joint you're going to,' Kurtiz explained.

Lawther said goodbye, and Susie said she would see him off at the station, and went to 'phone home.

He ate in another restaurant, this time with Kurtiz, and the still affectionate Susie. Again they drove about the city, now a rainbow-hued fairyland of coloured signs and flashing lights. They came at last to the Grand Central, and he discovered it to be a railway station, so vast, so cleanly white and cathedral-like that the swarming crowds in it were soft-footed and silent, and not a train visible.

Kurtiz made some negotiations, and they descended in an elevator, to find a train more massive than any Davie had ever seen. The cinema gave no idea of their size. There they handed him over to a Negro attendant. Davie saw money being slipped to the man, and heard the instructions, 'This is Davie Crombie, see? You look after him, and see that he gets off at Tanooda.'

And the rich, warm drawl in reply, 'Yessir, sure, I look after him real good. I'll see that he's O.K.'

Then Kurtiz took Davie aside. 'Now son, don't worry none. I done business with lots of you Scottie boys. You'll make out good, so send us your orders, we'll wire costs on all calls grossing over fifty dollars.'

Susie flung her arms round him. This kiss was even franker than the first, and Davie frankly returned it. Then, when they broke apart, he held her shoulders. 'Susie, you're a bonnie lassie' – the day had given him new confidence. 'One of the nicest I've met. Thanks for being so kind to me.'

'Who wouldn't be gone on a honey lamb like you?' she cried, then exclaimed to Kurtiz, 'Isn't he cute, don't you just love the way he talks?'

He was then shepherded aboard, and exchanged last words at the window. 'Lawther or me'll visit you summer or fall,' Kurtiz said. 'We see all our customers once a year.'

'Bring Susie with you,' Davie said, and saw her face flush with pleasure. 'That would be grand, honey lamb, if only he would.'

Like a giant awakened reluctantly, the train snorted in protest, clanked, emitted a few bass rumbles, then drew away into the darkness. Davie watched his friends out of sight, then let the attendant escort him to his seat.

2.

Even the trains in America were different. Kurtiz had called this the parlour car, and now Davie smiled to himself, remembering how they had regarded him as a piece of freight in their conversations. 'Sure, we're shipping the boy out on the Double Century, thataway, the kid won't be hanging around Cleveland, or changin' depots by night.'

Had that been yesterday, or only this morning? It seemed a lifetime ago. Quiet in his seat, Davie tried to grapple with the shattering impact of America. His mental confusion might be compared to a digestive system conditioned to deal adequately with plain simple fare, being called on to cope with a gargantuan banquet of exotic food. His senses reeled in an effort to assimilate the New World.

'Relax,' he told himself. Already this country was enlarging his vocabulary. 'You're here because there's a job for you to do.' Then a troubled inner voice added, 'and in debt for three and a half thousand dollars.'

The journey gave him ample opportunity to study the people he had come to work among. Thin men in loud check suits, their hands flashing rings, trailed wraiths of fragrant cigar smoke behind them. Little podgy men, in darker clothes, twinkled rimless eye glasses at him, and fumbled with silver cigarette cases. And the women! Their dresses and coats were wonderful, but anyone wearing such thin silk stockings and painting their faces up – why! They'd have been classed as besoms at home, no matter how nice they were.

He had already noticed one thing Americans had in common. They all talked in high-pitched nasal voices. Maybe the Yanks had to talk like that to make themselves heard.

Then the big Negro attendant came along the passage, his white coat and cap emphasising the gleaming ebony of his round face. To the orders given as he passed along, he answered, 'Yessir – directly, sir,' in a voice so richly baritone it sounded like music. Then he stopped and leaned over Davie.

'You all right, boss?'

'Yes, I'm fine, thanks.'

'Sure I can't get you sompin – a drink, a glass of ice water?'

'No, honest, I'm fine.'

'O.K. then,' his manner changed. He ceased to be a servant doing his job, and became a friend. 'Why don't you relax, get some sleep, issa long way to Tanooda.'

When he had passed down the car, Davie turned his face to the window, staring into the darkness, striving to see something of the new country. It was raining heavily. In the lights cast by the train on the trackside, banks and fences went blurredly by, with the rain shining like slanting steel rods. Beyond that, darkness, save now and then the lights of an isolated farm house, and once the glow of a burning trash pile making visible a group of men working at a big circular saw.

At times he dozed, waking stiff and uncomfortable. He ate at intervals, then dozed again. Now all track of time was lost. Was it yesterday, or the day before that he landed? Must be the day before, for now his second night on the train was approaching. Cities, towns, and villages flashed by, sôe with names that rang like songs.

On the edge of a doze, the train wheels beat a mocking tattoo on his mind. 'In the red, in the red' and always he woke with a jerk to resume his gaze at the American scene.

Once they passed through a place that might have been home. A level crossing spanned the street like Station Road. He noticed the swing gates were different, and several cars were parked, waiting for them to open again. Children waved with enthusiasm, and he saw two boys, hands deep in pockets, wearing expressions of ferocious boredom, waiting for the train to pass.

That night, Chae and he had watched the express from Aberdeen. Well, he could tell Chae all about eating on the train now, and the pink-frocked girl . . . ? Susie would have fitted perfectly.

Now the train wheels were chanting, 'Neveneck, Neveneck' and then, with a sinister note too, 'Three and a half thousand, three and a half thousand.'

Now it was dark again. He woke from a troubled sleep to find the attendant shaking his shoulder, 'Hey, Mr Davie – Tanooda next stop.'

3.

There was no platform, and it was quite a climb down from the car. His clubs and suitcases had been restored, and the rain beat about his shoulders as he made towards a dimly lit building. A tall figure emerged. A voice hailed him. 'That you, Davie?'

'Aye, Mr Cunningham.'

'Well, now, glad to see you. Have a good trip? Never mind that now – let's get out of this rain.'

He ushered him out to the yard, and stowed the luggage in his big car. The headlamps lanced the darkness, with the rain like steel darts flung by the wind at their beams. 'I got you in at a real nice place, she ain't a professional roomer, so you'll be looked after O.K.'

Sitting in the car, there were a thousand questions Davie wanted to ask, but this was not the moment. So far as he knew, this man was his boss, as Mr Johnston had been, and he'd only seen him twice or three times when he was home at New Year. Best to wait, hear what he said, about the debts and the job.

The canvas hood of the car flapped in the gusts, and a splatter of rain escaped the celluloid side curtains. Tanooda wasn't like New York. Though some of its shop windows were still lit, the broad main street was all but deserted. The headlamps swept round a curve, revealing a white-painted house standing among sodden shrubs, and small trees. Cunningham stopped. 'Here we are.'

Davie discovered he was tired and stiff. He noticed that the house had neither gate nor railings, the pavement started where the garden left off. Then he followed Cunningham up a paved way to the house. It was a wooden one with a covered verandah on two sides, and steps leading to the front door, which opened as they drew near.

'Ah, goot evening Mr Cunningham, and you too, David, is it not? – yes – Crombie – I must remember. Ach – such weather – these vile spring rains! But come in, yes, come in.'

'Aye, I've seen better evenings,' Cunningham said, shaking the rain from his hat at the door. 'Davie, meet Mrs Gertler.'

Traces of faded gold still showed in her white hair, which was dressed tight, so neat that not an end or tendril strayed. Her black dress proclaimed a figure still spruce enough to run upstairs without getting breathless. Lace at neck and cuffs relieved the black, and she wore a big cameo brooch. 'Come, your room is up here,' she said, 'you have a shower eh? And freshen up, then I have supper ready.'

'Aye, go and freshen up, boy, then we'll have a meal and a talk. I've got a lot to tell you.'

Alone for the first time since landing in America, Davie looked about him. The bedroom looked much the same as it would in a house at home, yet there were differences. The wooden matchboard walls, the luxury of electric light at the bedside, the fancy brass ornaments of the big double bed.

He looked at the pictures on the walls. One was a tinted photograph damp and mildewed in places, depicting the Chicago Exposition of 1901, the other a mezzotint entitled 'The Surrender of Appomattox'. Something in the lay-out, in the stiff grouping of horses and soldiers against their background held his attention. There had been a tiny reproduction of it in the history book at school.

The suggested shower was attractive. While he was undoing his collar, a train whistled in the distance. It turned his mind to home although the sound was different here, it had an eerie, lonesome wail.

What were his father and mother doing at this moment? Was it raining at home too? He put the beginnings of homesickness behind him, and made for the bathroom across the passage.

CHAPTER EIGHT

1.

'YEAH, Neveneck,' Cunningham said, and stretched his long legs to the stove. 'I laid out that course eighteen months ago, then the project folded, they ran outa dough.' He lit his cigar, and the blue wraiths of smoke curled up. 'Then this T. Warren Taylor comes along. He's meat packing, and investing top money in golf – at the moment. He sees the layout, gets set, and re-finances. Even the weather helped, with the open winter, they put on double squads, and now the club and course are due to open end of next week. You're just in time, boy.'

'Yes, but the money I'm owin' these folk in New York,' Davie began. The stone in Cunningham's ring flashed as he waved the objections away. 'Think nothing of it, Davie. I ordered as much again from Stone and Kibbits. Look, boy, this isn't a two-bit place like the old home town. This is going to be a number one club, there's real money to be made.'

'I've never owed money before,' Davie said. 'I hope it'll be all right.'

Cunningham sat upright in his chair. 'See, lad, you're getting the chance of a lifetime. When the project re-started, I was offered the green, and a seat on the governing board. But, well, I'm pretty nicely fixed where I am, so they co-opted me as a consultant and asked me to recommend a good pro, preferably a Scot. Get that?'

Davie nodded. He could follow Cunningham's reasoning but still wondered why he hadn't taken the job himself.

Steps sounded outside, and Mrs Gertler came in, to clear away. 'Radio says tomorrow will be fine – no wind, and rain gone.'

'Well, that course could use some sunshine,' Cunningham said, then turned to Davie. 'It'll sure shake you to catch the rate of growth out here once the spring gets going.'

Then he smiled at Mrs Gertler's back as she left the room. 'Came out here thirty years ago as a bride. Her man worked on the railways, and she still sounds a bit German.' He drew on his cigar, then went on, 'You know, there won't be many more jobs for Scottie boys out here as Professional Golfers, Davie – you'll be among the last.'

'But there's still plenty new courses being made.'

'Sure is.' The cigar was stubbed out. 'But the Americans are breeding their own pros now and they're better men than us.'

'Better golfers than us?' Davie was aghast at the heresy.

'Just that. They're more single-minded, and have greater powers of application, a better mental approach. Look at today's top men Hagen, Chick Evans, Diegel, look at Bobby Jones – we haven't an amateur to touch him. Scotsmen have done a lot to spread the game here, and it's still the fashion to have a Scots pro – but fashions die out, boy, so stick in, establish yourself.'

'I'll work hard, Mr Cunningham,' Davie promised.

'I know you will.' Cunningham smiled. 'Wouldn't have brought you out here if I hadn't thought that. Y'see, Davie, I had this Neveneck place in mind when I was home. Then, when I'd a talk with that Parson Lawson, and Johnston, I knew you could go places. You weren't just a good player, you know how to talk to folks, and you know how to sell, and that's important. Johnston told me you were attending at his counter trade.'

'Is that to be my job out here?' Davie asked.

'In a way. You sell all golf gear, and you teach.'

'I'm – I'm no very sure about how to do that,' Davie protested. 'I've never done any teaching.'

Cunningham grinned, and flicked an eyelid. 'Between ourselves, when I came out here first, I hadn't a clue how to teach.' He pulled out two books and handed them over.

'Read these. Coupla bestsellers on golf methods, they'll give you the hang on how to go about it. But read 'em in secret.'

Davie took the volumes slowly, wondering how many more surprises this evening had in store.

'I – I believe I could teach beginners all right,' he said slowly, still holding the books. 'But what if a really good player comes to me and asks what's gone wrong with his swing?'

'Trust you to see the tough spot right off.' Cunningham's grin was rueful. 'That ain't so easy, even for me, and I've been at it for fifteen years. Well now, in that case, you take he or she—'

'Do I have to teach girls and women too?'

'Sure, what of it? Some of them are darn good players. Well, you take 'em out for a round on the course, and watch closely for a few holes; say nothing. The less you say, the higher they rate you. Now, watching them play, you may be able to see what's gone haywire. But, if you can't, look smart, tell them to relax, and swing slower.'

'And is that all?'

'Well, if they do relax, and swing slower, like enough the fault will disappear, and if it don't, like enough you'll be able to spot it in the slower swing.'

Davie sat silent. The romantic glamour of being a professional golfer in America was dissolving into stern reality. So much to learn . . . the first glimmerings of a totally different way of life.

'Do you think I'll manage all right?' Davie asked. 'If I'd had a spell with you, as an assistant.'

'I sure could have used you,' Cunningham said, 'and I'll have to get me an assistant. I'm getting involved in all sorts of things now. I've another two courses to lay out this year.'

He paused, and smiled reassuringly. 'But I've managed to sell you to the Neveneck people, for this year at least, so work. Establish yourself. Boy, this is a great country. It pays well for real skill, but you gotta stand on your own two feet. Now, one or two little things you want to look out for.

Back home, you were a big shot, everyone said hullo to you. Out here, well, you won't get anything handed to you on a plate. Once the members decide you're an all right guy, and a straight shooter, you'll be O.K. You must watch one thing, keep your homely Scots accent. It's part of the fashion, they like to hear it.'

'But you talk American,' Davie pointed out.

'Sort of Scots American.' He smiled. 'Remember I've been out here fifteen years. The edge gets kinda rubbed off. And, now,' he spoke earnestly, 'don't get sore at this. You're a clean-looking boy, and you'll come into contact with lots of smart girls, the wives and daughters of your members. Now, things are different out here, the girls – well – they're friendly, and talk a lot freer.' He gave Davie a meaning look. 'Don't let that put ideas into your head. Sure, have fun, if you want to, but not with the girl friends of your club members, get it?' He paused. 'You'll get a lot of admiration, because of your playing skill – try not to take advantage of it—'

Now Davie smiled. 'You mean – keep the heid?'

'Exactly, a good Scots saying.'

Davie nodded, then asked, 'Who's Mr Van Den Berg?'

Cunningham's eyes narrowed. 'Taylor put him in as manager.'

'He phoned Mr Kurtiz in New York to ask if I'd arrived.'

'What was that to him?' The edge of anger was in Cunningham's voice. 'I told Taylor I'd have you here in time. Don't let that big Dutchman interfere with you, son. Just to use a good Scots word, thole him. If he starts riding you, tell me.'

He rose and stretched. 'Well, time I was hitting the road.'

'Is it far to Cray Creek?' Davie asked.

'Around sixty-five miles.'

'Is that no a terrible distance, so late at night?'

'Shucks, nothing to it.' He got his coat from the hall. 'Roads are pretty quiet at this time of night.'

They shook hands at parting. 'Now, Davie, stick in. For

the first few days, you're not likely to run into any trouble. Unpack your stock, and get your shop set up. You won't have much else to do. I'll be out to have a look before the course opens. If you have spare time and see a few members or visitors hanging around, bash a few balls up and down. Let them see how good you are.'

As he opened the front door, Mrs Gertler came out of a back room. Cunningham said a few words to her, then Davie followed him out to the car. The rain had ceased, but the wind still whipped fretfully at the sodden shrubs, spattering them with cold spray.

'Joe Danelli will call round for you in the morning,' Cunningham said finally. 'You can commute with him, and kick in for your share of the gas. Incidentally, you could do a lot worse than take Joe's advice, if you're in doubt about things.'

'Is he a good player?' Davie asked, and Cunningham smiled. 'I don't suppose Joe's ever swung a golf club in his life. He's the youngest of nine, and had a pretty thin time as a kid. But he's a worker, I'll say that for him. He was in the locker room at Cray Creek with me, then turned out to be such a good cook that he landed the job at Neveneck. You'll like Joe.'

Davie watched the tail light disappear round the corner, then lit a cigarette, and strolled along the main street. So straight and wide was it that the buildings seemed low and insignificant, though they were still lit with electric signs, shining defiance at the darkness.

Before he had walked a hundred yards, he halted. He had not marked the street where he lived, and if he walked too far, might be unable to find it again. Indeed, his new landlady seemed to have the same idea, for she was waiting at the porch when he returned.

'Ach, Davie, there you are. I was worried, you not in a mackinaw in the wet. Come in, I have coffee.'

The nightcap, kindly in intention, was a betrayal. He lay in the strange, big bed, in deeper comfort than he had known at home, but unable to sleep. A dozen doubts and worries nagged at his mind, persistent as a fly buzzing at a window, and the night sounds of the little American town intensified his strangeness and isolation. 'Out here, you gotta stand on your own two feet.'

In the red for three and a half thousand dollars besides the stuff Cunningham said he'd bought from the other firm. Where would the money to pay come from . . . ?'

Angrily, he told himself that such a frightened, doubting coward as himself didn't deserve the chance he was getting. Every development in this great country had been pioneered by men who took chances, not with dollars, but their lives, right from the days when the first white settlers had braved the Indians, and the privations of the wilderness. Neveneck was an Indian name . . . His mind went back over the years, to the day he had walked along wondering if the Indians played golf. Well, did they? Were there any Indians left?

Far off in the night, a train whistled, thin and lonely. Now, his mind tired out with thinking in circles went blank. He fell into an uneasy sleep.

2.

He woke to sunshine, bird song and the inviting aroma of frying bacon. That scalding hot water should flow from the tap – Mrs Gertler called it a faucet – he accepted as natural American. The breakfast she gave him might have been cooked at home, save for one thing, instead of porridge, he was presented with pancakes swimming in maple syrup. But the bacon and eggs were wonderful, and he discovered that coffee was the ideal drink to start the day, whatever it might do to him at night.

'Ach, yes, is exciting for you,' Mrs Gertler said, pressing him to eat more. 'The first day of a new job in a new country. Eat, David, food will stand to you. When will you be home?'

That was something he couldn't say. 'Ach, is no matter. You can telephone, and I will supper ready have.'

Now impatience gripped him. He waited for Joe Danelli, smoking an early cigarette, outside the house, enjoying the sun. He wished now that Cunningham had not been quite so cryptic about that. What did he mean by 'kicking in with your share of the gas?'

But Tanooda seemed a nice place. He marvelled at the clean look of the wooden houses, and the lack of railings. The air still felt damp, like washing, sweetly clean, but not quite dry. Pools in the gutters reflected the blue sky, and the very air sparkled.

Looking towards the main road he was surprised at the number of cars speeding along. Then a shiny one swung round and came towards him. Its driver, the only occupant, was a clear-skinned, pale young man, with gleaming black hair and brown eyes. He drew up and called, 'Hey – issa you Davie Crombie?'

'Aye, that's me, are you Joe Danelli?'

'Sure, issa fine. I am so glad to meet you. Sticka your clubs in the back and lets go.'

A great country this, where the cook at the golf club could have a car. Joe broke into his thoughts. 'Is grand morning, Davie, today, we do good business. Lasta Saturday, I do forty-five lunches.'

'But I thought the club wasn't open yet.'

'No, not till a week, but the dining-room issa making the lunches, and every day we do more.'

Now they were in the stream, swinging down the main thoroughfare he had glimpsed last night. Strange shop signs held his eyes. 'Drug Store', 'Liggets for notions and work wear', 'Delicatessen'.

Soon they reached an industrial zone. Several small, neat factories sat by the roadside, all carrying flamboyant notices boasting their prowess. 'We tool for Uncle Sam – We can do your job,' one said proudly, while another boasted, 'Show us something we can't do. We're getting swell headed.'

Joe saw his eyes on the hoarding. 'Issa truck highway, so always chance of buyers passing.'

Then the factories petered out into a straggle of less prosperous businesses, used car dealers, scrap yards, tired-looking saw mills. They turned on a side road, and overtook several big trucks, all loaded with green shrubs and young trees. 'Fora the golf course.' Joe said, 'they gotta be ready by Saturday, and the squad bosses are really drivin' – yessir! They gotta hustle on.'

The idea of making a golf course was one Davie found difficult to take in. He got no time to wonder, for now Joe turned into a smaller side road. It ran through a straggly wood of dwarf pines and licheny oaks, and bore a notice, 'Private road to Neveneck Golf and Country Club'.

A half-dozen big trucks were emerging, obviously on the way back to reload. 'I told you they had a hustle on,' Joe said, accelerating, and driving on.

Davie's excitement mounted. Soon he saw the roof of a large building, almost the size of the Wallace Hotel. It seemed to be plastered over, and painted a gentle cream colour. The roof was of dull red tiles, and workmen were fixing gaily striped sunblinds over the upper windows. The whole appearance of the building, with its arched supports to the wide verandah, was richly exotic, like pictures of places in Spain or Italy.

Joe parked in an area large as a football pitch, and as they got out he said, 'Van Den Berg issa no here yet. I do not see his car.'

Crowds of workmen were everywhere. Squads were planting trees and shrubs in front of the clubhouse, while others hauled further loads on low trolleys fitted with huge fat tyres to avoid damaging the turf. The trees were not the three-foot high specimens they thinned out from the plantations back home for replanting, some of them were twelve to fourteen feet high, and there were many.

'Your shop issa over there, Davie,' Joe said, pointing, 'but I no'a think she's up yet. You go over and hang around, I make

127

coffee soon, and bring you some.'

For a moment, Bert Sproggie and his morning brew over the smiddy fire flicked in his mind, then he hitched his kit to his shoulder, and walked in the direction Joe pointed. It was all so different to what he'd expected, yet, when he tried to recapture the mental image he'd built up, it was gone.

Past the last green; no hole cut yet, no flag in place, but a bank of young birches and dwarf pines had been set round the back. Their colouring made vivid contrast with the light sand of the gaping traps guarding the approach. Yes, it would be a beautiful golf course, but worlds away from the windswept links of home. It was like a city park!

A few steps on, he stopped and stared in amazement. A pointing sign on the path through a bank of new-planted shrubs: 'PRO SHOP: DAVE F. CROMBIE, PRO-FESSIONAL'. He started whistling 'Swanee'. He would stand on his own feet. Hitching his bag to his shoulder, he strode along the path to take possession of his kingdom.

But it wasn't ready yet. True, the site was there, and a tag said this foundation had been treated with Gibson's anti-termite mix, known coast to coast, but that was all. Beyond that, a big pile of cases were stacked under a tarpaulin, the stock Kurtiz had shipped out from New York.

What to do now? He leaned his kit against the stack, and lit a cigarette. Look for Van Den Berg, or just wait? It seemed daft to be idling with so much work going on around him. But before the cigarette was down to a stump, he heard the grind and snarl of a heavy vehicle. It swung into sight, a great eight-wheeled truck, its sides boasting, 'Climbers for Sectional Buildings, erected in an hour'. A blond giant of a man descended, and came towards him. 'Hey, son,' he smiled down at Davie. 'We gotta contact the professional, guy named Crombie.'

'My name's Crombie.'

'Hey – a lil' shaver like you – sorry Prof. No offence meant.'

'O.K., none taken,' Davie told him, conscious as he spoke

that while his accent was just the same, he must guard against slipping into the clipped American idiom.

'Well, Prof., we'll soon have you in business,' the big man said. Already the crane which was part of the great truck was whirring, swinging a complete side of his new shop into place.

Davie watched for a while, impressed by the speed they worked at, and the amount of planning which had gone into the operation. Every piece of his shop was complete in itself, and had been loaded in correct order for quick erection. Presently he asked, 'Can I help?'

'Sure, Prof., glad to have you,' the foreman smiled. 'Catch hold of that corner, 'n coax her into place as she swings round.'

Half an hour later, Davie was hoisted to a pair of brawny shoulders, and scrambled on to the roof to make a last minute adjustment, and put a carved ornament on the cornice. While he straddled the roof, screwing the decoration into place, the encouraging chaff of the men below ceased abruptly. Looking down, he saw a stranger, and knew at once that this was Van Den Berg.

He wore a cream silk shirt, open at the neck, sleeves rolled above his elbows. His trousers were sharply pressed, shoes brightly polished. His receding hair was carefully dressed. He wore an air of wealth and authority. Gold-cased teeth flashed as he said, 'Where the hella you guys been? This job was due on schedule yesterday.'

'One of the crew fell sick, we had to wire for another,' the foreman said. Van Den Berg grunted, his eyes on Davie. 'You Crombie?' he suddenly asked.

Still straddling the roof, screwdriver in hand, Davie felt anger at the brusque, boorish manner. 'Aye,' he said shortly, 'That's my name.'

'Not enough to do at your own job, so you hire out help, eh?' He turned to go, then halted in midstride. 'Good to know you're not a layabout. Maybe you're one of the smart guys who'll do any job but his own.'

He was striding away when Davie called, 'Mr Van Den Berg—'

He halted and half turned, 'Yeah?'

'Was there anything else you wanted me to do?' Davie found his voice thin with anger.

'Heck, no! What you do's your own affair, so long's you're on the job.'

Watching his retreating back, Davie knew his victory was hollow. He understood instinctively that part of the man's anger was frustration, because he had no direct authority over the club professional.

Scrambling down, he found Joe, now in a white chef's rig, with a tray, carrying mugs of steaming coffee. The workmen took theirs gratefully, and as Davie took his steaming mug, he asked, 'Did you see – –'

'Yeah, I saw him,' Joe said, and shrugged. Davie knew then that Joe, too, had felt the rough edge of Van Den Berg's tongue; like enough the overspill of the anger vented on himself. 'Ach – I'm sorry, Joe.'

'No – no'a worry Davee,' Joe smiled, 'today he issa a grouch.'

'That's being kind,' the blond foreman said. 'Damned sourpuss! Another crack, and I'd a pushed his face back.'

'He issa busy and worried about the opening,' Joe said. 'Some days he issa fine. I go now. In hurry.'

'Aye, sure, get back and don't give him any chance,' Davie advised. 'Thanks for the coffee, Joe.'

'Now, Prof,' the big foreman smiled, 'if you'll just have a look over the job, and give us your O.K. on the ticket.'

The whole affair had a touch of magic. Where but just two hours ago had been a foundation, now stood a shop, complete with drawers, lockers, shelves, cupboards – the foreman called them closets. Gravely he took Davie round, demonstrating that every window opened, every drawer opened easily, that sun blinds ran true on their rollers. 'And if you're satisfied she's O.K., Prof, just sign here.'

Tucking the sheet in his pocket, he patted Davie on the

back. 'You're in business. Good luck, son.'

Going outside, Davie picked up his golf bag. On the threshold of the empty shop, he paused a moment and smiled. In a way it wasn't unlike the romantic stories you read, about the lad carrying his bride over the door of her new home. Then he put the daft notion behind him. Removing his jacket, he rolled his sleeves, and began the task of unpacking the stock.

3.

The next few days were hard work from dawn till dusk. The American golfer used a great many more aids to the game than he'd known at home. And clothing! He unpacked cream plus fours, fancy stockings, studded shoes, and a variety of shirts, with sweaters in a variety of fabrics and colours. When it was done, the shop was a golfer's paradise. He found pleasure in making attractive displays with the stands for displaying clubs and balls, and the showcases for accessories.

The first morning he lost all count of time. Joe had to call, 'Heya, Davie – don't you ever eat? Come and get it.' He followed Joe across to the club, and in the kitchen entrance. Between thirty and forty cars were parked now, but he paused before entering the big dining-room, looking at it through the service hatch. A big spacious place, overlooking the last green, the tables gay with spring flowers, and snowy napery. Two white coated Filipino waiters were serving. 'Could I no just have a quiet bite with you here in the kitchen?' Davie asked.

'Go on, Davee, you havva right to use the dining room,' Joe insisted, but Davie flickered his eyes to where Van Den Berg was seated at a corner table, talking to an elegantly-dressed girl, whose hair seemed to be like burnished steel. Then he realised she was no longer young, that her hair was silver, though she had a girl's slimness, and wore striking clothes. 'She issa Mrs Taylor, wife of the big shot who put the dough up,' Joe whispered, following his eyes. 'O.K. cum-mon, and I feed you in here.'

Later that afternoon, Joe joined him. 'Use any help, Davee?'

In the act of unwrapping wooden clubs, Davie asked, 'What about . . .'

'Not to worry. No people living in club yet. No meals after lunches, maybe odd coffees.'

'Do you mean folk will live in this place like a hotel?'

'Sure, some. You no have the clubs at home?'

Davie shook his head. The clubhouse he knew was a strictly all-male resort, a store for clubs, and a place to enjoy a drink. 'Do – are there women members, too?'

'But sure, there will be big ladies section here,' Joe assured him, 'with dances twice a week.'

Davie said nothing. He needed time to digest this.

He was grateful for Joe's help. And Cunningham was right, he was a good worker. 'You looka after the club, eh?' he suggested, 'and I stow the soft goods.' And Davie agreed. But the Italian boy's help was greatest on the tricky business of mark-up for Davie was still thinking in terms of pounds, shillings and pence. They worked till the light began to fade, and Joe suggested, 'Davee – I thinka we go home, eh?'

No long light evenings here, and it got dark at about seven. They drove home together, and Mrs Gertler had a meal ready. She also had company. A bevy of ladies, all smartly dressed, who literally grilled him about life in 'Scatland'. The ladies' voices took on platform tones. 'Scatland is one of the cradles of the American race. You Scats have done much for America, and we sure wanna know about life back there. But while we're not a wealthy club, we wouldn't dream of taking your time . . . shall we say fifteen dollars? For say a half-hour talk!'

The remaining days before the club opened passed quietly; he worked till sunset each day, then Joe drove him home. Now his shop was ready, and even with the worry of his debts, he was proud of it. The Friday morning brought the last surprising touch. A big flat package was delivered, marked 'Glass, with care'. Opening it, he stared in amazement. It was a blown up press photograph of himself, driving-off to the long sixth, the night he beat Baxter in the semi-final. He was slightly off centre in the picture, caught at that 'Hands high' position, so loved by press photographers, with his weight on the left foot, body wound up, eyes following the flight of the ball. Around him, on the tee, were grouped his friends, Eck Black, Jim Marr, Bert Gallet. His dad, the kit of clubs slung on his shoulder, was caddying – with his brass collar stud showing. He hung it on the wall, at eye level. Cunningham must have got the photo before he left Scotland. 'David Forbes Crombie,' the caption read, 'born Angus, Scotland, 1905. Angus County Champion, 1923. Youngest ever Internationalist, St. Andrews, 1923. Reached last eight Scottish Amateur, 1923. Turned Professional, Neveneck, Ohio, 1924.' Looking at it, he knew the first waves of homesickness.

'Then he heard steps, and turned to find Van Den Berg at the door. 'Say, what kind of dump is this you're keeping? And the club opening tomorrow.'

'The lorry hasn't collected the cases yet,' Davie told him.

'Lorry – wwhat the – oh! You mean the truck? You Limeys sure are tightwads. What's the dough in a few cases. Break 'em up. Feed the furnace!'

'But they're charged five and ten dollars a piece.'

'So what!' He made to leave, then caught sight of the newly hung picture. He halted midstride, then crossed to examine it. 'So, Scottie, you were a big shot back home?'

The tone was much gentler, but Davie said nothing, being pretty sure the man already knew of his playing record. 'Yeah, maybe you have played S'Andrews, but you're not a big shot out here.'

Davie held his gaze firmly. 'No – not yet.'

There was silence between them for a moment, then Van Den Berg walked away.

Why did the man dislike him so much? The best thing that

could be said for him was that he made no effort to conceal his enmity. Could it be that Cunningham and he were enemies, and Van Den Berg was venting his spleen on him, because he was Cunningham's nominee? After all, Cunningham had hinted that his attitude might be unfriendly.

Outside the sun was shining. The gangs of workmen had thinned out to almost nothing now, and quite a few people were about, strolling around the course in little groups. Idle, with the sunshine there, and the broad fairways an invitation, Davie took his driver, and a pocket full of balls. As he opened his bag, a withered plant fell at his feet, the heather root Bert Gallet had given him 'To plant in front of your place in the States'. It might survive. Many of the shrubs around his shop had been planted in peat. He set it in one of the borders.

Then, club under his arm, he walked out along the first fairway. Hefting the driver, he found, as he expected, that his hands had gone soft. He pulled on a left hand glove, taken from his stock. At home, to wear any form of protection on the hands was regarded as a soft, cissy act. Spilling the balls from his pocket, he tried a swing. This would be the first time he'd played a shot in the New World. It would have to be a good one.

Then, from the little rise he stood on, he saw four people walking slowly across. They stopped, evidently waiting for him to play. He recognised two of them, Van Den Berg and the lady he had lunched with that first morning. Their companions were a thin, elderly man with a tanned, lined face and a slim girl, crowned with a mane of pale gold hair. He heard the manager's strident voice, 'Yeah, that's the Prof – playin' himself into shape.'

Knowing they were watching did not make him nervous. Instead, he found a new pleasure. Maybe the mental climate of America made folk more honest with themselves. All right, he would show off, enjoy this display of his skill. And that was something he would never have admitted, even to himself, at home. Deliberately he exaggerated. The smooth address, the slow, lazy back swing, the casual wind up, then, with perfect timing he lashed out . . . The ball screamed away over their heads into the blue. Comments drifted up as he placed another ball. The elderly man said, 'Wow – that boy packs a kick like a mule!' The older woman exclaimed, 'But I never imagined golf was anything like this, why he's as graceful as a ballet dancer!'

Shot after shot he sent whining over them, then he walked down the slope to retrieve the balls. As he passed the group, Van Den Berg hailed him, 'Hey, Scottie'.

Davie halted and half turned. In the brief moment, he realised the manager's voice was mild and friendly, and that the lovely, fair-haired girl was smiling to him. 'Can't you send a caddy to field 'em?' Van Den Berg asked.

'Aye, I could,' Davie said, 'but I'm enjoyin' the walk.' Then he touched his cap in quiet courtesy to the two women, and realised that the fair haired girl was still smiling to him.

That was his first meeting with Julie Buren.

CHAPTER NINE

I.

SPRING was blossoming fast, the turf was sprouting and knitting together, an altogether lusher, broader bladed, faster growing grass then he had known at home; the raw newness of the course was fading, trees and shrubs were rooting and sprouting.

On the opening day, the car park had been jammed; Joe had worked himself to a standstill, and Davie also, so much so that when Mr Cunningham called at the shop, accompanied by T. Warren Taylor, the man he had seen walking on the course the previous day, he had to snatch a word with them between customers.

Cunningham had touched his shoulder and said, 'Everything well in hand?' Then before Davie could reply, went on, 'A daft question, I can see you are doing fine.'

And, Taylor flicked his cold grey eyes around the shop, missing nothing, even going closer to look at the big photograph. His lined face softening, he smiled at Davie, 'Your shop is nicely laid out, a credit to the Club. Let me know if you want anything, Davie.'

With that they were gone, and Davie returned to his task of attending to several customers at once. One, a garrulous lady engaged in buying sports shirts for her family, assured him that she had searched Chicago for such garments, and a tall thin, bespectacled gentleman who was buying, under Davie's supervision, a complete new set of clubs, told him, 'Yessir, broke me up when I transferred out here, and no golf course; sold my gear and went into mourning, but now I guess I'll come on here for lunch two, three days a week, and have a half hour with you, get licked back into shape. Better

136

book it now, Prof, say Tuesdays and Fridays around one-thirty.'

Dusk fell, and the clubhouse lights were twinkling when at last Davie locked up his shop, and went to deposit the money in the safe until it could be banked. Already he was counting how much he could send to Kurtiz to reduce his debt.

Now Mr Van Den Berg was genial and expansive, until he saw the amount on the pay-in slip. 'Hey, Scottie, go easy,' he said. 'We don't want folks to get the idea this is a clip joint. You don't want to oversell, that won't do the club any good.'

Sunday was like any other day. The church bells rang as at home, and folks went to attend, as many in cars as on foot, and soon afterwards the car park started to fill up. Americans made it a day of recreation as well as rest. Davie sold his clubs and gave lessons, a pair of teenage sisters in particular trying his patience sorely. They were not so keen on the game as following the fashion. Slowly he tried to instil into each one the rudiments of a swing, only to have the other burst into a fit of giggles at her sister's efforts.

And, when he took his cash over that night, Van Den Berg said, 'You haven't done so good, you gotta sell, Scottie, or how are you gonna meet your overheads.' Davie closed his eyes and softly prayed for strength.

The days took on a pattern, and with no weekend to mark the calendar, he began to find it difficult to keep track of what day it was. Then one morning when it was a quiet period and he was writing out a stock replacement order to Kurtiz, a shadow fell across the threshold and a girl's voice, casual with a hint of mocking laughter in it, said: 'Morning, Maestro, could I have a little coaching please?' Despite the tone of request, he realised it was a command. This girl was used to getting her own way. Looking up, he saw the fair, slim figure and recognised the girl who had smiled at him that Friday before the opening. Seeing her again, he realised just how often he had thought of her since.

She was more lovely than he remembered. Her beauty caught his heart and throat, the fine-drawn perfection, her

137

wide-set blue eyes, high cheek bones and dazzling skin. Her clothes had the subtle simplicity of quality, and her perfume was elusive, like faint music heard at night. Now she smiled again. 'Well, left your tongue back in Scotland?' He realised that he'd been staring and felt his face flush, and knew that she was enjoying his embarrassment. 'Sorry, I was thinking.' He forced his voice to sound normal, 'I'm free until eleven, if that suits you.' Glancing at his wristwatch, he said crisply, 'What name, please?'

'Julie Buren.'

He entered it in his book, writing slowly, trying to control his racing pulse. He had never met anyone like this girl, her cool poise, coupled with the tremendous aura of feminity. 'You have your clubs. Fine! Will we go out to the nets?'

Walking behind her, he knew that this girl was used to having people fetch and carry for her. She had simply walked ahead, taking it for granted that he would pick up her clubs and follow her.

They stopped at the mat before the nets, and Davie took the mid-iron from her bag. Hefting it in one hand, he was surprised to find it weighed at least as heavy as his own. This slender girl, with those fine drawn hands and wrists could never swing this club and control it. He was on the point of saying so when Cunningham's words came to mind. 'The less you say, the higher they rate you.' So he handed her the club, 'Now, let me see your grip, please.'

'I'm not a beginner,' she told him, 'and, it's the woods I want help with.'

'We all need help with them at times,' he told her lightly, stalling for time. Was this the type of thing he feared? Having to correct some hard-to-spot kink in a top player's swing. 'The woods are the most difficult clubs to play.'

'Don't give me that line.' Her smile robbed the words of brusqueness. 'I watched you last week.' Her voice took on the hard edge of driving ambition. 'I'd give anything to drive the way you do – don't care what it takes in time or money.'

'It's my job to help you,' he told her gravely, 'but I doubt if you'll ever be able to hit the ball as far as I can. For one thing,' his voice became more broadly Scots, 'lassies are made different from men – and – well sheer brute strength does help.'

He saw her eyes flick over his arms, bared by the short sleeved shirt, and reddened as her gaze rested on his supple wrists and broad hands. 'You've got something there, Samson,' she smiled lightly, 'but apart from that.'

Davie, felt the drawled 'Samson' had an edge of sarcasm, but went on evenly, 'No reason why you shouldn't play a very good game, if your swing is right,' he told her. 'Now grip the club, and hit this one for me.' He laid a ball on the mat at her feet.

Her stance was sound enough, but stiff; she snatched the club away from the ball, her swing lightning fast; she struck the mat six inches behind the ball, and only sent it scuttering along the ground.

'Relax, swing slower,' Davie said, placing another ball. 'No hurry, this is the only game where the ball waits for you to hit it.'

But her swing remained as hurried as before, though now he saw what was basically wrong. The clubs she was using were all too heavy for her. With her fast back swing, the clubhead itself was taking control at the toe. Of six balls, she only struck one cleanly, despite Davie's instructions to relax and swing slower.

'Now, hold on a moment,' he told her, and hurrying to the shop, came back with a lightweight ladies' club. 'Try that,' he handed it to her, 'and swing very slowly.'

'The usual sales campaign,' she said in sarcastic mock despair. 'What's wrong with the clubs I have? Ed Fuegosi had them made specially, and when Pop saw the bill, he said I'd been gypped.'

'I'm not trying to sell you more clubs,' Davie said evenly. 'I think your clubs are too heavy for you, and if you agree, I can lighten them for you.'

She looked at him in surprise, but made no comment

beyond saying, O.K., Maestro, let's try again.'

Patiently, Davie covered every point, correcting grip, stance, attitude and shoulder turn. His thoroughness was his undoing. Setting her arms and hands right, correcting her stance, he bacame only too aware of her subtle perfume, and the warm velvet feeling of her skin. As he stood in front, setting her hands right, her silk blouse fell forward at the neck, and he became conscious of the fact that her firmly round breasts were not restricted in any way. At that moment she looked up and caught his gaze.

Davie's face crimsoned, and his embarrassment was not lessened when she chuckled throatily, 'Well, what do you know? The boy's human.'

He saw that she too was blushing, but her easy poise had enabled her to dissemble better and make what was almost a brazen remark, knowing her apparent self-possession would increase his discomfort.

Suddenly, she began to laugh, 'I bet the stories you tell behind the barn sound real funny in a Scottish accent.'

Now the atmosphere between them was changed. In some way he could not fathom, this girl was challenging him. Watching her against the dark green background of flowering shrubs, he wanted her to have the best that he had to give – his skill. Here was a pupil he could be proud of. He saw a picture in his mind of her lissom grace flowing in the arc of a perfect swing, lashing the ball away with the effortless ease of perfect timing, but she swung even faster than ever, and mishit the stroke again.

'Please, Miss Buren – ' Davie began.

'Maestro,' she interrupted, laughing mockery in her voice, 'couldn't you make it Julie, after what's between us?'

'Miss Buren,' he repeated firmly, 'you're not even trying to correct the faults I have pointed out.'

'I didn't ask you to remodel my swing, only to straighten out what's gone wrong.'

'There's a whole lot wrong. You'll never hit the ball consistently swinging as you are doing.'

'Is that so, Mr Clever?' Her cheeks showed two red spots. 'I've had coaching from Ed Fuegosi and Al Bartlett, two top players, and they both told me my swing would be O.K. once I got it set.'

'Ah, well, maybe so,' Davie sighed, 'but before you play the way you could play – the way I'd like to see you play – you'll have to listen to me, and start at the beginning – otherwise you're only wasting your money – and my time.'

'You've got a nerve!' she burst out at him. 'What's it to you how I spend my money, and as for your time, I'm paying you for it.'

'I did not mean to be rude,' he told her firmly, 'but when I take money from folk, I like to think they had some value for it. I can't take a fee for watching you practising your faults, it's just pure waste.'

'If that's the way you want it!'

He watched her stalk away, her straight back contemptuous, her stride smooth and unhurried. He had never met anyone like her; obviously well off, and a good bit spoiled by too much of her own way, yet she had character. He sensed that her anger wasn't all due to his criticism of her play. He sighed, and with the feeling of trouble ahead, went back to his shop. Ten minutes later, Van Den Berg walked in, and tossed a slip of paper on the counter. 'Now, look here, Crombie, I ain't gonna stand for my members bein' insulted. You're not on my staff, so I can't fire you, but—'

Davie's heart sank to his shoes. 'Insulted?'

'What the hell kinda sass is that to give the president's daughter, tellin' her she was wastin' your time?'

'But, Mr Taylor is president, her name was Julie Buren.'

'Miss Buren to you.' Van Den Berg glared at him. 'Ever heard of folk's being divorced? Or don't they bother gettin' married in your neck of the woods?'

'Now, please Mr Van Den Berg—'

'Please nothing, Crombie. Maybe you were a big shot back home, but while you're here – and I said while – you're gonna treat the members right. Any more complaints, and I'll phone Mr Taylor.'

The thought of losing his job was a horror, yet, despite this, he felt a rising tide of anger. In a quick flash of insight, he said, 'Miss Buren didn't complain.'

'No, but I saw she was good and mad, and when I asked how come she was through so soon, she said you couldn't expect a physics professor to waste his time teaching primary classes.'

Davie said no more. Alone again, he got some satisfaction in knowing his guess had been right. The golden girl had not said anything against him, merely that she had been unable to conceal her anger, and Van Den Berg's guess had been only too accurate.

He had a sudden horrifying picture of being packed off home, and the garbled accounts of the reasons which would be sure to circulate. 'He had the chance o' a lifetime, but just threw it awa' – had bother o' some kind wi' a millionaire's daughter.' The sneers and sniggers were easy to imagine, but he had no time to brood. Already he was due to play a few holes with a business executive, and try to cure his wild slice.

On the way over, he paused to look at the heather root he had planted. It was dry and lifeless-looking – maybe it could never flourish in alien soil.

But even the few holes he was trysted to play were cut short, when one of the Filipino boys hurried over to say a long-distance phone call was expected in ten minutes. Would Mr Lorenson please return to the clubhouse. The man thanked Davie with the quiet courtesy of top bracket Americans, paid for his shortened lesson and added a generous tip.

Alone, Davie sat down for a minute. He was too worried to play on alone, either for practice or pleasure. At home, his life had been made up of things – the craft of making clubs, the study of the game itself. Out here the main business was handling people, and that was a subject to which a man might give his life to study, and be no wiser at the finish.

Sighing, he looked about him. The course was set on gently rolling country, and Cunningham had certainly made the most of his layout. It was a beautiful place, already he was beginning to feel attached to it, despite the fact that he had not yet had time to play a complete round. Then, from behind the screen of trees circling the grass, he heard a voice raised in angry protest.

'Away ye silly lookin' gowk – pit it doon, pit it doon – ye'll strain aw' the threads.'

The broad Scots burr was a blow in the emotional solar plexus. It brought familiar things into strange close-up, yet at the same time, made home seem even further away. He went round, and immediately recognised the speaker with the tangled matt of hair, the high, flesh-covered cheekbones, the ruddy complexion, as a fellow countryman, from close to home.

'I think you're from my part o' the world,' Davie greeted him, and when the man turned, Davie saw something of his father, the brown, collarless neck, the too short trousers barely meeting the heavy boots. 'Aye, frae Letham – Forfar way.' Then his face lit in recognition. 'Here – I ken you – you're Crombie, the gowfer lad, I mind o' yer picture in the papers afore I came away. So this is whaur you are. Hoo are ye daein'?'

'Och, fine, just fine,' Davie said, and wished it was true. 'What are you doing?'

'Just my trade, the plumbing.' He fished out a crumpled packet, and they exchanged the modern equivalent of bread and salt. 'Even the fags dinna taste the same oot here – no sae good,' he said, and flicked the spent match away.

His sister had married an American soldier, and written home of the wonderful opportunities, and the money to be made. 'I didna bother at first, but wi' the auld folk awa', and me footloose, I cam oot here in January,' he told Davie. He was now completing the job of laying piped water to the greens. 'Och, it's a grand country, and the money's plentiful but it's different.'

143

'Aye, it's different,' Davie agreed.

The man from Letham flicked his cigarette ash, and rubbed the side of his nose. 'Funny, when you think o't, the things that *are* different are silly wee trifles, things that shouldna' bother you, yet they dae.'

'Things, like what?' Davie prompted him, and knew the gist of his reply before the words were spoken.

'Ach, like no bein' able to have the usual Seterday trip to Dundee, and a bit turn round the toon, then makin' for hame, along Dock Street, wi' a pint o' gude beer under yer belt, and a bag of sweeties for the neighbour's bairns in wan pooch, and a couple of Wallace's bridies in the other.'

'Aye,' Davie admitted, 'it's the wee things I never gave much thought to that I miss, same as you.'

'Weel, I have to get on.' The Letham man rose, 'But I'll gie you a bit look in when I'm passin', just to see how things are daein' wi' you,'

They parted with mutual good wishes, two pioneers in a strange land, two new citizens of a nation itself new, peopled from the beginning by the misfits, the radicals, the impatient progressives. And such was their driving vitality that already their skills were yielding a richer, fuller life than ever their own country could. Davie, from the moment of his landing, had been dimly aware of these things. Like the man from Letham, he too, longed for the familiar things so close to the daily pattern of living that it was only when he no longer saw them with the corner of his subconscious eye that he came to realise how much they meant to him.

2.

The gaudy stranger turned up that afternoon. He saw the long, white car, shinier and more festooned with lamps and gadgets than any he had seen previously. It turned in and parked close as possible to his shop, and he watched the lanky six-foot figure alight and stroll towards him.

Davie had never seen anyone like him. His cream plus fours were enhanced by diamond checked hose in startling hues. His black and white skin shoes were decorated with fearsome-looking studs, his cream sweater adorned with the crest of crossed golf clubs and balls. This ensemble was topped with a white linen cap. He walked over to Davie, and held out his hand. 'How ye doin', Davie – name's Ed Fuegosi – in the same racket as yourself.'

Davie shook hands. 'Glad to meet you, Ed. I've heard of you.'

'Yeah, yeah, I been around,' Fuegosi said complacently. 'Nice lill' set up you got here.' He led the way into the shop. 'Dropped over to ask you a favour.'

'It'll be a pleasure, if I can help.' Davie said.

Inside the shop, Fuegosi draped himself along the counter. 'You gotta whole range Thistle Brand irons n' woods?'

'Aye – hand made in Scotland.'

Fuegosi nodded. 'The suckers sure go for that line. Gotta guy wants a complete set. Kurtiz is outa stock – can you help out?'

'Certainly.' Davie started looking out the clubs. 'You said a complete set?'

Still draped along the counter, Fuegosi nodded again, then fumbled in his pocket, 'What ya marked 'em up to, Davie?'

When told the figure, he straightened up. 'Hey, son, you in this game for peanuts?'

'I thought it was a fair enough profit.'

'Well, so long's you're happy, Bud.' He scribbled, 'But I'm gonna charge him twice that. Here's your cheque.'

'Thanks' Davie stowed it in the till. 'Will I stow them in the car?'

'Let him sweat for a bit, puts a few dollars on the price. Cigarette?'

When they lit up, Fuegosi made a long reach and turned Davie's time book over. 'I see you've had the Buren dame?'

'Aye, this morning.' Davie was non-committal.

Fuegosi laughed. 'That dame sure is golf mad. Trots along

to every teacher in the county. Is she still swinging round her neck like lightning. I loaded her up with heavy clubs to try'n slow her down.' He laughed, 'Charged plenty for 'em, too.'

Davie kept his thoughts to himself, and his visitor did not seem to expect a reply. 'She sure is a looker,' he went on, 'but plays high hat hard to get. With her dough, I suppose she can afford to.'

And then Van Den Berg walked in.

'Why, Ed! You old son of a gun, how ya doin' boy?' They shook hands heartily.

'Fine and dandy, Bill.' Fuegosi was cordial. 'Dropped in to pick up a set of clubs from the Prof here, and give the joint the once over – quite a place!'

'Yes, Ed, we're real proud of our course,' Van Den Berg said. 'You must play over it sometime soon.'

'Glad to, Bill, glad to oblige anytime,' Fuegosi answered.

Van Den Berg's eyes went to the big press picture, then to the lanky Fuegosi. 'Hey, what about you and our Prof playing' an exhibition game?'

Slowly, with the bored air of a man forced to admire a child's toy, Fuegosi crossed and looked at the picture. 'Yeah, Davie and I could put on a show,' he said slowly, and a quick look passed between him and Van Den Berg.

'You game, Scottie?' Van Den Berg asked in a brisk, friendly voice. 'Guess the members would enjoy watchin' you two play – just a friendly game, you understand?'

'Aye, I'll be very pleased,' Davie said.

'Right, it's a date,' the manager announced. 'Next Saturday, play off around two, I'll have a notice put up right away.'

'I'll put your clubs in the car.' Davie collected Fuegosi's purchases.

'Heck, ain't you got a caddy handy?' Van Den Berg asked. 'O.K. then, if you don't mind, then come over to the club for coffee.'

Stowing the clubs, Davie found himself worrying over the manager's friendliness just as much as his anger of the morning. From the moment he had greeted Fuegosi, there had been an undercurrent that he felt was somehow against him. He knew Van Den Berg wasn't the kind of man to forgive and forget the Julie Buren incident. There was something here he had to be wary of, yet, for the life of him he couldn't think just what it was. And their small talk did nothing to quieten his uneasiness, for they were evidently friends of long standing, with the names of shared acquaintances cropping up in their talk.

After watching Fuegosi drive his flashy car away, Davie went into the clubhouse, and put through a call to Cunningham at Cray Creek. Waiting for the connection, he wondered if it was daft. How much of his worry should he tell Cunningham, the whole truth of the Julie incident would be embarrassing and Van Den Berg's enmity went further back than that. Then the operator's voice burred in his ear. 'You're through.'

'Is anything the matter, Davie?'

'No, no really,' then, after a pause, 'I had a visitor this afternoon, Ed Fuegosi.'

'That big bohunk.' Cunningham was scornful. 'What was he after?'

Told of the purchase, he said, 'Huh, get that cheque into the bank right off, in case it bounces.'

'I'm playing an exhibition game with him next Saturday,' Davie went on. 'Van Den Berg fixed it up.'

'Oh, no,' Cunningham said, 'Oh, Davie, you walked right into it.'

With this confirmation of his suspicions, Davie's spirits fell to zero. 'But I couldn't very well get out of it.'

'Has that big loud-mouthed Dutchman been kicking you around?'

'Well, he hasnae been exactly pleasant,' Davie admitted.

'I think I'd better come over and see you tomorrow,' Cunningham said. 'This is worse than you think.'

'But, Mr Cunningham – I – I never meant to bother you.'

'I'm not standing for these two making a monkey out of

you, and incidentally, out of me at the same time. Now, don't worry, boy! You couldn't have acted other than you did. There's more in this than you understand. Chin up, see you tomorrow.'

Davie went back to his shop more worried than ever. Dusk had fallen when he locked up that night. The clubhouse was bathed in light, casting golden pools on the paths and shrubs around it, the light reflecting back to cream-coloured walls and striped sun blinds. The picture breathed luxury and leisure. Sharp in his mind rose the image of the little grey stone clubhouse at home, stark in its setting by the cold North Sea. At home, men played golf for pleasure and relaxation, in a quietly dignified ritual. Here it wore a carnival air, and was allied to other social pursuits. Now the dance was in progress, the band playing. Some couples were already on the floor, he watched them glide past the windows, the bright colours of the women's frocks making contrast with the more sombre clothing of the men.

Then he saw Julie. Her soft pink dress left her throat and arms bare, and the swarthy young man she was dancing with emphasised her pale, blonde beauty. Aye, she was bonnie. He watched for a moment, then turned away to the car. Joe hadn't come out yet. He could take his eyes away from the scene, but could not close his ears to the music. The band struck up another tune, and the first few bars gripped him by the heart and the throat. It was a strident minor theme, rasped out in the gravelly snarl of trombones, allied to the thin whine of muted trumpets. It couldn't be – not that tune – 'I haven't seen you for a long time – I haven't seen you for a while.'

The tune didn't belong here. Then the brass went mute, and the saxophones slid into the broad melody of 'Swanee'. Heard thus, it had a mocking air, like meeting an old friend whom you'd always known in homespun, all dressed up in evening clothes.

Sitting on Joe's running board, a wave of homesickness poured over him, making him feel literally sick. The tune evoked so many memories he missed and longed for, even dafter things than the Letham man's list. The cool, salt-tanged breeze, and the way it riffled the grass. Sand gathering in the gutters after a high wind. The smell of fresh cut grass after a shower.

'Swanee' ended, and another tune started, still he sat, fighting back his weakness. Now he saw America for what it was to him – a challenge. It wasn't like home, it never could be. Home was a land tamed and ordered, where men contrived to win a sufficiency and were content, skill being a reward and an end in itself. Out here, skill was merely a means to riches, and power over one's fellows, yet, with the rewards so great, it was every man for himself. You stood up alone, and battled it out. Now his struggle was to be his own man, against Van Den Berg, Fuegosi, and anyone else who thought they could beat him.

All right, he was David Forbes Crombie, and not ill-skilled at his trade. Maybe they would get him down, but they'd have to sit on his chest to keep him there.

'Hey, Davee, you sick or sompin'?' Joe asked, breaking into his thoughts. 'I aska you three times, you no answer.'

'No, Joe – I'm fine.' Davie rose, stretched, and managed a smile. 'Let's go home.'

CHAPTER TEN

'YEAH,' Cunningham said slowly, 'Yeah – a pity.' He reached for the inevitable cigar, lit it, and sat quiet, mulling over the facts Davie had related.

'But I couldnae have done other than I did.'

'I know you couldn't, son. You wouldn't be Davie Crombie if you had, still—'.

Then he brightened, smiling, 'That Buren dame – did she give you the old come-on?'

Davie coloured, 'Aye – a wee bit.'

'She's not vicious, a nice kid really, just the Devil in her. Julie's got too much of her own way because of her money – all in her own right, too.'

Davie paused, then plunged. 'You and Van Den Berg are no exactly pals, are you?'

'No, Davie, we're not. I should have told you right at the start – didn't want to put you off before you'd even started the job.' He drew on his cigar. 'When Taylor put him in for manager, the Dutchman wanted to bring an American pro.'

'Fuegosi?' Davie ventured.

'You've guessed it. But Taylor wanted a Scots pro, and I knew you were the lad for the job – you can keep the head', he smiled, 'at least I'm pretty sure you can. Taylor knew that if they had a Scot, you'd be here, on the job, when a member wanted to buy a club, or take some coaching. Big Fuegosi isn't very bright in the top storey – girls and flashy cars are all he thinks about.'

'So you think Fuegosi and Van Den Berg have set this up, to make me look silly?' Davie asked.

'No, Fuegosi, he hasna the brains, but the Dutchman

reckons Fuegosi will win, and that's one in the eye for me, since you're my protégé – but it's not so much the play I'm worried about, it's the money.'

'Nothing was said about money,' Davie said, 'though I expect Fuegosi will get—'

'It's the members' money I'm thinking about,' Cunningham interrupted. 'The Yanks are great gamblers, Davie, they'll bet on anything. Local patriotism is fierce here as anywhere. They get het up far more easily than we do, and when you step on to that tee Saturday, you'll be carrying hundreds, maybe thousands of dollars of your members' bets.'

Davie drew a deep breath. This was an additional load he hadn't thought of. 'Is Fuegosi a good player?'

'He's all that.' Cunningham's voice was grim. 'Been State Champion twice, and what's more, he's a hardened professional up to all the tricks, whereas you're just a lad who's played with his friends for the fun of it, and won some events back home.'

'What do you think my chances are?' Davie asked bluntly.

'Candidly, son, about evens. I think you have the golf to beat him, and the brains to outthink him, but you're not used to conditions out here yet – and your hands will be soft.'

'Well,' Davie's smile was grim, 'at least I'll no start the game frightened of him.'

'That's my Davie,' Cunningham cried and rose. 'You'll be all right – wish I could come over and watch the game, but I'm just about run ragged over my place.'

'You said I'd have to stand on my own feet,' Davie reminded him.

'I sure did. Get in as much practice as you can – and play your own game – go for figures.'

One more unpleasant truth had to be faced. 'If he beats me—'

'Your members will lose their dough – so what? They'll all have lost bets before.' Cunningham paused. 'If you win, you'll be top of the world here. If you go down, well, at least you'll have their sympathy – reckon everyone always has a soft spot for the little guy.'

It was the last remark that stiffened Davie's back, and made him determined to win, or burst a gut trying.

2.

'Get in as much practice as you can.' That remark of Cunningham's sat on his mind after Cunningham's departure, and made him smile. It was a strange paradox that the skill which had made this new life possible now tied up his waking hours so tightly that he had no time to practise and retain his proficiency. That evening, in a store at Tanooda, he bought a warm Indian blanket, and a few small nightlights.

When he confided his intention to Joe, the Italian boy was worried. 'Van Den Berg no like it, Davie.'

And, Davie lapsed for a brief moment into colloquial American. 'That's too bad Joe – and am I breakin' my heart?'

That night, when he closed his shop, Joe gave him a meal in the kitchen, then, with a pitching club and his putter, the nightlights and a couple of balls in his pocket, Davie set out for the far limits of the course, to practise the short game in private.

The 'feel' of American grass was different, as was the grain of the greens. His little nightlight glowed like a stranded firefly in the hole as he played, chip and putt, chip and putt, till, at last, even in the changed conditions, the ball began running to his satisfaction.

He walked home over the darkened course, the lights of the clubhouse a bright beacon, past the screens of new trees, past a soggy banked creek, where bullfrogs croaked lustily, to his shop. There he rolled himself up in the Indian blanket and slept. He was up at the first streaks of grey Ohio dawn. Dew was heavy on the shrubs, and strange American birds eyed him sleepily, but were unafraid. Anyone who was about so early could harm no one but himself, seemed to be their

152

verdict.

Now he set out to learn the course, studying the best line from tee to flag, driving, then playing several second strokes, to make sure he had the distance right. Then, just in case his drive strayed a little, he carefully paced out the distances from here, and here, and here . . . By the time he had studied six holes, it was almost eight. He walked back, washed and shaved in the men's room in the club, then ate the breakfast Joe had prepared, and was back, spruce and ready, in his shop when the first member arrived. Next morning he would start at the seventh.

That night, enjoying the meal Joe had cooked, he got a report. 'The Van Den Berg, Davee – he noa act mad, just sorta double talk, not sayin' the names, but talkin' about turnin' the place into a flop house, and tightwads too mean to pay room rent.'

Davie merely smiled. Another small problem had to be solved. Fuegosi was a snappy dresser, and Davie had as much personal vanity as most young men, and wit enough to realise that neatness of person rated a man higher out here than at home. Even if he didn't win, at least he'd try to prevent his audience passing comment on his appearance. The current fashion of knickerbockers, known as plus fours, he knew were not for him, he hadn't the height or build. The flannels he had brought from home were stout and service-able, but their grey shade was hardly attuned to the American scene. He chose a pair from his stock which were of a finer texture and a brighter shade and a white poplin shirt, collar attached, but he preferred wearing a tie to leaving it open at the neck. At home, the loose ends seemed to distract his attention, and pinned down, were apt to bulge up when he stooped over a chip or long putt. Greatly daring, he tried a bow tie. A 'Cheetie Bow' it would have been called back home, and its appearance greeted with derisive cries, yet it suited him. He felt right, with the taut, firm feeling he liked to have playing in front of a crowd. A manufacturer's sample pair of shoes described as 'Genuine Scots Auchterlonie moccasin brogues' were comfortable, their fringed tongues falling over the lace fronts, adding a picturesque touch.

Now he only had to replace the blue blazer he wore at home. It had to be something dark. At his practice session in the dawn, he had worn a white sweater, and all the time had been conscious of his white clad arms distracting his eyes from the ball. He took a blue denim garment called an overshirt home to Mrs Gertler, who, he discovered, ran a home dressmaking business for the ladies of Tanooda, and got her to cut it short at the waist, then blouse it by adding a broad band of shirred elastic.

3.

As the date drew near, tension mounted. Cunningham's words rang in his mind. 'You're a professional now, you play to win.'

It was the first exhibition match ever played on the course, and had been billed as far away as Cray Creek. Since Fuegosi commanded a good following, it was likely to be the biggest gallery Davie had ever played to. And the golfers who purchased or took lessons all had the match on their minds. 'Sure am lookin' forward to seein' you do your stuff Saturday, Prof. Guess after seein' you I'll feel like throwin' the clubs away.'

Davie would be encouraging. 'Och, now, you're only a beginner. Remember I've been at this game all my days.'

'And I reckon that's about the only way to be any good, born with a golf club in your hand, yessir!'

Then on another occasion. 'Think you can lick 'im, Scottie? He's a whole heap bigger'n you – sure don't seem fair.'

And Davie, reassuring himself as much as his questioner, 'Ach, size is no all that important.' Then, with a touch of pawky humour, 'I should be more accurate than he is, after all, I'm a lot nearer the ball.'

This inevitably delighted his listener. 'Atta boy, Scottie, I'll be rootin' for you!'

From Joe, he got regular reports of dining- and locker-room gossip. He was not a gambler, consequently knew nothing of the intricacies of betting, though he understood the significance of long and short odds. Thus to learn that he was quoted at eight to ten, while Fuegosi's price was around twos to evens, was just about what he expected.

'And Van Den Berg, whena the members issa talkin' he back you, then goes to phone, and lays off on his pal, Fuegosi.'

Then, on the morning of the match, Joe unwittingly gave him a piece of news he would rather not have heard at least not until afterwards. 'Davee, I think the Berg Boy be kinda quiet today, yes – Mistare Taylor issa coming to see the match.'

Davie had not told Joe about the manager's outburst after the Julie Buren incident. Indeed, in the stress of trying to play himself back into form, and do justice to his job at the same time, he had almost forgotten it. Now no matter how he tried to forget it, the thought leered like a ghost at a wedding.

The car park filled to overflowing. The crowds began to gather at the first tee, and filter along the fairways. It was a gayer dressed, more noisy and volatile crowd, with more women present, than at home.

Davie waited quietly beside his shop until he saw Fuegosi more elegant than ever stroll nonchalantly through the crowd. Then Davie nodded to the boy he engaged to carry his clubs, and walked across to the start.

Van Den Berg climbed to a bench behind the first tee, and greeted the crowd. 'Well, good afternoon, folks, the governors have asked me to say how pleased we are to have you here as our guests at Neveneck, and we sure hope to show you some good golf. The players are Ed Fuegosi, our own State Champion, who has a fine record in National events, he finished equal eighth in our Open, and our Home Pro. Dave Crombie, fresh out from Lill old Scatland, but with a top record as an amateur. This is his first pro game over here, so I'll dry up now, except to say, go ahead, you two fightin' cats – tear one another apart!'

This produced laughter and applause from those near enough to hear him, then Fuegosi advanced towards Davie, hand extended in beaming good fellowship. . . . Had Davie not got his grip in immediately, his hand might well have been pulped, as it was, his fingers were numb when released. Aye, Fuegosi was up to all the tricks.

As host, he pointed out the best lie to the flag, and the American played first. Much later, Davie realised that he became a professional that afternoon, and his graduation began from the moment he had to coax the blood back into his numbed hand. Rather to his surprise, Fuegosi played a spoon from the tee, the club which in later years became known as a number three wood. To Davie's pleasure, his own drive bounded some fifteen to twenty yards further on, thus forcing the American to play his second shot before Davie did.

It was strong, finishing behind the green, whilst Davie's iron landed barely six yards from the hole. Fuegosi chipped back to within three feet and Davie's try for a three, possibly due to his first hole nerves, ran two feet past. The lanky Yank got his putt down easily, and before Davie could walk forward to sink his little one, Fuegosi contemptuously knocked his bell away, conceding a half.

Again Davie politely pointed the road to the flag, and this time, Fuegosi used his driver, Davie's drive being five or ten yards short of his opponent's. Now he was right behind Davie, as he prepared to play his second, and seemed very interested in the club selected.

It was only when he saw the American take his own mid-iron and play a shot similar to his own that Davie understood why Fuegosi had used a spoon for the first tee. That had been his estimate of how far he could outdrive him. A complete stranger to the course, he aimed to place his drives just ahead, and thus be in no doubt as to which club to play next.

Elated by the discovery of this professional quirk, after another halved hole, and another conceded putt, Davie went through the polite motion of pointing the line, and after watching the American lash a long drive in the direction indicated, smashed his own tee shot away across to the opposite side of the fairway. Maybe he was leaving himself a difficult second stroke but thanks to his dawn practice, he knew how to play it, whereas Fuegosi now separated from him by the fairway, and the milling crowd, would have to figure it out for himself. Yet Davie walked off the third green one hole down, caught napping by the oldest, corniest trick in the bag.

He had putted to within two feet from the edge of the green, and Fuegosi had holed out from six feet in one more. As good etiquette demanded, Davie had remained standing from where he played, so that he would not walk over the line of Fuegosi's putt, or be within his vision to distract him. With his own ball so near the hole, he had hesitated when the American holed out, expecting the putt to be conceded. But Fuegosi took his own ball from the cup and turned away, very concerned, lighting a cigarette from the match his caddy was holding. In nervous embarrassment, conscious of the crowd's eyes, he played hurriedly . . . the ball ran six inches past.

Well, that was something he'd learned the hard way. On the fourth tee, he mentally wiped the slate clean. All right, play it Bert Sproggie's way. Forget what the other man's doing. Play your own game. Go out for figures, and empty your mind between shots. But that one-hole deficit was hard to make up. But for his one lapse he knew he was playing the game of his life, at the peak of his power and strength. He could sense the sympathy of the crowd, and knew from their comments that they marvelled at his ability to almost match his six-foot opponent's tremendous hitting. Yet he reached the turn still one hole in arrears. But for that, the crowd's sympathy would have been heady wine. As he walked through a lane of spectators, strangers would touch his arm,

'Go on, son – go it!, we're rootin' for you.'

For a few moments at the tenth, Davie's hopes rose. It seemed he could pull the game back to square. Due to a freshening breeze both had under-clubbed. Fuegosi was in a sand trap, and Davie short of the green, leaving him a pitch and run shot over an narrow bank. His pitch was a picture, it landed square, then ran straight for the hole, coming to rest against the flag stick.

The American played a spectacular explosion shot, raising a great feather of sand. His ball flopped to the green, leaving him a putt of six yards or so. Before lining it up, he asked for the flag to be removed. The crowd was tense, silent. If Davie's ball dropped when the flag was withdrawn, he would be deemed to have holed out at his last stroke, and thus won the hole.

Carefully, Van Den Berg, acting as referee, drew out the stick, but the ball merely teetered and stayed out. The crowd's breath drawn 'Aaaah' of disappointment was some consolation, yet, despite his feeling of being robbed by a rub of the green, when Fuegosi slotted home, his long putt for a half, Davie cried, 'Great stuff!' And led the applause, but he was still one down.

Going to the eleventh, he made the frightening discovery that despite the protective glove, his hands were giving out. Already he felt the raw soreness in his fingers and the fleshy pads at the base of them that foretold blisters.

Cut and thrust. Probe, try and gauge the other fellow's weakness. But hole after hole was halved in par figures. If this standard was maintained he would break seventy – for the first time in his life – yet he was still one in arrears!

The turning point came at the sixteenth. Their drives were on opposite sides of the fairway, and, waiting for Fuegosi to play, he wondered what the hold-up was. The bulging crowd hid what was going on. Then he saw Van Den Berg hurrying towards him. 'Come and have a look, Scottie, we're a bit balled up here.' Fuegosi's ball had landed in an absolutely unplayable lie. A hazard had been cut, and a big crescent of turf removed. Then a decision must have been taken to place the trap elsewhere. The turf had been replaced, all save the corner of a large sod. It had not been pressed down, and in the pocket it left, the Yank's ball was firmly lodged.

Fuegosi looked up as Davie came forward. 'Say – what's the local rule?'

Davie shook his head, and Van Den Berg spoke. 'Heck, guess that's something we haven't gotten around to yet. What's your say-so Scottie?'

For a moment Davie was tempted. Here was his chance to retrieve the situation. He could rule that the ball must be played as it lay, or penalty stroke incurred for lifting and dropping it. He hesitated a moment, then gave the ruling he deemed right and just. 'Ground under repair, Lift and drop – no penalty.'

Conscious of the crowd's murmurs, he walked away, then found the manager at his back. 'Hey, Scottie, don't you want to win this game?'

'Aye, I do,' Davie said coolly, 'but I want to win making the best play not from the other chap's bad luck.'

'Luck's part of this game, ain't it?' the man demanded . 'Plumb crazy – lettin' the club down.'

The tone was his usual angry snarl, yet Davie detected a note of unwilling admiration. The man had divided loyalties.

Then, almost before he realised it, they were on the seventeenth tee – and he was still one down, with only two holes to play.

The second last hole was Cunningham's gesture for a 'Tiger' finish – springing from the road hole at St Andrews. The sluggish creek hole of the Bullfrogs thrust out an elbow here, and the green was sited high on a plateau beyond the upper arm of it. Against the wind, it was just a possible two-shotter provided you were willing to take the risk, and could hit far enough to carry both arms of the water.

Fuegosi played safe. A long iron to the left. Now Davie pondered. Either play safe, or take the risk. Turning to his caddy, he had the fleeting impression of turning in time, he could see his father pulling the brassie out, saying, 'Go for it boy, take a chance.' He took the driver from his bag, and lashed a long shot away down to the right, committing himself to the dangerous chance of carrying the water hazard – and reaching the green in two.

Tension mounted in the crowd. They started the rush and scramble for vantage points. He knew qualms of doubt, facing the long second which must reach the narrow ridge of green, but put it behind him, steady now, easy, don't tighten up. It was a long carry, high arced brassie shot, fading slightly as it dropped, to bounce twice then race on to the green. Now he felt satisfied. His gamble had come off, and he wouldn't have many more full shots to play. His fingers were feeling like raw flesh.

Watching the ball's long flight, the crowd was silent, then as it ran on the green, a man behind him yelled, 'Yippee – he made it!'

As though the yell was the starting gun for a race, next instant he found himself carried along in a stampede to reach vantage points on the green. By the time he reached it, they were five to six deep all round.

Fuegosi's third shot left him perhaps three yards away. He might well hole it. Carefully, Davie lined up his ten-yard third shot, and Bert Sproggie's words came back to him. 'When a lad comes along who can get down in one putt on nine greens outa eighteen, he'll be the world's top golfer.'

All right, Bert, let's hope this one goes down. Relax, steady, . . . let your breath out slow . . .

He didn't need to look to see if it had dropped. His eyes landed on a tall, balding man in a light tweed suit, wearing rimless glasses. He was stooped forward, hands on knees, face rapt in agonised concentration. Then, simultaneous with the crowd's yell, Davie saw the man's face split into a grin of pure delight. 'Whoopee!' he yelled, then flung his arms round the man next to him, cuddling him in ecstasy.

All this he saw in a flash of arrested motion, as though a

cine-camera had stopped momentarily, then he was again engulfed in a swirling mob, racing to see the last act of the drama.

Now, for the first time since the game began, it was Davie's honour, his turn to play first. Now they were all square, and waiting for the crowd to settle, he remembered Cunningham's voice saying 'They get het up far more easily than we do.' All square now, still anyone's game, save that for the next slip there was no reprieve.

The crowd made a loop from tee to green, the nearer end pinched in to get a good view. The balcony of the clubhouse was crowded, every open window carried its quota of faces. The Filipino waiters, the porters and boys, even Joe in his chef's rig-out, were standing, all on boxes and barrows to see better.

Davie hefted the driver in his raw, aching hands; relax, his mind said, don't tighten up; easy, wait for it. Struck clean as a whistle, the ball screamed away over the crowd, every head turning to watch its flight. Where it settled left him an easy shot to the green. While Fuegosi's drive was still in the air, the crowd dissolved into a scurrying mass, eager to see the finish.

Both their seconds were picture shots. Fuegosi's a yard or so inside his own. The serried ranks around the green waited in tense silence as Davie lined up the putt. Confidence begets confidence. His last putt had gone down . . . calm and steady, he stroked it away. The ball raced over the green and scuttled into the can as though it had never any intention of doing anything else.

The crowd gave tongue in a quick burst, then, in fairness, went quiet as Fuegosi prepared to play.

All right, Davie thought, now you sweat it out. Maybe you'll get it down, but you can't beat me now. Then, looking at the man, he felt confident the match was already won. Fuegosi was trying too hard. His knuckles showed white on his club, a tiny muscle in his jaw was twitching. His ball trickled half-heartedly towards the hole, and stopped six inches short.

Pandemonium broke loose. Even as Fuegosi advanced to shake hands, the crowd were spilling over the grass. The big American was smiling, the gallant sportsman in defeat. He patted Davie on the back and from his smiling mouth came the greeting, 'Little Limey squirt!' in a venomous snarl.

Now Davie was surrounded by a wildly cheering mob, all trying to shake hands, to pat his back, to touch him wherever they could reach. Tall ones at the back to touch his clubs, or the top of his head. 'Atta boy!' Someone yelled 'Crombie of Neveneck – Rah – Rah!'

With his caddy, he was half led, half carried from the green. Now the balding spectacled man was close beside him. 'Sure knew you could do it, Scottie, I got tens – here – ' He stuffed a wedge of dollar bills into Davie's pocket.

That started a flood. Everyone near him began stuffing money into his pockets, his bag, inside his blouse, under his cap.

Slightly dazed by his victory, and embarrassed by the crowds of strangers stuffing money into his clothes, he became aware that one of the Filipino waiters was trying to attract his attention. 'Please, Mister Crombie, Mister Taylor wishes to speak to you.'

The joy went from the day. In an instant, he felt flat, deflated. Was all he had gained to be negatived because of his brush with an over-rich spoiled girl? He walked blindly up the steps across the verandah. Women turned and smiled to him, clapping their hands as he passed. Men who could reach him patted his back. 'Great boy, Scottie, we're proud of you!' Going up the broad stairway to the executive suite, he felt his studded shoes rasping the carpets. He should have changed them.

Waiting for him in the governor's room, with its panelled walls and panoramic view of the first and last holes, Mr Taylor was cool and remote as ever.

'First, David, my congratulations on a very fine win – a great boost for Neveneck – and its new pro.'

Davie coloured. 'Ach, maybe I was just lucky,' he

muttered.

'You were not.' The voice was cool and crisp. 'You took a carefully calculated risk, and brought it off. I admire a man who can do that.' He paused, 'Don't please judge all American golfers by Fuegosi. A good player, but a poor sport, and no gentleman.'

There was nothing much Davie could reply to that. Taylor went on, 'And now I should thank you and apologise. To thank you for a service you rendered me indirectly, and apologise for an unpleasant incident that was none of your choosing.'

For a moment, Davie could not follow his words, or grasp their meaning. Then he began to understand.

'Integrity, David, is one of the essential qualities men – and nations – must have if they are to survive and prosper. Unfortunately, when we prosper, we are apt to become surrounded by people who have a personal axe to grind, and whose self-interest is to make us lose sight of the obvious truth. You dealt my daughter's self-esteem quite a jolt and did her good!'

'I never realised at the time that I was maybe rude,' Davie began, but Taylor cut him short with a gesture. 'I'm glad you didn't.' His eyes met Davie's and held them. 'I'd like to think you carry that code of conduct into all your activities and associations.'

Davie hesitated a moment. 'That's the way I was brought up, Mr Taylor.'

The lean, brown face lit in a smile. 'I'm glad of that – typical of you Scots – ' He broke off as someone tapped at the door. 'Yes, come in.'

Cunningham entered, his face beaming. 'Come in Andy, just having a chat with your protégé here, though he doesn't need anyone to sponsor him now.'

'I'll say he doesn't.' Cunningham put an arm on Davie's shoulders. 'Just managed to catch the finish of your game. I'm proud of you, boy – and what a score – sixty-eight – you've sure made my pet course look silly.'

'He sure has,' Taylor put in. 'Maybe you'll have to think of toughening it up a bit, Andy.'

'Maybe,' Cunningham was thoughtful. 'Then maybe no. I'll say this, Mr Taylor, I don't think even Hagen or Jones would have licked this boy today, the stuff he was shooting.'

'I'm inclined to agree with you,' Taylor nodded. 'We're lucky to have him – and now, David, you'd like time to freshen up, then maybe you'd care to join Mrs Taylor, Andy here and myself for dinner – '. His eyes twinkled. 'Reckon Julie'll be along too. We intend to bask in the reflected glory of being seen with you, and are staking our claim first.'

His worries melted away, and he went through the club, smiling and acknowledging the cheers and backpats, the invitations to eat and drink.

The waning sun was still glorious as he returned to his shop, pausing to look at the clump of heather he had planted in the shrubbery. It was growing. The little trifle set the seal on his happiness. Now, he suddenly understood why staid, grown men, could leap in the air and shout 'Yippee!' for the sheer joy of being alive. He felt like doing that now. 'Swanee River' began sounding in his mind.

That night, his raw hands bathed and dressed by Mrs Gertler, he lay in the big bed, and watched the stern faces of Generals Grant and Robert E. Lee at the surrender at Appomattox, he wrote home.

Dear father and mother, sorry I haven't been able to write sooner, except for that postcard from New York, but I've been real busy since I got here. I'm not with Mr Cunningham after all, but have got a job as full blown pro at a green on my own. It is a lovely place, and I have a big shop where I sell clubs, bags and balls, everything for the game – even trousers and shirts. The name of my Club is Neveneck, and today I played an exhibition match with another pro and managed to win. I'm sending Ma a handbag, and Dad a wee short coat they call a Mackinaw out here. He can carry it with him, and maybe it'll stop his

164

cough in the bad weather. I'm real happy, and like it fine, though I miss you both very much. Give my regards to Bert Sproggie and Eck Black, and all the folk I knew, and all my love to you both from your son David.

And, on the edge of sleep, he saw again the windswept Angus coast, a club head glowing to birth under the magic of Bert Sproggie's hammer, his father plying the hoe among the loose soil in the garden. He saw the boundary fence at the sixth, and the flag winking away over the burn at the tenth, South America.

CHAPTER ELEVEN

I.

'WHERE do we go from here?'

Julie had said that first in the beginning of the summer. It was just a popular saying; a cheap verbal shuttlecock to be tossed airily back and forth. But as the months went by and the Yanks began talking about the 'Fall', the remark became a mental hazard in Davie's mind.

America was grand, he was getting on fine. True, he still had odd bouts of homesickness, generally after a letter from home, and Van Den Berg still found things to complain of. He was debt free and found that the only difference it made, was that he worried over other things instead.

Where do we go from here? In his heart he knew the answer, yet realised that it meant taking a bigger gamble than any chance he had taken before. Plain stupid, he told himself sternly, half the folk at home would give their back teeth to have his job yet he wanted wider fields to conquer. The life of a teacher professional was a good one, with good money but it was dull.

Thinking back, he tried to isolate the incident which had sparked off his discontent. Had it been Julie? Maybe it was being with her, talking and listening, catching chance remarks she made about distant places. He tried to argue himself out of the idea, and imagined discussing it with Bert Sproggie. His advice was likely to be: 'Away and do what you've a mind to, for if you don't have a bit try when you're young, you're not likely to when you're old.' And against that Chae Whitton would say, 'He's a fine one to be taking advice from – a drunken old smith who never has a penny to rub against another.'

And Davie knew what his dad would say, thinking back to that night when he'd beaten Baxter. Strange to think of that reckless streak in his dad.

Had Julie really touched off his discontent? No, she had never said a word until last night, and then her words had fallen on fertile ground.

Julie! . . . even to think of her gave him a warm, happy feeling inside. Right from the start he had been on his guard with her and even now, knowing her so much better, he always felt a tingle of expectancy, she was so unpredictable. Who would have thought she would have come back the way she did a few days after his game with Fuegosi. He had been on his knees, arranging a rack of shoes, when he heard her step, and saw her shadow fall across the threshold. She smiled, seeing his attitude, 'Morning, Maestro – is the penitent's bench full up?'

All right, what if she was spoiled and wilful, who could resist the gay beauty of her? He turned and met her mocking smile, and answered in the same mood. 'No, always room for another sinner at the end of the row.'

He knew by the impudent glint in her eye that she was about to say something intended to make him blush, to offset her casual apology by getting him at a disadvantage, and renewing her challenge, 'And properly dressed this time,' she went on, as he entered her name in the book.

Lifting his eyes from the page, he saw that she had turned away, and was examining a rack of iron clubs. Had she turned to conceal her own embarrassment?

'Fine,' he said. 'That will help to keep my mind on the job.'

She turned and made a mouth at him. 'So discouraging for us poor girls – and we try so hard.'

'Better to save your energies for the game.' He picked up her clubs. 'Let's go.'

'And start at the beginning,' she finished for him.

Her father must have given her a real talking to, he decided, for now she listened, and really tried to follow his teaching. An hour later, he had to admit she was an apt pupil, possessing the co-ordination of mind, eye and muscle which are the necessary natural endowments of any good golfer. The ball began to leave her club with a sweet 'click', and thud against the net.

'Easy,' he kept urging her. 'Relax – no tight muscles anywhere – swing the clubhead – think of it as a brick tied to a string.'

'Yes, Maestro.' She bobbed him a mock little curtsey, 'And then—'

'Away and practise, the way I've shown you, slow and easy and every time you get up the top of the swing, say to yourself, "Wait for it" then bring me your card the first time you break ninety.'

'No more lessons?'

'Look, Julie,' he used her first name before he realised it, and flushed.

'Keep at it, girl,' she cried in delight, 'you're breaking him down.'

'Look, Julie,' he repeated firmly, 'golf is a game you only have to start right – the rest you find out for yourself. Come to me once a week for a few minutes, just to check that you are not slipping back to your old ways, the rest is up to you.'

2.

That was the beginning. She brought him a card of eighty-eight then, six weeks later, one of eighty-four. 'And not allowing myself even the shortest putts,' she declared proudly.

'That's the way,' Davie nodded, 'I always think if a body is honest with himself in small things, he's—'

'Oh, Davie,' she broke in, 'I sure love these homespun sermons, all wool and a yard wide, don't you ever have fun? Are you really an old sourpuss?'

His mind slipped back to another life. New Year morning at the Johnstons' the farewell party at the Club.

'I like a party fine, if that's your meaning,' he told her, 'but this job doesn't give me a lot of free time.'

'You work too hard and too often,' she said. 'Look, Hagen and Chick Evans are playing a demonstration game at Blue Mountains, Sunday, let's go and watch them. Take a day off.'

He only hesitated for a moment, then, 'I'd like that fine but what will Mr Tay – your father say?'

'He'll give three cheers because I'm with you, he thinks you are a good influence.'

Such was his acclimatization to the social habits of America that he never gave a thought to the fact that Julie had dated him or that girls at home would never act that way.

She called for him in an enormous car with a bright-faced Filipino chauffeur sitting in the back. She saw the quick glance he gave towards the rear. 'No, I don't think I need a chaperone,' she read his thoughts, 'but we might want to come back with friends so Jake comes along to take the buggy home.'

Davie knew how to act in this democratic country. 'How are you, Jake?' he asked.

'Just fine, Davie,' the boy smiled back. 'Gee but you sure are a fine golfer, yessir!'

'Ach,' Davie said, 'I'm no better golfer than you are a driver, I bet.'

'Heck, anyone can drive a car,' Jake told him, and when Davie smiled and said 'Not anyone. I can't for one,' both Julie and the chauffeur cried out together, 'What? You can't drive!'

'Until I came out here I'd hardly ever been in a motor car – let alone drive one,' he told them.

'Well, what d'ye know?' Jake said in amazement, and Julie gave a crisp instruction.

'Jake, on the way home, we'll take side roads, and you'll start teaching Davie.' She turned to him 'it's kinda hard to take in, I've been driving ever since I could reach the pedals.'

She drove fast. Used as he was to the daily trip out and home with Joe, this smooth-running juggernaut which seemed to seize the road ahead, and fling it behind them with incredible speed, as driven by Julie, made him curl his toes in nervous fear for the first half-hour or so then, like everything else in this amazing country, he got used to it.

Blue Mountains Club was larger and more luxurious than Neveneck, like a huge hotel set in the midst of what looked like a great formal garden masquerading as a golf course. He was amazed to find that admission was being charged, but even as he pulled out his wallet, he was forestalled by Jake, who had in some unobtrusive fashion managed to park the car and obtain their tickets.

'Jake looks after things when I bring him,' Julie said. 'He'll see to the lunches as well.'

Davie gave himself up to pure enjoyment. It was almost a forgotten pleasure for him to be watching a golf match, and despite the novelty, he found himself assessing the play from a professional standpoint.

The course was beautiful. It looked a really stern test of the game but he soon discovered that it wasn't as difficult as it looked. It was designed to flatter the average player. Great sand traps yawned in front of every hole, yet there was always an easy road to the flag. Every green sloped towards the player, and the turf was so saturated with water that the ball could be pitched right up to the pin.

But it was thrilling to watch these two current masters. It was, altogether, a bigger crowd than he had ever known at home, more women among them, and more colourful and richer in dress. The players chatted and wisecracked with the gallery between strokes, two kings holding court, yet he could sense the edge between them. They might pretend it was fun, yet both of them were striving to give of their best.

The crowd bulged and eddied and swayed around the players. Every now and then, someone would touch his elbow, he would turn to find one of the Neveneck members smiling, 'Busman's holiday, eh, Scottie?' Then one said, 'You won't learn much here Davie – bar tactics – these guys got nothing on you.' Their names were headlines in the sporting press, and so glamorous, that he never thought to compare his own game against theirs. Now, as he piloted Julie through the crowd, with the quiet Jake ever an unobtrusive yard or so behind, new thoughts began running in his mind. He began to play along with them, to think what he would have done with each stroke, then watched how they tackled them.

Carefully, he began pacing out the length of their strokes, difficult though it was to count accurately in the moving crowd. Hagen and Evans certainly seemed to have more length off the tee than he had, but above all he noticed their supreme self-confidence and complete ability to keep casual and relaxed.

It was Julie who finally clothed his thoughts in words; they had reached the half-way stage; the players were taking a breather, and having their hands bathed and refreshed by their caddies. A red-faced man, acting as combined referee and master of ceremonies, stood up on a box and gave a resumé of the game and each player's figures so far.

'You can shoot stuff better than that any day of the week,' Julie said suddenly, linking her arm through his. 'You ought to be out there playing, not just following.'

Suddenly with the swift change of mood and subject so typical of her, Julie led him away from the crowd. 'I just wish you could see the National Links at Long Island. I bet they're more like that home course of yours.'

3.

' – better stuff than that any day of the week'. Not really true, but he could shoot stuff just as good, maybe, given the constant practice and experience. Julie's comment remained in his mind. Had she realised its impact, and deliberately changed the subject? Given a chance to make a disclaimer, the remark might well have been forgotten.

Through the long summer days, of teaching, coaching,

selling, then sleeping and starting again, it proved a constant nagging goad. Occasionally it would be nourished by some of the club's best players, who would invite him to make up a foursome. He and whoever was his partner delighted in conceding half a stroke to their opponents, and, generally, on the home stretch, Davie would have what he called 'a daft turn' and shoot three or more birdies in half a dozen holes, inevitably winning the game.

'No use you guys ever thinkin' you can beat the pro – ' his delighted partner would say. 'Next week Dick can have a shot of bein' his buddy and after that, it will be Elmer's turn, that way all of us will have a chance of winning sometime, meanwhile you guys pay up and like it.'

And whatever stake there was would be settled, and the little farce of engaging Davie in talk on some trifle or other while the money they insisted on paying him for his golfing company was tactfully slipped into his bag.

At first, the idea of being paid for playing a friendly game made him vaguely uncomfortable. Andy Cunningham was almost impatient when he mentioned it. 'Heck, son, you came here to make money, didn't you? Don't you understand that if you weren't so well liked by your members, you'd never be asked to join them in a game and, knowing you, I'll bet you're coaching them most of the time, true?'

'Well,' Davie admitted, 'when I see one of them doing something wrong – it's my job.'

'Sure,' Cunningham nodded, 'and just as I pay the doc when I'm sick, or the dentist when I've toothache, they're paying you for your services. Ye' know, Davie son, there's not many teaching pros who can shoot the brand of golf you do any day of the week.'

This near duplication of Julie's words came back again that night, when under the delighted eye of Mrs Gertler, he put on his new dinner suit.

Now the countryside was gay with the flowing reds and yellows of the Fall Summer was ended, and at the end of October, the course would close for the winter.

'Where do we go from here?' Another teaching job down at some winter resort in Florida? One had already been offered to him. And as a counter to that easy road, Julie's words came ringing back.

'Davie,' Mrs Gertler's voice broke in, 'I am telling you how nice you look, almost could I wish to be young again, you are a beau to be proud of.'

'What – ' he turned to her. 'Sorry, I wasn't thinking.'

'But you were,' she smiled archly, 'thinking of your Julie Buren, oh what a sweetheart for a young man!' Mrs Gertler rolled her eyes.

'Julie's not my – ' Davie began, then stopped. Just how could he describe his friendship with her. Their Sunday outing had been the first of many. They visited golf matches, sometimes merely for the pleasure of playing on a strange course. Free and friendly, she would link her arm with his, sometimes with the almost natural gesture of a child, she would take his hand. Somewhere along the road of their friendship, her feminine challenge had receded, though never for a moment did he cease to be conscious of her charm. In her gay off-hand way, she had assumed control of his further education. He could now drive a car, and make at least a fair showing on the dance floor, and now he was ready to appear at the Club's Fall Dance in his first tuxedo.

Yet, held back by child-deep restraints, he had never attempted to carry their relationship further, to 'slip around the corner for a spot of necking,' as Julie would put it. He was always aware of the power her wealth gave her, and that her stepfather was his boss, and, in a way, his friend.

He went out to Joe's car, lent with good will for the occasion. In two weeks' time the course would close. He had to decide – 'Where do we go from here?'

His faculties for appreciating life's good things were altogether sharper now. Moving about the crowded club, greeted on all sides by the members, he thought of the few dances he had been to at home, and mentally contrasted the little church hall, with its varnished planked walls, and knotty floor with the Club's lavish flower decorations, polished golden floors and first-class band. Aye, America had it all. Yet home had something too. What if the church hall smelled of varnish and disinfectant, it was, somehow, just as you felt it should be. Maybe the folks at home did not have much, but they made the best of it.

But home hadn't anyone like Julie. Tonight she was lovely, silken soft in floating gold and silver, with an exotic lustre that was somehow completely American. In spite of the people who claimed her, she seemed generally close to his shoulder. They danced a waltz to the tune of 'Wonderful One', then an enthusiastic Charleston to the current rage of 'Yes Sir, That's My Baby'; then with flushed cheeks, Julie suggested a cool walk in the quiet night air.

A fat harvest moon rode high, and the grass was dewy underfoot. The rich scent of autumn was in the air, as they strolled over the moonlit fairway, past the last green. Davie could feel the warmth of her bare arm through his sleeve, and her subtle perfume rose over the scents of sleeping flowers and fallen leaves. She stumbled, and he put out his free arm to steady her. The movement brought them face to face. Her hair was a nimbus of misty gold and the stars shone in her eyes.

'Julie – ' he said huskily, and drew her into his arms.

Her arms went gently round his neck. It was a long, quiet, kiss, but it made the blood pound in his ears. 'Julie, dearest Julie, you're bonnie – '

She took her hands from behind his neck and laid them on his shoulders. 'I think you're swell too, Davie,' she whispered.

He felt the soft swell of her breasts against him and her perfumed hair brushed his cheek. 'I – I wish,' he began, and his voice choked.

'What do you wish, Davie?' she whispered and laid her head against his cheek.

'Oh – I – just wish—'

'Shall I tell you what I wish?' she asked and he nodded.

'I wish my guy to be the greatest golfer in the world, and he could be just that – if he wanted to.' She put her hands back on his shoulders. She seemed to be shaking him, but so gently that it might only have been the quiver of excitement with her or even his own trembling.

'But I've got to—'

'All you need is some big-time experience on the tournament circuit. You're as good as any of the big timers.'

His mind confused by her rapid switch to such practicalities he protested. 'But, Julie, that takes money, and I've got to earn my living.'

She shook his shoulders. 'Wasting your time teaching duds to play.'

'I – I would like fine to play the big time,' he admitted, 'but, to make anything of it, well you have to be constantly at it – it would cost—'

'Cost nothing' The edge of impatience hardened her voice. 'I could stake you.'

He felt the primeval male urge to be free and master, untied and unbeholden. Yet he knew the offer was meant kindly – always having too much money, it meant little to her.

'But, Julie,' he said firmly, 'I couldn't let you do that, it wouldn't be right.'

For a moment, he saw a flicker of anger tighten her lovely mouth, then, in a flash, it was gone. She kissed him again, gently. 'Oh, my real homespun Davie, with your stuffy Scots ideas. Just for the sake of a few dollars, a guy who would lick the world has to waste his time teaching beginners, and selling golf gear.'

She tugged at his arm. 'Let's go back and dance. It's damp and cold out here,'

Somehow it didn't seem like Julie, to give in so easily. He fully realised that she was used to getting her own way. But the seed had fallen on well-tilled ground. If he could manage to play a season or two at the tournaments. Crazy to think of it, with a good job as he had here. Still it was tempting.

Now the season was really finished. After Saturday, the course would close down until April.

Cunningham was visiting, giving Davie help to check up and assess the balance of his first season. In some strange way, their relationship had changed, and it was Andy Cunningham who had brought the change about. As the summer months wore on and Davie stood ever firmer on his own feet, the older man had gently admitted him to a friendly equality.

In a sudden moment of deepened perception, Davie saw his daily round. His well-appointed shop, with its lavish stock of merchandise, Andy Cunningham, his friend, lounging in one of the easy chairs provided for his clients, a big sheaf of papers in his hand, and the inevitable cigar clamped in his jaws. Andy Cunningham, exiled Scot, who had conquered the New World, a visiting ambassador at the court of a friendly power, dressed in expensive, easy-fitting clothes, with a big car to carry him wherever he wished, whenever he wanted to go. Now Cunningham made the characteristic gesture of taking out his cigar, and rubbing his jaw with the heel of his hand.

'Say, Davie, what have you been living on all summer? Heck, if I could cut my overheads to this chickenfeed, I could have been retired by now. If I'd wanted to.'

Davie hesitated, then, 'To begin with, Andy, I lived thin because of the money I owed for stock. Then, well after that was paid, I was so busy here that I hadn't time to spend much. Besides I had everything I needed.'

Cunningham nodded. 'Maybe that, but don't forget you came out here to make a better life for yourself. Now, get this straight, not every lad from back home falls into an outfit like this. I expected you to do well; but it sure shakes me the way you've piled it up in one season. You'll have to spend it around, boy, that's what money's made for.'

'You mean spend money for the sake of spending it?' David said.

'That sure scares that canny Scot!' Cunningham watched the fragrant blue smoke curl lazily up, then turned and grinned at him.

'Son, this country is booming because folk don't salt their dough away, but spend it to make things better for themselves. They're always confident that there is more where that came from. Maybe the balloon will burst one day, but there's no sign of it yet. So do your bit towards American prosperity, spread it around.'

'But what should I do?'

'Heck, Davie, d'ye expect me to show you how to suck an egg? Buy yourself a car, go down to Florida, take a vacation and get yourself some fun. If you feel you must work, take that job with the hotel and only work when you feel like it. Then come back here in the spring.'

This was it. Now he must tell Andy.

'I'm – I'm minded to have a shot at some of the big tournaments, the big time stuff.'

Cunningham stubbed out his cigar. 'Here we go – another contender for the British Open!'

'But I'd have to go home to try for that,' Davie stammered.

'That's the goal for every guy on the tournament trail,' Andy said. 'They play out here for the big dough so's they can go back to the old country – and play for peanuts.'

'If there's no money in our Open, why are they all so keen on it?'

'Distant fields are aye green,' Andy lapsed into his native speech. 'The tradition and glamour of it, I guess. What's put this idea in your mind – the Buren girl been working on you?'

Davie had now acquired enough self-possession to restrain his blush. 'She hasn't exactly discouraged me.'

'That baby would settle for fame at second-hand, I reckon, so long she was part of it. No, Davie, I'm not knocking your girl friend, she's a nice kid, but let us hope that it's Crombie the man she's after not Crombie the golfer.'

Davie met his eyes, and held them. 'Do you think Crombie the golfer might ever amount to much?'

Andy shook his head in doubt. 'Hard to say. It's a tough game, the tournament circuit, Davie, d'ye know what you're in for?'

'Not exactly, but I can guess. Andy, tell me honestly, do you think it's not worth it.'

'If you can hit the top and stay there, boy, it's Klondike so far as the money is concerned. But it is brutal – dog eat dog – and the also-rans on the edge of the breadline! They would be far better off doing your job, teaching and selling.'

'Andy, I'm twenty-two now, and playing pretty well. Do you think I'd be throwing my future away?'

'Hell, Davie, if you can hit the top ten, the sky's the limit so far's your future's concerned. The golf business is on the up-and-up. Golf is a big public spectacle now, and in the years to come, even bigger. The manufacturers and merchandise guys are gonna organise bigger and better shows. Don't you see it's their way of spreading the game? If you want to sell more golf goods then you need more golfers. They organise a big show and advertise it. Along comes Mr Citizen and his wife. Nice afternoon in the country, hullo what's this? Let's watch this golf game – got it?'

Davie nodded.

'Now, even to a non-player, good golf is thrilling. It's a game of individual effort, man against man and nature. It's got excitement, tension, drama. And can you imagine a better place to spend a nice afternoon than out on a good course?

'Pretty soon, Mrs Citizen begins thinking what a nice refined and healthy game it is, and how she'd like to see Henry playing, so much better than yelling his head off watching baseball, or hanging about a pool-room. And Henry having a whale of a time watching some player lambasting the ball from here to breakfast time, and seeing himself doing the same, 'I'd sure like to take up golf,' he says. 'If only we had a course handy.' Get a dozen or two citizens

178

together, thinking the same way and bingo! There's a new club formed, and the tournament sponsors have got themselves customers.'

Davie listened to this simplified formula for expanding the market and realised the truth in it. 'Looks like there'll be plenty of competitions to play in, then,' he said, 'if you have the time – and the money.'

Andy fumbled in his case for another cigar. 'Trust canny Davie to stopt the snags right off. Aye, it needs money to start with, a lot more than you have salted away, for it will take you at least eighteen months to break through, even if you have the top stuff in you.' He lit up, and put the spent match away. 'I suppose you turned down the Buren girl's offer of backing?'

'How did you know she – ?' Davie said, then stopped.

'Heck, quite a few top men have been staked to start off by folks who believed in them, but not for me, no sir!'

'Nor me,' Davie said, 'but I'd fair like to have a try.'

Andy got up and laid a hand on his shoulder. 'I think you'd best do that, Davie, if you have a mind to. If you can stick it out, you might well break through and would I and everyone who knows you be real proud!'

Davie drew a long slow breath. The die was cast!

'How do I get started?'

'You still go down to Florida. Get hold of Bob Sloan. He's a Scot from our part of the world. Last I heard he'd retired from playing, and is working for a new outfit who are organising big tournaments for various sponsors. I'll give you a note for him.'

'And where do I find him?'

'Bob's a convivial soul, go on a club and pub crawl till you find him. Lots of our lads go there for the winter, and play the circuit, they make enough to cover their expenses, and go back to teaching come spring. You'll spot them, and if you can't, well, stand by the door and start singing 'Loch Lomond'. Before you've got through a couple of lines, every Scot in the place will have joined in.'

When they parted, Cunningham wished him luck.

'I've got to hand it to you, Davie, you've got guts. Maybe I'd like to have done the same at your age, though conditions were different then, and I'm too old now. Anyway, I reckon there's easier ways of getting stomach ulcers. I'll be watching the papers and rooting for you.'

It was the afternoon of the day the course was closing. Davie had a visitor. 'Just come over to say cheerio and good luck, Scottie.'

Busy putting dust sheets on the stock, Davie did not pause. 'Thanks, Mr Van Den Berg,' he said.

But the man did not leave. He stood silent for a moment, then said, 'Reckon you think I was pretty rough with you?'

Davie realised that Van Den Berg was embarrassed. He turned and gave him a grim smile. 'What do you think?'

Van Den Burg made a gesture. 'I'd been working all hours getting the course and clubhouse ready. I'd got used to working with Fuegosi – thought you were another stand-offish Limey. Then I began to see you were a decent guy, that everyone liked you.'

A warm tide rose in Davie. He held out his hand,' Thanks, Bill.'

The handshake was firm. Then Van Den Berg put his free hand on Davie's shoulder. 'Good luck, Davie boy. I've talked to the governors. You'll still be listed as attached to Neveneck; if you break through to the top, will every member here be proud. I can just hear them boasting, 'Davie Crombie – he's our club pro, but we couldn't expect him to waste his time at the nets and in the shop – we always reckoned he was a world beater.'

'You understand, Bill, I've got to try.'

'Davie, if I had half your skill at the game, I'd be doing the same. You'll always be welcome here.

For a moment, Davie was doubtful. Was he doing the right thing? But the die was cast. He had to pit his strength and skill against the best there was.

CHAPTER TWELVE

1.

IN January 1927, in the clammy heat of the American Deep South, Davie hit rock-bottom in the hard, cut-throat world of the big golf business. He stood alone, looking at the completely impersonal scoreboard. The press might get lyrical in their write-ups of smiling Walt Hagen, and wise-cracking Chick Evans, but here, they were listed just as Hagen, W. and Evans, C. No matter who'd won, it wasn't Crombie, D. F.

He paid off his caddy, hitched the bag to his shoulder, and made for the car park. His auto was a veteran now, worn out with his wanderings over the American continent. Sitting on the cracked running board, he took stock of his position – he was as near broke as made no difference.

Give up the tournament racket? Go back and maybe get a teaching pro job somewhere? He was still listed as attached to Neveneck, and they still paid him a modest retainer, though his shop and stock had been taken over by a tall, young American, who realised his limitations, and was content to teach and sell.

But Davie wasn't going to give up. He'd been conned over the appearance money and that would have to be paid back for the sake of his self respect. He'd seen Julie once last September and got a card at Christmas, and she'd been so dead keen for him to take the tournament trail. Had Cunningham been right – not the man but the golfer?

Yet, despite the lean times, and always ending up halfway, he was still stubbornly certain he could stand up and slog stroke for stroke with the best. He was competition-wise now, tournament-salted. He was stupid over Julie as he'd been about the Johnston girl. The less he saw of Julie, the more he longed for her. When things had been really tight, he'd filled in with odd jobs, coaching, selling golf gear in the sports departments of big stores. He was always asked to stay on, but when the date of a big event came round, the urge to try his luck was irresistible and off he went again.

When he started his car, the engine belched smoke, and made asthmatic protests. The prize money was in his wallet – equal seventh – one hundred dollars, and that added up to cheap rooming-houses and hamburger meals.

On the way through the town, he collected his mail. Two were from home, one in strange writing, the other from his father. The third was marked 'Golf Sport Inc'. They still kept up the appearance of sending the money through that organisation. He felt like tearing it up, and throwing the fragments in a trash can, but poverty ever humbles pride and he put the cheque carefully in his wallet.

His thumb was under the envelope flap of his dad's letter when he saw a cop waiting across the street, ready to give him a ticket. He put the letter in his pocket, and drove out of town.

At a roadside café, he lingered over his meal, and read,

Dear Davie, Hoping this finds you well as it leaves me at present. I had a bad turn with my chest at the back end, and am fine now. It's grand to know you are getting on so well, seeing so much of America. Bert Sproggie was asking for you, and says it's the life for a young man and he envies you and says he knew all along you'd do well out there.

Poor Bert is far from happy as Johnston is fair letting his business go to smash, after the let down of his family. His son got a lassie into bother, and he ran away to London, and the older girl has been chasing the Menzies lad a fair scandal. Well, she got him, they were married last month, but his father has been thrown out of the foundry. Some trouble about money from India, and the girl thinking she was getting the foundry, and the Menzies lad with a job up in Dundee as a clerk. The only one of them worth a snuff is the wee lassie, Beth, the most sensible one of the lot, but not much she could do, and her growing up so bonnie.

Now for the big news, the course is to be remodelled, and that will make it top championship standard. The great James Braid was here, and walked over the links with me – a perfect gentleman, and real interested when I told him about you. There is talk that the Open Championship will be played here once the turf is knitted together. We have six of a staff now, and the Committee has put water in the house. Your mother sends all her love, we are both keeping fine. Your affec. father.

The sheets of cheap paper in his hand, Davie saw the kitchen at home, and his mother knitting by the fire, his father labouring with a spluttering pen and a penny bottle of ink. Davie sighed. If he had stayed at Neveneck, he'd have had money in the bank now, able to do something for his father who was obviously not in the best of health. He opened the strange envelope. 'Dear David, Thank you very much for the lovely Christmas card to Dad – we don't live at Balgowan now, what with Rodger away, and Mary married. The house was too big for mother to look after, since trade is slack, and Dad far from well. We have a nice house on the new council estate, and Dad keeps asking Bert Sproggie about you. We hear you are doing very well indeed. Yours sincerely, Elizabeth Johnston.'

His mind saw Beth in her gym slip and white blouse, warning him from the stairs; the same wee lass in tears – then pulling angrily away from when he told her she was too young to be thinking about things like that. Aye, she was the nicest of the lot, but that was long ago and far away.

He felt fresh, with the heat waning with the sunset. If he drove most of the night, and slept in the car, that would give him an extra day's practice before the big money tournament started at Indian Trace – practice to try out the discovery he'd made last week. The discovery that might shoot him to the top if it really worked. To combat the big hitters, courses were being continually stretched. That meant more length from the tee and his lack of inches made that difficult until he made his discovery. He was confident that in all other aspects of the game, he was as good as anyone and several of the leading sports writers agreed. 'Crombie – the perky little Scot, cannot be held back from top money and first place much longer. His golf is superb, he is a likeable chap – lack of competition experience and maybe his lack of inches – yet, his very cockiness, his lips ever pursed to a whistle, makes him beloved of the crowds – mark our words – he'll break through soon, and once there, he'll be hard to dislodge!'

That had been six or seven months ago and he hadn't broken through yet. Then Davie made a resolution. The Indian Trace event was a big one and prize money was high. All the stars would be there, and today America's best was the world's best. If he couldn't do well in this one, a second or third, he'd go back to teaching and selling. At least he'd eat better, and be able to save a few dollars. He set out to drive by night.

He drove steadily on, slowing only at intersections to check direction. As he drove along, his mind went back to his first game for prize money – soon after he'd left Neveneck. It was in Florida, the late fall of 1924. It was a one-day event, $500 top prize, hardly enough to attract the top men, but quite a field of really top class players lined up that morning. He'd thought the heat in Florida would be troublesome, but a cool breeze blew in from the Gulf of Mexico, bringing with it a soft, pearly grey sea mist, that reminded him of home. And the ball ran for him. Nothing went wrong. The shrubs lining the fairways resembled the whin and gorse bushes he knew from home. He tramped along, whistling 'Swanee', and the crowds encouraging 'Go it, Scottie boy, you're making the rest look silly.'

He'd won that event by two clear strokes, and when the time for the presentation came, the hardened regulars looked sourly at a raw first-timer walking off with the money. The event had been sponsored by a shoemaking company, and when he came on the platform to receive his prize, it was discovered that he was wearing the firm's product, the 'Genuine Scots Auchterlonie Moccasin Brogues'. The sponsors were delighted. That rated a bonus of another hundred dollars. Davie signed their form without another thought, and went on his way, whistling.

The shoes were worn out now on the turf of a thousand fairways, still the money had been useful, he could have used it now. For he hadn't lifted another first in the two years' hard slog with barely eating money to show for it.

The appearance money was the thing that rankled. He'd finished equal eighth in an event in New York State, and been summoned to the organiser's office.

'Seems like things aren't too good for you, son,' a man who introduced himself as Bob De Cuyster said. 'Yet you're a natural – the crowds like you.'

'I like playing – competing,' Davie said. 'I'm trying to prove I'm as good as anyone.'

'There's a whole lot of good boys tryin' to prove the same thing,' another stout man put in. 'They can't all be winners, son, but we like havin' you around. You got fans even if you're not hittin' the top.'

'So we're adding your name to the list for appearance money,' De Cuyster went on. He handed over a list of the forthcoming events. 'For every one of these that you tee off in, we'll pay you – ' he named a modest sum. 'It'll at least see that you eat. If you hit top money, well we don't pay, you won't need it. But win, or lose, we want you playin'.'

Davie had signed their forms without a thought. So the months of hard, unrewarding effort went past and then that day at the end of the big tournament in Chicago, which was still so vivid. He'd gone down to the men's room for a shower. It was tiled, underground, with it's double row of washbasins down the centre. One side was filled with competitors, all cleaning up. The mirrors above the basins made them invisible to him, as he used a basin on the far side. But their words came over clearly, 'Yeah, I'd sure like to have some dame screwy enough to stake me—'

'You mean Bill Cowdersby?' another voice asked.

'Sure and he'll never make it. Couldn't hit a bull over the butt with a banjo and he's not the only one.'

'You mean the lil' Scots guy, the whistlin' iceberg?'

'Huh, he's not big enough for an iceberg, he's only a snowflake.'

'And on some crazy dame's payroll?'

'Guess so. Back of the barn talk says it's some meat packin' millionaire's daughter. Determined to make a world champ outa him but his Scots pride gotta be saved – yessir! They give out through Golf Inc., call it appearance money.'

The words crawled like maggots through Davie's mind. He dried his hands, and left the room. Now he lived for the day when he could hand Julie a cheque, and say, 'Thanks, that money was helpful when I needed it, but I've made the grade, thanks for the loan.'

A huge truck with blazing headlamps pulled his mind back to the road. How many miles to Indian Trace now?

On the spacious practice ground next morning, he started with his driver, and a dozen balls. More length from the tee to ensure his second could be an iron, even his rivals admitted his accuracy in that sphere. But more length wasn't enough, he had to have accuracy from the tee as well. That day, he hit hundreds of practice drives. Evening found him tired, but satisfied. He went back to his cheap motel whistling 'Swanee'. From now on, he'd either be top of the tree – or give it up.

2.

Pete McAran was a journalist with one ambition. He wanted to be a sports writer. The editor kept him pinned down to street stuff, with an occasional foray to features or off-beat stories. Now, with the big event at Indian Trace starting today, he was sent off to cover that giant terrapin story, and after him studying the form of all the entrants. That lil' guy Crombie now, it sure had to be his turn soon. Pete felt a sort of affection for him; after all, Pete reasoned, his name had a 'Mac' in it, so, way back, his folk must have come from Scotland too. So Pete took a chance. Got a phoned cover from a buddy about the terrapin, and praying that the editor wouldn't phone him at the point for an expand, he went off to Indian Trace. But once there, Pete got scared. If he were found out, he'd thrown his job away unless he pulled off a scoop – and that wouldn't be easy, golf tourneys were big news now.

Then, when he saw the scoreboard, Pete's hopes rose. Crombie, D. F. was leading, end of second round, by two strokes. This was it. If the lil' guy won, and he could get the news in first, old Spittinblood wouldn't give a damn where he was calling from. So Pete started to reconnoitre. It was no good hangin' around the Press Tent. The big guys would have the phones tied up. Then he made a discovery and patted himself on the back for his smartness. At the top of the club stairs they had a phone, and stretching the cord to its limit and looking sideways from the window, you could see the last fairway, the last green was just under the window at the corner.

So Pete went out on the course, and gathered enough background material for a column. Some of it would come in handy if he'd have to stall for time on the line. All the galleries were talking about Crombie, 'the Whistling Snowflake', and big chaps were puzzled, saying it just wasn't physically possible for a guy his size to drive the length he was doing. Then, on the greens, he was slotting the ball home from all angles. At the end of the third round, he was four under par, and five strokes clear of the field.

Then Pete smelled another story, when that fair-haired honey tore up in the Cad with the Filipino chauffeur, asked where Davie Crombie was on the course, and went straight there. Who was she? Ask some of the gossip writers. She was the daughter of that meat packing millionaire, the guy building the new course at Pampoona Beach? What's her name? Burring – Bunning? Oh, Buren, she sure is rooting for that Crombie guy!

Pete waited in impatience, then, when Crombie got to the turn on his last round in a three below par of thirty-three strokes, he made for the clubhouse, and stood by the phone, occasionally stretching the cord to reassure himself he could see all the last hole from the window.

When the moving mass of Crombie's gallery dissolved from around the seventeenth green, scrambling for the last tee, spreading along the fairway, Pete lifted the phone and called his paper.

He asked for the newsdesk, but it was old Spittinblood's voice who growled at him 'McAran, what the hella you do'n at Indian Trace?'

'Never mind that now,' Pete's voice was shaking. 'Get this headline, Crombie breaks through! The lithe, little Scot, whom leading sports writers have said was bound to break through sooner or later, today justified their prophecies. On this super course, extended to punishing length, and playing to a star-spangled field of the World's best, 'the Whistling Snowflake', as the crowds call him, spreadeagled the entire entry—'

'Quit stalling!' the voice growled in his ears, 'gimme the score.'

Pete extended the phone cord to his utmost, and looked down on the mass of people surrounding the last green. A spruce little figure clad in the now familiar dark blue jerkin, was carefully lining up an eight-yard putt. Pete drew a deep breath and took a chance.

'To his magnificent rounds of sixty-eight, seventy, sixty-eight, he has clinched his victory by another sparkling round of sixty-eight.' A thin sound of handclaps and cheers drifted up. Pete looked out of the window – the little guy was just taking his ball from the hole. 'Hold it! He'd slotted in a long one – sixty-seven, making a winning total of two seven three.'

'O.K., Buster, you made it, now I'm gonna ask you again, two questions – how come you've beaten the lot – not a word from the tickertape yet, and second, what the hella you doin' at Indian Trace?'

But Pete had hung up, and was gazing out the window, taking in the frenetic scene round the last green. That Buren dame sure was pettin' the Crombie, arms round his neck, kissin' him, then takin' his arm, leading him off the green, and a horde of guys round him, all making their pitch. He can't even get his card signed. Now the radio guy had got hold of him, his jaws snapping like a pair of scissors, and hanging on to Crombie's other arm so that he couldn't get away before they'd interviewed him.

3.

Dozens of strange men were shouting questions at him, thrusting papers at him, and pens to sign with. The world was unreal, the only reality was Julie's arm through his – the scent of her, bringing back Neveneck. Suddenly, Davie found his hands trembling, his knees shaky. Still not grasping the full results of his success, he allowed Julie to lead him into the sanctuary of the clubhouse, where he sank gratefully into a chair. The struggle to maintain control, to concentrate, to appear ice cool, concentrating, whistling – knowing that one slip could lose him the event had exhausted him.

Julie saw him shaking, his face white. 'Relax, Davie dear, you've won, take it easy.'

But Davie couldn't calm down. He needed time to unwind. 'It's all these men, Julie – something I don't know what to do about – all wanting me to sign contracts. What cigarettes do I smoke, what shaving cream do I use, what about a licence to make jerkins like the one I wear, would I talk on the radio, write golf articles?'

189

'Relax, Davie,' Julie kissed him again. 'You've broken through to the top so, of course, they all want you to sponsor things and write, and go on radio.' She signed for a waiter to bring him a drink, but when it arrived, it wasn't a waiter who brought it, but a keen-looking man in a business suit, with another stouter man, dressed much the same behind him. 'Glad to know you, Mr Crombie.' He proffered a glass. 'And not rotgut, the finest produce of your native land, next to the golf, of course ha! ha! I represent the biggest marketing company in the Mid-west, and we'd like to sign you up, why, there's a heap of good products you could—'

'Davie's not talking to anyone right now.' It was Julie who spoke. 'Come back tomorrow and see his manager.'

'But I haven't – ' Davie began, then her soft hand stopped his mouth.

'Could we contact Davie's manager now?' the second man asked. 'Long distance phone, maybe?'

'Sorry, gentlemen. Davie's manager is on a plane right now, flying up here, and he's gonna be mighty busy when he does arrive. Davie has two big exhibition games to play next week, and another big event on the following week – why we're working now on the script for his coast-to-coast radio talk. Just leave your card, boys. Davie's manager will be in touch.'

They withdrew defeated, but immediately, there was another knock on the door. 'Please, Mr Crombie – presentation of prizes – crowd's getting impatient.'

'But Julie, I haven't got a manager,' Davie repeated.

'But sure you need one, why, country boy, you can't even begin to handle this.'

Davie was recovering, but still shaky. For over two years, all his drive, energy, determination had been concentrated on winning. Now he stood aghast before the commercial monster that threatened to devour him.

'A manager – but who?' he asked.

'Bill Van Den Berg,' Julie said promptly, and stopped his protests with a gesture. 'I know you didn't get on with him.

He's sorry he rode you as he did. He admits now that you're worth a dozen Ed Fuegosis. He hasn't enough to do at Neveneck, he'll jump at the chance of managing your affairs.'

A louder, more impatient knock at the door, 'Please, Mister Crombie – presentation.'

Julie bent over him smiling. 'We'd better go, Davie, or they'll think you're throwing a temperament.' She straightened back an errant lock of hair, adjusted his bow tie, then pulled him to his feet. 'Cummon, Maestro, come out and meet your fans and don't forget the cute lil' Scots accent when you come to make your speech.'

And the roars of the crowd swelled up as he mounted the platform, holding on to Julie's hand as though it was a lifebelt.

After that, Davie let Julie take over. His battered old auto was left in the car park. 'The used car boys will give you a few dollars for it,' Julie said, in the hotel lounge that night. 'Take the Cad, with Jake to drive to the next event. From now on, Davie, you just concentrate on hitting the ball – let other people do the rest.'

'Now Julie, that money you were paying me – ' Davie fumbled for his cheque book.

'Forget it. Old man Taylor was even keener than me to stake you. Why blame us for wanting to help write a new chapter in the history of American golf? It was only peanuts anyway.'

Again her gesture stopped his protest. 'That stuffy Presbyterian conscience of yours. It has to be placated some way.'

Her business-like manner was a new Julie. He pushed away his doubts and the warning lurking in his mind. After two years of comparative loneliness, her company, in any mood, seemed wonderful.

Later in bed that night, tired, yet wakeful, he started as his door handle turned, then sat upright almost in fright when Julie came in, and closed the door behind her. 'You shouldna come in here!' he protested.

'Shucks, who says?' She was scornful, then her lovely eyes twinkled mischievously, 'after what's between us.' Then, as though to quieten his nervous attitude, her manner changed. 'And you're doubtful about needin' a manager? Look at this.'

It was a copy of an evening paper, and carried a half-page advert. '*Top Golfers Wear Only Genuine Auchterlonie Scots Moccasin Brogues* says Golf's pint-size Maestro, Dave Crombie, top money winner at the all star Indian Trace Tourney. They really helped me win, he says. They'll improve your game too!' The letterpress was finished with a full length portrait of him, followed by a list of stockists and prices. 'How much did you get for this, Country Boy?'

'I – I was wearing a pair that day I won the event down in Florida. I gotta hundred bonus.'

'Yeah because you were wearin' em,' Julie said, 'over two years ago, and I'll bet you signed on the dotted line. And now they'll make thousands, and you won't get a red cent. Boy! Do you need a manager!'

Then her mood changed. 'Never mind, Davie, you're still tops with me.'

She shed the silk robe she was wearing, and Davie saw she had nothing but a cobwebby garment beneath it. As she reached for the light, he made a last protest. 'Julie – I like your father – he's been good to me – how can I face him if . . .'

'I'm fond of the old man Taylor, too.' She snapped out the light, leaving only a reflected glow from still burning signs. He heard her shoes being kicked off, and the slither of her last garment falling. 'But I'm grown up, Davie – I've the right to do as I please—'

Now she was at the bedside, her fingers fumbling at his pyjama coat buttons. 'Davie, dear you're all tensed up – and you're human – and a man—'

Her breasts were against his chest, her arms round him. All his moral principles vanished in the fires of his need. His sleep that night was dreamless exhaustion.

Next morning she was gone when he woke. He hardly knew how to treat her when she came down a few minutes later, radiant as ever. 'Wow, Davie – that was glorious, wasn't it?' she said, then resumed her old, teasing manner. 'And next time I come along for a little lovin' in the night, if you make any protests, Buster, I'll bat you one.'

Then their breakfast was interrupted by a desk porter bearing a double handful of letters, telegrams, and messages phoned in, all addressed to Mr D. F. Crombie. Davie stared at them in dismay, but Julie pushed him aside. 'Eat your ham and eggs, Davie – and forget 'em – not your worry.' Then she spoke to the desk clerk who'd brought them in. 'Get on the phone to Mr Bill Van Den Berg, at Neveneck Golf and Country Club, and tell me when he comes on.'

Then she smiled again to Davie, 'All you've got to think about is hitting the ball – let Bill sort these out when he gets here.'

And, as Davie ate his breakfast, the saying of Cunningham's rose in his mind, 'The Yanks love a winner.'

CHAPTER THIRTEEN

1.

The Golf Mechanic was an annual journal designed to help the less proficient players. In pictures and prose, it dissected the styles and swing, the methods and movements of the top players, pointing out the tricks and mannerisms, the anxious-to-improve might adopt with profit.

In the 1928 edition, Lee Bendon wrote:

> Dave Crombie, the 'Whistling Snowflake', the Gallery's idol, is undoubtedly the master shotmaker on the present American scene. He is the exception to the rule that a good big 'un always beats a good little 'un – And, while it is interesting to note just how he has overcome his lack of inches, the study is profitless – no one could copy him. No one can hope to attack the ball in the Crombie style. The method is his alone.
>
> The advantage of a tall man, is, naturally, the extra leverage he can bring to bear by reason of the larger diameter circle his club head describes. As will be brought out by the slow motion film.
>
> Crombie has offset this by flattening both top and bottom ellipses, and thus stretching it sideways. On the back swing, with club vertical, hands at shoulder height, there is a decided rock sideways of the trunk from the hip upwards, and this, with the completion of the back swing in this plane, gives a terrific wind up preparatory to hitting.
>
> The downswing starts in the usual Crombie manner, until the hitting area is reached, then the trunk snaps back to the vertical, giving extra, added force to an already

mighty wallop. But the terrific force he has generated must be curbed slowly, else he would be swept off his feet. At the moment of impact, the trunk sways back, away from the line of flight, and, at the same time, the hands go straight out and up, still with both elbows straight. Then, as the hands reach the apex of their swing, the body snaps back to its upright plane, the elbows bend, and he comes round to that lovely hands high pose so beloved of photographers but with the little extras he alone can give, like that tiny snapping twitch of the right shoulder, and his habit of turning his head along with his shoulders in the follow through, and following the ball's flight with the corners of his eyes.

To players and non-players alike, to watch Crombie drive is a thrilling experience. Laymen, knowing nothing of the game, see him, and talk about the poetry of motion, the ballet-like grace of Dolin and Martinez.

To the average golfer, and among the horde include this humble scribe, watching 'Snowflake' play makes us sit by the fairway's edge and weep in impotent frustration. To many of us who ought to have nobler and more worthy ambitions, the ability of this pint-sized Scot to literally bash the ball out of sight and then very summit of human achievement.

And his admiring fans troop after him. Ever his galleries grow larger. Already he's the Year's top money spinner on the tournament trail – because he has perfected his method. To play like Crombie is every aspiring golfer's dream. Well, given time and talent, it might be done but don't try to copy Crombie. The method he uses is strictly his own.

2.

Dick Lawther, formerly of Algolf Inc. and now travelling exhibit manager for Stone and Kibbits was bored. The wind whipped and cracked at the canvas of the big top. Now and then, the canvas eaves lifted, and the wind made scattered attacks on piles of folders and leaflets, sending them spinning and flying like leaves in an autumn gale. Business was quiet this morning. It always was on the last day of a big event. At the start, the casual buyers were around, and you did good business. Then, as interest in the play got going, folk wanted to be out on the course watching. Things tailed off until on the last day not a thing moved until the event was over, then every single thing the winner used or wore, from cigarettes to underwear, would sell out.

He wandered around his stand, flicking imaginary dust from displays of numbered irons and fancy golf bags, then he brightened as two figures strolled casually down the central aisle. 'Hi, there,' he greeted them, 'Cummon and take a weight off your feet. I've just sent the girl out for coffee.'

The two men were obviously bored with each other's company, yet not too eager to accept his invitation, maybe because they guessed what the conversation would be.

'Well, how come you two couldn't make the last day's play?' he twitted them, then, immediately regretted the words. After all, they were both customers. He tried to soften his words with a bright smile.

Big Ed Fuegosi ground out his cigarette, then sat heavily in the only easy chair. 'Little Limey squirt!' he growled, then lapsed into angry silence.

Al Bowdler perched on the table. 'Guess we haven't much chance of winning anything much these days – just a couple of stooges in Crombie's Circus.'

The coffee arrived. Lawther presided, opening a big box of cigarettes, 'On the house, boys.'

Conversation lapsed in smoke, then Lawther said, 'Funny, that little guy has come a long way in four years, and I met him the day he came off the boat, just a simple Scottie straight out from the sticks.'

'Pity you didn't souse him in the East River,' Fuegosi growled, 'then we'd alla had a chance to pick up some dough.'

'Be fair, Ed,' Bowdler said, 'you gotta admit he's good – too good for me, at any rate.'

'It's the crowd swarmin' around him that gets my goat,' Fuegosi said. 'Is he still totin' that trailer outfit of his around?'

Lawther pointed out beyond the rear of the marquee, 'Parked out there on the edge of the lot.'

'And he's even sponsoring the trailers.' Fuegosi's voice sounded as if that rated as the final seal of commercial flummery.

'They're marketing two Crombie models, the Circuit and the De Luxe as used by the Maestro himself, can you beat it? With all the dough he's makin' – livin' in a trailer, lousy little tightwad.'

'You sure love him, Ed,' Bowdler laughed. 'He's no tightwad. It's just that livin' high don' mean a thing to him. He's dead scared of plushy hotels and snooty head waiters, besides, he likes privacy.'

'I'll say he does,' Fuegosi put in. 'And what do you bet that De Luxe outfit of his has a double bed in it. Guess that'll be a must, with the Buren dame floatin' around.'

'Well – what do you expect? He's a quiet little guy, but not a queer or a fairy. Anyway, you know what he does when he has free time? Sits in his trailer and reads American history.'

'That's it, that's it!' Fuegosi snapped from boredom to attention. 'I allus knew the guy was a nut! He ain't human.'

'And he even cashes in on that,' Lawther was frankly enjoying Fuegosi's futile rage. 'Everywhere he goes, they ask him to say a few words on the air. In that soft Scots voice of his he talks about the early Scots golfers in America and lays it on about the debt his part of Scotland owes to the States for giving so many of her young men their big chance to teach the game over here.'

'Clever,' Bowdler put in. ''Cause there's always the other side, just how much we all owe to the Scottie boys for spreading the game over here, and giving us a livelihood.'

'Livelihood. Hell!' Fuegosi exploded. 'And him takin' first

in the six leadin' events this spring.'

'Maybe so but I don't see you doing much about it, Ed.' Bowdler was frankly fed up. 'After all, we sure started level with him.'

'You give a bellyache,' Fuegosi snarled, and rose. 'For ever larding up to that little Limey squirt.'

The other two exchanged glances as they watched the angry man stride away, 'Ed's sure gunning for the "Snowflake",' Lawther said.

'Ed would be a better golfer if he had something less solid to keep his ears apart,' Bowdler answered. 'Maybe that's why the little guy does so well – he thinks . . .'

Lawther nodded. 'I've heard him on the air once or twice, he's good – asking anyone who can tell him anything about pioneer Scots pros to write to him.'

'Goin' highbrow – aiming to write a book?'

'Could be, but I don't think it's Davie who's so hot after the dough. That's part of Fuegosi's beef. Davie's manager, big Bill Van Den Berg, used to be a pal of Ed's, and Ed's real sore because Bill can't see past Crombie now.'

'I can't say I blame him – quite straight, I like Crombie. He's a real nice little guy.'

Lawther nodded. 'I hadda long chat with him the other night. He recalled the day I met him at the ship, and he's just the same old Davie. Not so strange and scared as he was then but he still wears the same size of hat.'

Bowdler gave a wry smile. 'I honestly wonder if folk would say that of me if I was in his shoes. He's right on top and making scads.'

'I don't think he gives the money much thought,' Lowther said, 'He's always thinking about improving his game and giving the customers value for their tickets.' He looked through the open flap of the marquee, and saw a dark mass of people far across the course. 'Here he comes now, by the size of the crowd.'

Bowdler rose. 'I'll slip across and see the scoreboard.'

He was back in a minute, 'Three under fours at the

198

fifteenth. He'll break seventy.'

'Looks like he'll do it again?' Lawther asked.

Bowdler grinned. 'Can you see anyone catching him now if this wind keeps up? He always says the wind don't reach down far enough to bother him.'

'Gee, I sure wish we were carrying one or two of his sponsored lines,' Lawther said ruefully. 'Then I could sure do some business, as it is – might as well shut up shop.'

'Too bad.' Bowdler's smile was a taunt, friendly though it seemed. 'Sure shows lack of foresight on your part. Why didn't you sign him up that day you met him at the ship?'

'Hell, how was I to know?' Lawther called after him as he walked away.

3.

By spring 1929, they were calling any big event 'Crombie's Circus'. There were restaurant and trade show tents; golf book stands, hot dog stalls, and all the other amenities the great American public deemed necessary for its refreshment and entertainment. And always in a quiet corner of the lot, two big cars with trailers attached. Crombie and his staff.

One of the trailers served a dual purpose, connected as it was to a nearby telephone standard. By night it was Big Bill Van Den Berg's sleeping quarters, by day, his office. He was talking rapidly into the telephone.

'Yeah, I've got all the papers ready. Sure he'll sign, just that I ain't asked him yet. I never discuss propositions when he's playin' a tourney, eh? What say? Forget it! No, if you and I are to do business, it must be on the level. He's too decent a guy to put anything across on. Eh? All right, you gotta point, sure, there was a time I didn't like him – a man can change can't he? Sure I'll call you back.'

As he replaced the phone a shadow made him look up, it was Julie. 'Hi – how's our boy doing?' he asked.

'How do you expect our Davie to do? A new course

199

record, and in this wind! Three strokes ahead now, if he doesn't crack this afternoon, he'll walk away with it!'

'Have you ever known him to crack up?' Now it was Van Den Berg's turn to make mild reproof for lack of faith; then his face clouded. 'Say, he hasn't been complaining about that pain again, has he?'

Julie shook her head, but her eyes were thoughtful. 'No, says he's never had a twinge since that last turn. Maybe that diet he's on has done the trick.'

'Huh, that pap won't give him the strength to shoot figures,' Van Den Berg said. 'But maybe it was only indigestion. Say, see where the British Open's to be played next summer.' He handed her the newssheet, 'Ain't that Davie's home town?'

Julie wrinkled her brows. 'Car – gee – these hard Scots names, but that's Davie's home town all right.' Guess only the folks who live there can pronounce it.' Then she caught the gist of Van Den Berg's thoughts. 'Gosh, if Davie should take a trip home and win! That would really set him up.'

'Top of the world,' Van Den Berg's tone was crisp. 'No other title carries the weight of that one. The guy who can lift the British Open is King Pin Golf.'

'Davie could do it, couldn't he, Bill? He's ready now?'

'All the ready he'll ever be. Reckon on present form, he's unbeatable, and that would set us going on the exploitation. What a boost. If he was Open Champ, we could make ten sales of sponsored lines to every one we're makin' now.'

'Bill, he's got to enter. He's just got to. He's due a trip home now, and I'm coming right along.'

'What's ole Pop Taylor gonna say?'

'Reckon he'll come along too, if he can make it. Gosh, won't it be wonderful, seein' oup Davie on his home territory, and hearing them all speak soft like him.'

'If that boy could go home and lift the Open on his own course – what a story! He could write his own ticket for radio and press stuff. And with us due to float the new consolidated firm to boost sales, why it's just comin' at the right time!'

But Julie was suddenly thoughtful. 'Bill, do you think he's been looking – well – kind of tired, lately?'

Van Den Berg shook his head doubtfully. 'A little maybe, but I reckon it's mental tiredness. I'd say he's in pretty good shape physically – in spite of his spot of stomach trouble.'

4.

Cool and refreshed after his shower in the clubhouse, Davie walked across to his trailer. He made a habit now of wearing a light coloured jacket between rounds, thus his fans and followers, so used to seeing him in the navy blue jerkin, were often unaware of him passing among them.

Inside, he relaxed, closing his eyes for a few moments, then opened them to look thoughtfully at two new books Julie had brought. He hesitated between *With Sherman in Georgia* and *Pittsburg Pioneer*, wondering which would provide the best entertainment in his short rest before starting the last round of the event. His doubt was resolved by the club waiter entering with his light snack lunch. He was halfway through the inevitable ice cream sweet when Van Den Berg poked his head in the door, and said: 'Hi, mail for you.'

'That's fine,' Davie smiled. 'Give – ' The sight of his father's writing made him pick up the letter opener, then he laid it down. 'What have we for the weekend?'

'Not too bad,' Bill always said that, even if the schedule was tight. 'Man from Finkelmeyers is here – final fitting of the noo style jerkin – you know, West and Cattle States events, with the fringed seams.'

Davie shook his head ruefully, 'The things I do to make money.'

'It's gonna sell and make work for folks. Tonight's usual radio talk script all ready, if winner this afternoon.' He paused waiting for Davie's reaction. 'Extra few minutes sportscast on the event and your feelings. Then tomorrow, two sessions of one hour each autographing gear at Linker and Kelman's then principal guest at Sussiequeue Club, givin' talk on golf in the old country. Sunday, demonstration game at Arrowhead Blue Club, followed by film show and talk on game to members.'

'Aye – quite a full weekend,' Davie said, his eyes on the letter. 'Anything else to tell me?'

'Sure, next year's Open is on your home course – gonna emter?' His tone clearly anticipated an affirmative reply and he seemed puzzled when Davie hesitated. So much so that when Julie came in, he turned to her, 'Hey, Julie, Davie don't seem to be keen to try the British Open and on his own course, too!'

'I – I want to think about it,' Davie said. 'I'd love a trip home and a try at the Open, but – well – all the folk I know – if they read about me out here – they'd be expecting great things from me at home. I – I wouldn't like them to be disappointed.'

'Listen to doleful Davie,' Julie scoffed. 'Of course, you'd win or be pretty near the top and think of the business it would bring.'

Looking at the glowing vivid face, Davie was conscious of a bleak ache of disappointment. With all her money, Julie was ever open to plans for making more. He reproached himself for the thought, she was doing it for his sake, still . . .

On sudden impulse, a rebound from his thoughts, he said, 'And if I lift the British Open, could we consider some more permanent arrangement than our present one?'

A year ago he couldn't have come out with that, now he put it over in Julie's flippant manner, oblivious to Bill Van Den Berg.

'If you win – we might get round to it, might be fun,' she said, then making mock gestures of maidenly confusion, 'Oh – la – Sire – really you must see my papa.' Then with a quick return to her old manner, 'And I guess he'll give three cheers.'

'If you two are startin' a neckin' party,' Van Den Berg said, 'I'll be moseying along.'

'Wait, Bill,' Davie said, caught off balance by the result of his impulsive words, 'that sponsor tie-up agreement you wanted to sell me . . .'

'I'm not selling you anything, Davie, it's sound right through. Julie agrees with me. It's a cinch!'

Davie pushed away his glass of milk and lit a cigarette and leaned forward. 'O.K. I'm may be sort of dense, just the slow country boy. Give me the gist of it again.'

'It's like this, we gotta fat bank balance and it's idle earning only peanuts, right?'

'If you call the interest only peanuts, right,' Davie agreed.

Van Den Berg uncrossed his legs and leaned forward. 'O.K. we lift the idle money, and use it as a down payment to buy ourselves a sizeable chunk of real estate. Then we make a noo arrangement with all our sponsors, and use their money to meet the interest and mortgage charges. You're not using that dough, so you'll never miss it, and meanwhile, the income from that real estate buy will provide you with plenty to meet higher overheads, leaving all the purses you win to play around with. Its a cinch, boy! I called Lindstrom and Crone, the investment brokers, not ten minutes back. I got all the papers from them this morning.'

Davie thought for a moment. 'Seems to me we're delivering ourselves to the bank, body and soul. What if the sales from Crombie lines drop, and don't make enough to cover the mortgage charge?'

Julie laughed; Van Den Berg made a gesture of despair. 'Listen to him! We're on the up and up, Dave. Even if sales dropped ten per cent they'd still cover, and if you can lift the British open, I reckon we could make an even bigger estate buy from increased sales alone. Get wise to yourself! The sky's the limit, Dave.'

Davie was confused. It was pure gambling, though the Americans called it selling forward.

'What are you worrying about?' his manager asked. 'I've

never given you a bum steer yet.' And Julie broke in, 'It's sound business practice, and property is a good investment in any language.'

'Aye, I dare say.' Davie was thoughtful, then his eyes caught the unopened letter, with promised respite from the problem. 'Where's your dad now, Julie?'

'Why – at the hotel in town. He'll tell you the same as Bill, if you ask him.'

'I wasn't thinking of asking him about that.' Davie was still thoughtful. 'Would you try and get him on the phone for me, Bill?'

Van Den Berg saw him fingering the letter. 'Sure, Dave, I'll try to get him now.'

Julie knew him well enough to understand that a letter from home meant so much to him, that he liked to enjoy it in private, withdrawing into himself into a world of memory. Suddenly she understood the doubts and conflict in his mind. To return to his own land was something he wanted to do but returning to attempt a major title in the playground of his boyhood that was another matter. Maybe he realised that his vision of home was too rosy tinted and dreaded disappointment. She put her arms gently round his neck and kissed his cheek. 'Oh, Davie, you're sweet but far too canny – that's a word I've learned from you.'

Bird-light of step, she was gone. He grinned to himself and slit open the envelope.

Dear Davie,

Well, here we are again, with the summer near hand on us. But a fine mild spring and I'm glad to say no signs of my chest trouble, that's a blessing, maybe I've really got rid of it now, but your mother says the best thing you can send me is a new set of pipes. The Americans can make anything, judging from the presents you keep sending and your mother is aye having folk into see them, proud's a peacock.

You have no idea how proud your mother is bringing in strangers if they come and ask about you, and Bert

Sproggie is forever bringing bits out of American Mag-
azines from the club about you, always winning and the
holiday folk buy him a glass now and again in the club
when he brags about you bein' his apprentice laddie.

I'm thinking it's a blessing poor Bert has that much to
take up his time for he is out of work now. Poor Johnston
has smashed at last and the business closed up and his braw
house, an awful talk aboot the place and the poor man in a
home outside Forfar. His son has run away and the oldest
girl is living in one o' the council houses and her man a
clerk in Dundee as I told you before. The only one worth a
snuff is the youngest one, Beth, who did the best she could
and saw the lawyers and so on. A sorry business and the
men all out of work.

But the course is all new and you'll find it fine. The
Open is here this year, and we're all hoping you will come
over and have a try, every one of your old friends would
go fair delighted if you could win. The rebuilding has
meant a lot of extra work and with the Open coming on,
we'll be right busy all the time now getting it ready, so
hope my chest doesn't come on again. Write soon and say
we'll see you this Summer. Your affec. Father.

Within him, burning but unacknowledged, was the Scots
passionate love of home. What if it was a poor country and its
folk prone to gossip? Come spring and early summer its
beauty was something every exile longed for, and its people
were kinder than you ever could imagine.

He rose at a hail from the other trailer, and crossed over.
Van Den Berg motioned him towards the telephone. Mr
Taylor was on the line.

'Hullo there, Davie, nice of you to call me. Just seen your
third-round score – can you do it again in the last
round – and win?'

'Och – I'll try – I think so.'

'I know you'll try all right, and when you turn in another
wonder round, I expect you'll tell the press you've been
lucky. Now, son, on, can I help you with anything?'

'Aye, you could do me a big favour. Could – could you find a job for a good greenkeeper?'

'Heck, Davie,' the little far-away metallic voice chuckled in his ear. 'Don't tell me you figure on retiring?'

Now it was Davie's turn to laugh. 'No, not yet a while. It's my dad, his health's not so good, and the doctor says he would do better in a warmer, drier climate. I'm thinking of bringing him out here. Ohio would suit him fine. It's not that he needs to work, for I could keep him in comfort, but he's—'

'Wouldn't be happy unless he had a job to do. I get you, son. Is he a good greenkeeper? Hold it, that's a silly question and him your dad. Let's see now, when do you figure on having him?'

'Oh, late July, August maybe.'

'Bringing him back with you after the Open?' Good, now let's see. Yeah, I've got it; we'll pack him right down to winter in Florida. I gotta noo place there, where his job will leave him lots of free time. Then, come spring, we'll get him to take over Neveneck – the head man there is moving over to Blue Mountain.'

'That's just what I wanted.' A warm glow filled Davie. 'Thanks Mr Taylor.'

'Listen, son. If your dad's anything like you, I reckon the boot's on the other foot. Don't worry any more, it's all set. Now go ahead and shoot another sixty-eight. Bye.' The line went dead.

'Guess you got good news,' Van Den Berg said, and Davie turned to him. 'Bill, that scheme of yours, get the papers ready and I'll sign.'

It was ungrateful of him to lack faith in the future when this country had done so much for him.

'You won't regret it, Davie, I'm sure of that. Just sign here and here.'

'And, Bill – the Open – cable my entry.'

'Atta boy,' Julie cried, 'and cummon, you're on the tee in five minutes.'

PART THREE

THE MAN RETURNS

CHAPTER FOURTEEN

I.

BILL Van Den Berg was a good organiser. The big car, complete with chauffeur, was waiting when they docked at Southampton. The driver was only to give Davie a chance to become used to driving on the left, and manipulating the gear and brake with the opposite hand. It had been decided that he should do the driving, for with no playing and the leisurely journey north, his hands, if not used, might go soft.

They saw Mr and Mrs Taylor off on the London train, and made arrangements to meet them later in Scotland. It was mid-June, cool, breezy, and given to sudden sharp bursts of rain, which made the green of field, tree and hedgerow sparkle with diamonds. Julie developed a habit of drawing her elegant tweeds around her, and saying, 'Gee, but it sure is airy in your little neck of the woods, Davie.'

Davie, besides having the pre-occupation of driving a strange car on the wrong side of the road, found other things buzzing the fringe of his mind. Was it only imagination or had Bill and Julie's voices suddenly become more nasal and American-sounding since they landed?

But he was on his way home. Every turn of the road, every town and village passed, brought it nearer, although, at Julie's request, the journey was slow and far from direct. This was for his sake, for he had been a bit stale lately, and in the last three events, had only rated one first and two seconds.

So they went slowly north. Julie loved the trip. She'd discovered a new word, and rather overworked it. Stratford-on-Avon began it. 'Gosh, I just love it, isn't it quaint?' she cried in rapture, and Davie, now seeing it for the first time, felt it incumbent on him to show a mildly modest and deprecating air. This was his own country or at least part of it. Maybe his detached and proprietorial air was something of a front, arising from a feeling of irritation with Julie's raptures. They savoured somehow of a teenager in a toy shop, pretending to patronise things long desired, but never owned.

And Bill Van Den Berg, too, was proving something of a disappointment. The first thing to annoy him was the almost complete lack of newspaper interest in their arrival. He was inclined to regard this as a personal slur, and all Davie's reassurances did not assuage his feelings.

'After all my advance work, to meet this flop,' he kept repeating, 'ain't this darn country interested in nuthin' but cricket?'

At each overnight stop, he collected mail, and in their hotel room at Carlisle, Davie found him puzzled. 'Just can't get the hang of things,' he growled, 'sales down ten to fifteen per cent. Maybe it's only seasonal – still . . .'

'Nothing to worry over,' he assured Davie, 'not a thing. There's still more'n enough to cover the bank call – just that it doesn't make sense.'

But when they crossed the border next morning, Davie's heart sang. His rise of spirits infected both his companions. He was home again, breathing the air of Scotland. He drove happily along, whistling 'Swanee'. Tonight he would sleep beside the cool North Sea, smelling its salt, hearing its music and the soft burring speech of his folk. In the Crawford Hotel where they stopped for coffee, he could have cuddled the little waitress; hers was the first Scots tongue to please his ears since further back than he could remember.

In their afternoon coffee stop at Perth, Davie drank tea, because he was home again, and an incident occurred that set Van Den Berg up happily.

The waitress who served them hung about their table, then at last said, 'Are – are you no Davie Crombie?'

'Aye, that's my name,' Davie said warming, 'but I don't seem to mind of you.'

'You wouldnae,' she told him. 'I'm Meg Patullo's sister. But they're aw' prood of you. Ye've done great things in the States.'

'And he's gonna do great things over here,' Van Den Berg assured her.

She gave him barely a glance, her eyes were on Davie. 'Well, welcome home and good luck,' she said, then, 'excuse me, I'll have to phone – somebody you know.' With that she smiled and hurried away.

Van Den Berg smiled and rubbed his hands. 'This is better. She'll be snoopin' for a local paper, we'll get a write-up outa this, just you wait.'

'Can you imagine it,' Julie cried happily, 'she talks just like our Davie, Gosh! How quaint to hear her.'

In the pale gold of a fine afternoon, they rolled along the fertile Carse of Gowrie; great clouds piled high over the Firth of Tay, and the light was like mother of pearl. 'This your country, Dave?' Van Den Berg asked, and on Davie saying yes, 'Heck, I can understand you being homesick. Reckon this 'ud get anyone.'

'And look at the little houses!' Julie cried. 'All made of stone – aren't they just too quaint!'

Outside Invergowrie, they came upon a cyclist. A dark girl who hurriedly dismounted from her machine, and signalled them to stop. She was petite, and more than pretty. Davie, as he braked the big car to a halt, thought her face vaguely familiar.

'Hullo there, honey,' Van Den Berg called from the back seat. 'In trouble – can we help?'

Her eyes gave him no more than a passing glance, rested for a moment on Julie, then settled on Davie.

They were dark eyes, serene in their expression. 'Davie,' she said quietly, then, at his puzzled glance, she repeated it with a note of reproach. 'David Forbes Crombie – do you not remember me? I'm—'

Then he remembered the voice, 'Beth – wee Beth!' he cried in delight, and jumping out of the car, siezed both her hands. 'But you've grown up!'

'What did you expect me to do?' Tart though her tone was, he knew she was pleased by the warmth of his welcome.

'But you've grown up!' he repeated. 'It's kinda hard to grasp. When I went away, you were just a wee lassie in a gym slip and now . . .'

'I want you to meet my friends.' In quiet pride, he introduced them, 'Miss Julie Buren, and Mr Van Den Berg, my business manager.'

'My, but you've come on,' Beth said, 'but then you aye intended to.'

'And, are all the Scots lassies as bonnie as you?' Van Den Berg asked, his voice a raw parody of music hall Scots. 'Any friend of Davie's is a friend of ours. I'll stick your wheel in the trunk, Miss Johnston, and you'll ride into town with us.'

Davie was glad Bill's heartiness had covered the bleak smile Julie had given Beth.

'Thanks, Mr Van Den Berg, but I came out here to tell you something.' She turned to Davie, 'You know how rumours get about?'

Davie nodded and wondered what the trouble was. He saw speculation in Julie's eyes, and said, 'Beth and I are old friends, her dad used to be my boss.' The moment the words were out, he saw the pain in her eyes, and cursed his tactless tongue.

'It's the boys in the club, and the town folk,' Beth went on gravely. 'Somehow or other, the news is going about that you're due in on the 6.25 train. They've all clubbed together to give you a sort of welcome home. I know you wouldn't want to disappoint them. Well, they'll get you all right, no matter how you arrive, but it would be nice for all your friends if you were to arrive on that train.'

'But how did you know to meet us?' Davie asked.

'Jennie Patullo phoned me from Perth,' she told him.

'Guess the little lady's right!' Van Den Berg cried. 'And it was real smart of you to tip us off. Guess we'd better get on the train, Dave.'

'Aw gee – have we gotta get out of the car, and travel in some whistle stop tanker?' Julie asked.

'Don't you want to see Davie gettin' a real, royal welcome?' Van Den Berg asked. 'And you'll travel with us too, Miss Beth.' He turned his charm on her. 'You'll wanna be in on the party – an old buddy of Davie's.'

'Thanks all the same,' Beth flashed a quick look at Julie, 'but I'll have to get back to the office, if you'd just drop me as you pass.'

2.

With every glimpse of a well-remembered scene, a shop on a corner, the arch of the docks, the long vista stretching to the station, the smaller buildings, the narrower streets, Davie's joy in returning mounted. He steered the big car through the traffic singing 'Swanee' in his mind.

They dropped Beth at the office where she worked. She had sat in the back seat, and though he had a thousand questions he wanted to ask her, he was, in a way, almost glad he had no chance of quizzing her. Sooner or later, some innocent question would have brought him to her father's misfortune, and brought back the look of pain to her fine, dark eyes.

They had hired a driver from a garage in the town, and sent him on his way. Then, carrying only the few things Julie had bought, they made their way to the East Station.

'Gosh, isn't it quaint? It looks hundreds of years old!' Julie exclaimed, but Davie said nothing. He was lost in the delight of finding that the engines and coaches looked exactly as he remembered them, save that they seemed smaller. They travelled along the sand flats of the Tay Estuary, past West Ferry past Broughty Ferry, then Barnhill and Monifieth. To Davie every minute was a new pleasure. Everything was as he remembered, save that it seemed smaller and a little shrunken.

And the flags on the garland of golf courses strung along the line winked a welcome. 'Heck, you boys ought to know the game,' Van Den Berg said. 'Ain't nothin' else but golf courses along this section.'

'And nae links anywhere in the world to beat them!' Davie cried in happy pride.

It was an evening of pure gold, cloud high to a dark blue sea, and white breakers creaming over the bar at the river mouth. The two lighthouses on the Ness peered over the hutments at Barry Camp, and Davie craned his head eagerly to catch a first glimpse of home when they passed the pine wood bordering the ninth. The woods rushed by in a blur, then, like the whisking aside of a curtain, they were gone, revealing the wide panorama of golf course, laced with outcroppings of heather and gorse, carnival gay with striped direction poles and twinkling flags. 'This is – ' Davie cried, and his voice choked on a lump in his throat. 'That's the tenth, South America, they call it,' he stammered. 'There's our house,' he pointed out the cottage.

He was afraid that Julie might call it quaint, but she smiled and said, 'Talk about the old Kentucky home, only Davie has golf links stead of roses.'

They raced along. Passing the house, he caught a glimpse of a familiar figure, furiously beating at a rug on the farthest corner. He smiled, knowing a new and tender affection for his mother, engaged in a last-minute attack on any scattered fragments of dust and disorder with the effrontery to linger in her house on the eve of his homecoming.

They passed the starter's box, then the brakes went on, and the train began to slow. Past the backs of the houses facing the front, past Clubbie Johnston's, closed and silent now, past the rear of the Wallace Hotel, a glimpse of the picture house and the shoe factory, then a grinding halt at the station, with the familiar crossing gates a barrier to a motley crowd and the platform packed with people.

Van Den Berg knew the drill. 'Let Davie get out first, stand on the step. Let 'em see you, then Julie. Don't rush it – let them come to you.'

The platform was a sea of questing faces. As he stood at the carriage door, a voice yelled, 'There he is – Davie – Davie!' They surged forward. Big Riddoch, he wore Sergeant's stripes now, spread his arms to hold them back. Davie saw Eck Black, and thought he caught a glimpse of Bert Sproggie. Then be became aware that the Reverend Lawson, and a stout man in a bowler hat were in front of the policeman.

'Welcome Home, David.' Lawson wrung his hand. 'This is Mr Sanderson, our Provost.'

As he shook the man's hand, and listened to his pompous speech of welcome, the thought flashed through his mind that there had been some dissension at the last council meeting as to whether he should be accorded a welcome or not and this was the compromise. He should be welcomed, but by a provost without his chain of office.

'Pride in your golfing prowess shared by the whole town . . . even greater glory . . . all our hopes for your success in the coming championship,' said Mr Sanderson. 'And now your friends must be getting impatient.'

That was an understatement. Hardly had the provost mouthed his last words when the crowd surged round Davie and his party. Jim Marr and Bob Gallet were the first, pulling Bert Sproggie, struggling to get his skull pipe into his pocket, and a little, stooped brown-faced man whom Davie with a shock of horrified surprise, followed by a surge of compassion, realised was his father. He looked tired, yet his eyes were proudly bright, and his lined face radiant with happiness. In love and pity, Davie threw aside the social inhibitions of home, and put his arms round his father. 'Oh, Dad!' was all he could say. Everything seemed smaller than he remembered, but his father had shrunk more than anything. 'Davie, oh son, it's grand to see you, and looking so well,' his father said, and kept patting his shoulder.

Then Davie turned to Bert Sproggie. 'How are you, auld yin?' he asked putting an arm on his shoulder and giving him a friendly prod in the belly. 'Och, no so bad,' Bert smiled, 'kinda stiff wi' the rheumatics at times, Davie.'

'Listen to him,' his father said, 'well past sixty now, and still lashing them oot like a lad. In the semi-final of the links this year!'

'What else is there for an auld man to do,' Bert asked, 'except sign on at the dole?'

The press round them grew thicker and more insistent. Seeming strangers turned welcoming faces and outstretched hands toward him, then the strangeness dissolved to reveal the familiar face of an old acquaintance, weathered and mellowed by the passing years.

Davie presented Julie and Van Den Berg to his father and Bert. The gentle courtesy of both men, who removed their caps before shaking hands, pleased her.

She turned bright-eyed to Davie. 'Gee, but there sure is something to this old world tradition stuff and manners. You're a coupla real pets!' Then to Davie's amusement, she gave each of them a quick kiss on the cheek.

'Well, folks, whatta we waiting for?' Van Den Berg asked, to regain control. 'Let's go.'

As they turned to leave the station, a bright banner caught Davie's eye. Strung across the bridge, it read, '*Welcome To All Our Visitors For The Open.*'

Even as he saw this, a couple of enthusiasts, undeterred by the efforts of the police sergeant to reach them were busy lowering another crude, hand-painted effort. This said, '*Welcome Home To Oor Davie – And We Hope You Win.*'

They passed through a lane of welcoming people to the street, where the car was waiting. Men jostled to open the doors. 'Sit right up atop the hood, Davie. Take Julie with you,' Van Den Berg ordered.

The canvas hood was folded back. His dad and Bert sat in the back seat with the Reverend Lawson between them, their heads just above Davie's knees. Van Den Berg got in front with the driver, and quite uninvited, Eck Black squeezed in beside him. Old friends like Chae Whitton and Ron

McLeod, trying to snatch a word or a handshake, were still clinging to the car, on the running boards, when it started. 'Stay on, boys,' Van Den Berg called, 'not so far to go.'

They moved along the front, slowly, making for the Wallace Hotel. The crowd gave way reluctantly, their cheers held a note of relief, for so many were clinging to the vehicle that it looked doubtful if it would carry them.

Children scampered alongside the car, shrilly boasting their triumphs. 'I touched him twice. I'll bet he's the greatest gowfer in the world!'

'Ach you – he used to work wi' my Da – my Da kens him.'

And thus the cavalcade swept to the big front door of the Wallace Hotel. The manager and a waiter in a tail coat were at one side, and a smart receptionist in a black satin frock on the other, welcoming them like a guard of honour. Eck Black got out, and swaggered up the steps. 'Welcome party for Mr Crombie,' he called out, as if he owned the place, and Bert Sproggie, helping Julie down from her perch, said to Davie, 'Listen to him, if it wasnae for you bein' along wi' him, he'd be sneakin' in the back door!'

'Poor Eck's a bit like mysel',' Davie's father said. 'He needs a bit moral support afore he can walk intae a place like this. I've never been ower the door.'

Bill Van Den Berg was perfectly at ease. 'This way, folks,' he called out, making for the cocktail bar. 'We'll soon have 'em set up.'

Eck Black became truculent. 'Who are you, and who invited you, onywey?' he demanded. 'Davie's oor pal. It's us that's welcoming him.'

With quiet self-possession, Davie moved into the threatening breach. 'Bill's my business manager, Eck. He generally arranges parties for my friends.'

'Well, he's no arrangin' this ane,' Eck said, 'for we've done that already. Cummon, this way.'

Mr Lawson crooked a hand under Davie's elbow. 'Don't let Eck upset you,' he advised. 'He's been the moving spirit in all this. It was to be in the club, until they heard of the lady in the party. It took quite a bit of organising to shift it here at such short notice.'

And there was a table laden with paper thin sandwiches, sardines on slivers of toast, and fancy bottles and polished glasses. The talk swelled to a babel of sound. Davie's hand was shaken till it ached, and when the glasses were charged, they stood and pledged him. 'Welcome Home, Davie, and gie us a Scots Open Champion next week.'

'Aye, the whole world's here to try and lift it – the Yanks are here in droves, but Davie'll keep it at hame for us.'

'Does Davie no count as a Yank now?'

'Did you ever hear such a haver? How can he be even half a Yank? I used to go to school wi' him.'

In one corner, Julie was holding court, the centre of a delighted group. She thought she was drawing them out, to enjoy their broad Angus burr, so like Davie's, while they did everything possible to make her talk, equally enthralled by her glowing beauty, her exotic clothes, and her American drawl. 'What a dame!' one lad exclaimed. 'Braw as the women you see on the pictures, and quick in the tongue as a dose of salts.'

The magic of homecoming burned in Davie. His father proud at his elbow, he held court like an emperor returned from exile. Then his father touched his elbow. 'Can we no slip away, son? Your mother will be wearying to see you.'

'Sure, Dad. I'm wearying to see Ma again,' Davie agreed.

Eck Black came back from a visit to the gents. 'Hey, you should be flattered, Davie.' He laid a heavy hand on his shoulder. 'Half the toon's ootside, waitin' to get a glimpse of you.' Then he plunged back into the crowd round the table.

'Ach, I'm no keen on facing any more crowds,' Davie said, and Bert Sproggie was ready with help. 'Away oot the back and slip through the fence at the end of Clubbie Johnston's place.'

'Don't tell me that fence is no mended yet!' Davie cried.

'Looks like it'll never be mended now,' Bert said sadly, and downed the last of his glass.

So again, in the blue and gold of the waning day, with the homing gulls making a living frieze against the sky, Davie walked home with his father, their shoulders touching. Now the world was quiet, Davie drew the cool, salt tanged air deep into his lungs, and smelled the old familiar scents. Away to the North stood the Sidlaws. His eyes swept there, across the fields, the links, the woods, and sand dunes.

A myriad of images flashed across his mind. He saw manicured golf courses in Kansas and Texas, in Indiana and California, in Maine and Ohio. Visions of ornate clubhouses, hordes of richly dressed people with sleek cars – all the panorama of his American years, slick and embellished with the gadgets of gracious living, yet none could compare with this. This was where his heart would ever be. This was home.

His father was stuffing tobacco into his pipe. 'I'm thinkin' you've seen a fair wheen of places since the last time you and I walked hame, son,' he said, and put a match to his pipe.

'I have that, Dad, but I'd settle for this any time.'

His mother met him at the door. No fuss or flurry. She put her arms round him, and laid her cheek against his for a moment. 'I've ham and eggs ready – the eggs are no bad but the shop stuff is never as fresh as straight frae the hen, nothing like keepin' yer ain poultry.'

But before he sat down, his hands must be washed in the tiny scullery, so that he could enjoy the running water put in by the committee. The warmth of the homecoming still in him, Davie sang 'Swanee' as he stood at the sink.

Turning as he wiped his hands, he found his father and mother were watching him at the door, his dad smiling, but his mother close to tears. 'Eh, dear, Davie, ye near hand deeved us daft wi' that song afore you went away. Then when we missed you so sore, we'd have given anything just to hear you at it – and to think you're still singing it!'

They sat and joined him at the meal, and when at last the big cup of tea was on the ebb, Davie broached the subject which, since seeing his father, had assumed a real urgency.

'Dad, would you like a job out in America – same as here – greenkeeping.'

'Me – oot in America – you're kiddin', son.'

'No, I'm serious, Dad. Mr Taylor – a wealthy man, has been really kind to me. Asked if I could find a really good greenkeeper when I was home. I told him about you, so he said to offer you the job, and bring you back with me.'

He saw the wild, terrible joy burn briefly in his father's face, and then die out. 'It's real kind of your friend, son, but I could never manage wan o' thae fancy places like the pictures you sent home.'

'Don't talk daft, Dad!' Davie's voice held the rasp of authority his successes had earned. 'Golf courses are only grass, no matter where they are. You'll have a lot less bother gettin' growth out there, wi' plenty of weed killers and fancy tools, aye and squads of men to do the work. You'll be the gaffer. You could do it standin' on your head.'

'Davie, don't make fun of me. Do you honestly think I could make a go of it? I'd hate to let you down, and be a disappointment to Mr Taylor.'

'Dad, I've been the length and breadth of the States now, and I know you could manage fine.'

His father's pipe had gone out. With shaking fingers he fumbled for matches. 'Whit de ye think, Mary – would you go to America?' His voice trembled with excitement.

'I think it's the best thing that ever happened, James Crombie, and if it's a warm, dry climate, the sooner the better, for it's the rime at the back end that upsets your chest.'

'And the climate is just what you're needin', Davie assured him. 'And the first go off, Mr Taylor wants you down in Florida for six months.'

'Florida!' they both echoed, lost with the wonder of it.

'A new course he wants Dad to sort of set in order for a start,' Davie concluded.

'What sort of place does he want me for after that?'

'Head man at Neveneck, my old club in Ohio, a lovely

place,' Davie assured him. Then his mother leaned forward. 'Is there a hoose, or do we—'

'There's a fine house, about five minutes from the course, and about an acre of ground with it.'

'Oh Davie, would I be allowed to keep a few hens? A real fresh egg's such a blessing and I love havin' hens to look after.'

'You could keep as many as you like, and a pig forbye.'

'Ech, dear, but it sounds just grand, son.' His father sighed. 'But just where's the money to come frae. That's the problem. It costs a wheen o' siller for twa tickets tae America.'

Davie smiled and lit a cigarette. 'That'll be my part of it. I'll pay you both out.'

'Och, but that's no fair. You've done so much, and aw the grand presents you've sent—'

'Dad, I could ship you and Ma out to the States, and it wouldn't mean any more to me than the shilling a week pocket money I got when I started to serve my time.'

They stared at him, as though the extent of his success had just become plain. 'Dad – Ma – ,' Davie said, 'wi' the income I have now, I could keep you both in comfort but you wouldn't be happy not without something to do.'

Now his father's delight mounted to a climax. 'Davie, son, I'll dae it. Yer Ma and me are real grateful. I'll write your Mr Taylor tonight, and tell him. But Davie, I'll have tae give the committee a month's notice. It's the least I can do for they've been real kind to me.'

'And so they should.' His mother's voice was indignant. 'He's worked like a slave since they re-laid it, fair run off his feet, and near hand chokin' wi' his chest. And this Julie girl, is she your lass, son?' Before Davie could answer a knock sounded at the door, and Bert Sproggie, his pipe dangling, stuck his head in. 'Only me, Davie. I brought your clubs along. Dearie me, this is a fearsome size o' a bag you've gotten noo.' He laid it carefully down. 'Does yer caddie no expect cuddy money for humphin' this aboot?'

'Ach, the size o' the bag is to help prestige,' Davie said. 'And believe me, the Yank caddies are well enough paid.'

'Deed, they'd need to be. Well, I'll be away.'

'Whit's the hurry?' Davie asked. 'Have you no time for a crack wi' an old friend?'

Davie saw his father and Bert were embarrassed for some reason.

'I'll tell ye whit's the matter!' His mother's voice was suddenly shrill. 'The two auld fools, efter bein' the best o' friends aw' the years you were awa', cast oot three weeks ago, and have hardly spoken since!'

'Ach, we were at the station meeting him,' his father mumbled.

'Cast out?' Davie smiled. 'Whatever in the world about?'

'Aboot who was to caddy for you in the championship. Did you ever hear the like? Yer Da said it was his right, seein' he did it when you were just a laddie, and Bert asked hoo could he caddy, and him so busy on the course, and forbye, you would need his help and advice – daft auld scunners!' his mother concluded.

Davie burst into laughter not far removed from tears. Suddenly he realised his new status, as head of the house. He put a hand on each of their shoulders. 'Will I knock your daft heads, together?'

' 'Deed, Davie, I wouldnae be oot the way o't,' Bert mumbled. 'If my rheumatics came on, I could never humph that bag of yours, and forbye, yer Da has the right.'

'Bert, I could never manage the time, and me so busy on the course. And you're right, Bert. He'd be better wi' you cairryin – a seasoned experienced player like yerself.'

They laughed together, a little shamefaced, then his dad said, 'There's enough in the bottle to wet oor whistles.' Then calling Davie over to get the glasses, whispered, 'No a word tae Bert aboot us goin' awa' tae that braw job in America. I wouldna like Bert tae feel oot of things, and him, poor soul, on the dole.'

Afterwards, with pipes and cigarettes going, they stood

out in the gloaming, where the fifth fairway ran across the front of the house, and the tenth green nodded to the far gable end.

'I'd near hand forgotten how lovely the late evenings are,' Davie said. 'It's dark in America about seven.' And the evening was still, save for the distant murmur of the sea, then far away a train whistled. He knew he was really home. The trains in America never made music like that.

CHAPTER FIFTEEN

I.

EVERY sport and pastime wherein man pits his skill against his fellows, or against nature, has a natural climax. The golfer speculates who'll be this year's Open Champion.

Many of the games that originated in Britain, are shared by other countries. The Australians send over teams to give the old country a drubbing, and the Americans forever seek to carry away British titles, not for the financial worth of them, but for the honour and glory, the prestige it brings.

So now to the little township on the Angus coast the crowds came hurrying. First the press men, from the four corners of the world, hungry for personality paragraphs, sending back local talk, reports on form, hints of likely winners. And all this from the press tent, with its untidy web of telephone wires. The news broadcasting van was there, with an attendant coterie of immaculate but bored-looking young men, who stared at everyone and everything with the languid disdain of their kind. There was also the trade show, with its big marquee, the dining and refreshment tents, and the big open space for parking cars.

To Davie it was a familiar scene although a little more discreet, a little less raucous than the American version. But for the links committee, and the greenkeeping staff, it was an anxious time. Night and day, they almost lived on the course, cutting, raking, tending, smoothing. 'Do you think the rain'll last long?' 'Deed, pray it doesn't or we'll have floodin' round the low places.' 'If only the wind would swing round – this west wind's aye wet.' 'And if it blaws frae the east, it's no better, dries up the greens like fire.' Press down every divot, brush and cosset every tee. See to it that the greens are living velvet, with never an errant blade of grass to divert a ball, and maybe rob a man of the title. Rake the flowing sand in every trap, leaving never a heelmark, lest a player have cause to complain. And live ever in fear of the unpredictable. Let some big hitter from the States hit a screamer down the wind, and be trapped in a bunker meant for a loose second shot, and halfway across the world, his words would erupt in headlines, 'Bill Blank says Championship Course unfair to long hitters.'

Davie watched his father toil and marvelled that such stubborn endurance should dwell in the thin, stooping body. 'I'm all right,' he would say. 'I'll be for hame soon, after I've seen to the two bunkers at the sixth. Ach, it's an anxious time, but I'll get a rest after it's by with.'

And the old men with lined cheeks, sat on grassy hummocks and around the first tee, appraising form, and predicting the likely winning figures. It was generally agreed that unless given a week of windless weather, with enough moisture to hold the ball on difficult greens, seventy was not likely to be broken. Given the usual drying wind, and the putting surfaces fast anything was likely to happen. And while admitting that there were a lot of grand players among the Yanks and the other foreign lads, those new-fangled steel shafts were likely to prove the fair ruination of the game.

2.

The Championship was due to start on the Monday. His practice complete, Davie went in search of Van Den Berg and Julie on the Saturday afternoon.

He found his manager rather quieter in manner than usual. 'Julie gone off to some place around the Highlands with some folks,' he said. 'You ain't sore, Davie?'

'Why should I be?' Davie smiled.

'Guess she was taken with their titles. One of the guys was Sir something or other, and the other was the son of a Lord.

Looked a proper bunch of deadbeats to me, and the women folk with them dressed up like the follies of 1910, but Julie thought they were the cat's pyjamas.'

Davie got the impression that he was talking about one thing in order to avoid some other topic. 'Everything all right, otherwise?' he asked.

'Why sure, Davie, sure. You're finding the course O.K.?'

'Need you ask that and me learned the game here?' Davie said. 'I'm for a final round now, with the wind dropping. Are you for walking round with me?'

'I'll join you later – just waiting on a cable from home,' Van Den Berg said, and Davie felt that there was an edge of anxiety in his voice.

Maybe it was only his imagination, Davie told himself, as he walked over to where his dad was waiting.

People were pouring into the town. Crowds gathered continually at the first tee, and departed in droves to follow their favourite players as they set out to play their last rounds before the match.

'My, your bag's no as heavy as I thocht,' his dad greeted him. Davie smiled but said nothing. He had lightened it by removing some of his clubs, and the sets of waterproof overalls he usually carried.

It was a fine, mild evening, with the wind dropping and the great cloud masses slowing down. The years fell away. It was just a friendly game, played for the fun of it, despite the great crowds watching. His dad loved every minute of it. He was back in the centre of things, holding the flag, advising, pointing out the best line. And when strangers spoke to him between strokes, saying, 'Crombie's a glorious golfer, he'll not be far away at the finish, starting favourite isn't he?' Jim Crombie answered, 'I'm no qualified to say, for I'm prejudiced, he's my laddie, my son!'

And Davie quietly watched his father glorying in the strangers' reactions. 'Eh, but you must be a proud man.'

But the fickle breeze backed to the east, piling up masses of moisture. When they were far from shelter at the eighth, a torrential cloudburst opened on them, the rain fell in sheets.

'We'd better take shelter,' Davie said, struggling to open the big, coloured umbrella.

'You'll have to play on next week,' his dad said, 'whatever the weather, just play on, Davie. It'll no harm me, I'm out in many a worse.'

So they ignored the weather and played on, still followed by a crowd of the faithful, some with umbrellas, many with light raincoats over their heads. At the tenth hole, quite close to home, Davie saw his father was white and shivering. 'This is plain daft, come on, Dad, into the house with you.' The rain was still heavy.

'Ach, I'm fine, summer rain'll no harm anybody,' he said stoutly, but Davie insisted.

After a hot bath at the hotel, Davie was none the worse. He listened to Julie's rapturous account of her journey to the Highlands and her eulogies on the new friends she had made. 'Can you imagine it. Davie, Lord Glenlonie's title goes back over seven hundred years, and that old castle of theirs!'

First thing in the morning, when he hurried to the house, his mother's anxious face greeted him. 'I don't like the look of your dad, Davie, I think we'd better get the doctor.'

'Ach, you're fussing about nothing,' his father's voice was thin and strained. 'I'll be fine in the morning, just a wee bit of a chill. I canna be laid up now, wi' the Championship starting tomorrow.' He coughed with a painful racking sound.

Fear catching at Davie's heart, he hurried to the nearest phone. The doctor, after examining the sick man, was noncommittal. 'We'll keep him in his bed. Trouble is, he's not in too good shape generally, hasn't the resistance. I'll look in again tomorrow.'

Davie tried to placate his father, and assure him he would explain to the Links Committee.

'Now promise me, son, you're not to worry about me, and let it upset your playing.' The sick man's voice was insistent. 'This is nothing out of the ordinary, though I never had a bout like this in the summer.' The knotted brown hand, thin and wiry, and burning with heat, reached for his. 'You're not to think about me, you've got to keep your mind on the game, the whole town wants you to win.'

'I think the sonner I get you away to Florida, the better,' Davie said, assuming a cheerfulness he did not feel. If only he had stayed at Neveneck, his dad might have been out in America now, a fitter, healthier man. If only he hadn't taken the waterproofs out of his bag, he might have protected his father and prevented this . . .'

But he had to play, and play his best. Empty your mind, Bert Sproggie used to advise. Don't think about anything between shots. But if he tried to empty his mind, the picture of a sick man, fighting for breath, immediately filled it. But the habit of grim determined effort was strongly part of Davie now. Despite the gnawing fear for his dad, he shot seventy-one on a fearsome course stretched to punishing length.

And the crowds continued to pour into the little town. The organising committee held hurried conferences, and increased their army of stewards and marshals. Vast galleries blackened the wide acres of the course, straining the arrangements for spectators' control almost to breaking point. 'Please, gangway for the players, please!' Waving their little flags, trying to confine the mobs behind the painted lines, futile Canutes resisting the waves of humanity.

And on Tuesday, a day of fickle wind and passing showers, Davie tramped along between lanes of massed onlookers, and duplicated his round of the previous day, to lead the qualifiers, and send the whole town in a frenzy of hope that he might pull it off. And half a world away, men sat behind their desks and asked their secretaries to phone the news agencies for the latest scores. 'Gee, our lil' snowflake's doin' well – think he'll pull it off? I remember watchin' that kid out at Long Island once . . .'

At home, the old men, the wiseacres, shook their heads doubtfully. Aye, two grand scores, but had he shot his bolt too soon, burned himself out in what was only the preliminary?

And Bert Sproggie, carrying the big bag, as proudly as a squire, the helmet and shield of his knight, 'That's my boy, just take it easy. Dinna' worry over your dad. Just ca' awa' for another four rounds like that, and we've got it.'

When Davie was with his dad that day, the sick man rallied. 'You're doing grand, son, I want you to win, and Davie, could I get the bed shifted round, then I could see the tenth, and maybe a glance of you driving to the eleventh. I would fair like to have seen you playin'.'

So with the help of Bert Sproggie and Van Den Berg, they moved the bed across the room, and propped him up on pillows. His father had a quiet night, and next day, Wednesday, the first round of the event proper, his heart happy with relief, Davie went to town.

A gallery of thousands watched, herded by a small army of marshals, all local men, who were inclined to treat any spectator who stepped out of line, as guilty of sacrilege. 'Play fair, sir, it's our Davie, you want him to win, don't you? Give him a chance.'

And so with Bert Sproggie at his elbow, Davie romped round whistling 'Swanee' between his teeth. His return was a magnificent seventy, to lead the field by one stroke, with a dozen of the world's finest players grouped behind him, only seven strokes separating them.

But that night, his dad's temperature shot up, and the doctor came hurriedly. 'Aye, it's pneumonia, I was rather afraid of that. He's fightin' it certainly, but I'll look back first thing in the morning.'

At Davie's pleas, Bill Van Den Berg arranged for a specialist from Dundee, and since it was not advisable to move the patient to hospital, he installed a nurse in the house.

On the Thursday, although the news Van Den Berg brought was reassuring, Davie's score went up to seventy-three, and he dropped back to fourth place on the score board. When Davie went into the bedroom that evening, he found his father only semi-conscious, and rambling in his speech. Bright fever spots were on his cheeks, and his tired voice mouthed the worries on his mind. 'That Bob Lawrie's a lazy devil. I told him time and time again to rake those two bunkers at the seventh. Johnnie, see that he takes his besom with him after he's swept the tenth. The twelfth's just as apt to have water on it, and watch that bit of low ground in front of the tenth – with the west wind a lot o' them will play short – see all the divot marks are filled in.'

Davie stood by the bedside, his heart wrung with pity. After a few minutes, the rambling ceased, the tired eyes opened, 'Aye, ye're there, Davie, and doin' well – leadin' the field at the end o' the first day – that's grand, grand!'

He had lost twenty-four hours. Davie found he could not speak, and the nurse mouthed a silent order not to disturb her patient. Now the thin hand, fired and dry with fever, came out and fumbled for his. 'I want you tae win, son. I've thocht o' nothin' else ever since the course was remade. Promise me ye'll no worry aboot me. I'll be fine. You bring that cup hame wi' you, and set it where I can see it. That will have me on my feet again in no time.' The tired eyes closed, and Davie, obeying the nurse's gesture, tiptoed away to the kitchen, and did his best to comfort his mother.

The last day of the event broke fine and clear, but with a steadily freshening breeze blowing from the east. That certainly made easier the westward facing holes, but made cruel, punishing work for those facing the east, particularly the homeward ones. Only fifty out of over two hundred players were left to fight it out now.

Today, two rounds had to be played. This was the climax – one or two slack strokes, and your chance was gone. Nerves were strung and stretched to snapping point. Word came that his father had passed a fair night, so Davie stepped on to the first tee with an iron resolution in his heart. Every familiar face he saw in the crowds following him carried the same unspoken wish. 'Davie – can you do it?' The press were commenting, 'The home challenge of native Davie Crombie has receded somewhat. Hagen, Jones, Chute and Gudahl lead the American thrust, with our own Padgham alongside, together with Moreno of Spain and Jurado of South America just following, and still dangerous.'

With his placing, the gallery had shrunk a little, but it was still large enough to make the marshals work hard. All right, this is it. Fight it out. And, for some reason, the ball ran for him. With Bert Sproggie alongside him, puffing a little, but jubilant, Davie whistled 'Swanee' between his teeth, and reeled off par figures like a machine, slotted home several long putts for birdies, and finished with a triumphant seventy, despite the freshening breeze.

This brought him back to top place. The sages confidently predicted that if he could repeat the same figures in the afternoon, it was in the bag. Clubs and shops in the town made quietly certain that flags and bunting were to hand. If Crombie pulled it off, the town would certainly go on a spending spree – the few who had any money to spend, anyway.

But the breeze was freshening. It was a wind now, tousling the hair, plucking at the light summer frocks of the women. With another round to play in the afternoon, Davie had no time to go home in the interval, though he got word from Van Den Berg that there was no change in his father's condition. Had he been less worried, he might well have noticed that his manager was more serious and thoughtful than usual. But his experiences of the tournament trail had made concentration automatic and he started the final round oblivious of the crowd and the weather. He saw only the distant flag and thought only of how to reach it, getting the ball down in the fewest possible strokes. And not only was he playing his best, but he was lucky. A well played stroke can still hit a tuft or hummock, and shoot off the line. A tiny blade of grass can divert a long putt, and cost strokes, but nothing like that happened. He reeled off perfect figures, and reached the turn in thirty-five strokes.

His friends in the vast crowd were biting their fingernails with the tension, and women were tearing and riving at handkerchiefs. Now he faced the last nine holes and the famous South America, with the wind ever freshening, and the dreaded burn, like the river Styx, flowing across the front of the green. Word came to him that Chute, the American, was leading at 285. If he could get home in thirty-six strokes, he could win.

The terrific wooden club strokes, lashed into the teeth of the wind, carried him into the heart of the green. He was standing beside his ball, the packed gallery tense and silent, waiting for his partner to play. Davie looked past the crowd, over their heads, towards his home, only a few yards away.

He saw the big car, parked beside the far end. He saw the door open, and the doctor come out, followed by the specialist from Dundee. He saw his own doctor shake his head sadly, as though answering the other man, then his heart went cold inside him, his stomach numb. He saw a hand appear at the window where his dad's bed had been, and the blind was slowly pulled down. A few seconds later, the same hand pulled down the blind of the kitchen window.

And something inside him died. The sun still shone, the wind set dancing the willow trees about the green, the crowd around him gravely intent on the game. What did it matter to them? Oh, dad, my dad, and you gone!

Bert Sproggie, the big bag slung from his shoulder, had seen nothing. Now he held the flag and nodded to Davie. His turn to play. His dad had wanted him to win, his friends wanted him to win . . . the crowd was waiting.

Somehow or other, he holed out, and the crowd, released from tension, went plunging and racing to get into position for the next hole. Relax, empty your mind, but grief isn't like water that flows from your mind like fluid from a jug. Grief is a hard, cold lump inside you. Now Bert had news. 'That's Sarazen in at 287, and Padgham at 288. You've only the Chute lad to beat – that would allow us a couple o' fives, and still win.'

Davie heard the words with only part of his mind. Bert was still heart and soul in the business on hand. Should he tell him? No, play on, empty your mind. How he played out that round, he could never afterwards remember. His body made the strokes, some part of his subconscious mind figured out the tactics. The press spoke of his poker face, and ice-cold concentration.

They surged around him. Frou, frou, went their feet, then the rhythm broke as they jockeyed for a place before he made a stroke. Then the feet started again, frou, frou. Hole after hole went by. He was aware of Bert, his face becoming ever more jubilantly excited as he reeled off par figures.

And Davie stalked along in a daze of grief. Oh my dad, why could you not be given the chance to walk at ease in the sun, and know the places I've seen. So hardworking, so patient, and kindly. The very turf beneath my feet watered with your sweat. You lifted me on to the back of Clyde, the grey plough horse, and let me ride him. It was so high, I was frightened. You laughed and put your hand up to steady me.

Then, when you took this job here, and I started swinging at a ball, you cadged old clubs for me, cut down the shafts, putting on grips with bits of string, working by the light of a guttering candle end. You even made a kitbag for me, because we were hard up, but you didna want me to lack anything the other boys had, if you could make it. I mind of it yet, made with a strip of sailcloth, and an old leather strap.

His mind jerked back to the present; frou, frou went the crowd's feet, and every now and then the insistent cry of the marshals. 'More room for the players, please – keep behind the white lines – back on the right there.'

Bert Sproggie beside him. 'Aye, yer spoon, Davie – a nice canny lick now – keep right if you can, and she'll break offen that bank toward the flag.'

The world was a lane of people, six, eight, ten deep round and along the fairway, clotting into a dark mass round the greens. They were no longer individuals, just a crowd, dead silent while he or his partner made a stroke, then released to running, plunging life the moment they struck the ball.

Now at last they stood on the eighteenth tee. Now he only

needed five to win, but the last hole was a tiger, a terror, with the wind still stiffening from the east, making the flags snap and whip at their mastheads. Spectators were barred from the first and last fairways. So now they were shepherded along the far side of the boundary line.

'A guid job we're no pushed for a four here, Davie,' Bert said, on the tee, 'for this one needs two helluva good licks to carry the water, with that wind.'

The burden of grief pressed even more heavily now, but still he said nothing. Facing up to the last drive of the event, Davie tried to keep his mind blank, to relax, wait for it. The well-grooved swing of constant practice did not desert him. The ball screamed away bullet straight to its mark, but it was still a long, long way to the green.

The crowd massed along the fence, tense, silent, waiting. 'Take a cleek, Davie.' Bert was puffing now, his second hike round the extended course with the heavy bag was beginning to tire him.

'Play it safe, son, ye can afford a five – play short.'

But Davie scarcely heard him; time and memory mixed and mingled. Was he a man of twenty-four, or a boy of eighteen? Once before he had stood on this spot, and faced the same problem. Before his eyes, the pot-bellied figure of Bert Sproggie melted, and was gone. His dad stood there. 'Take yer brassie, son – tak' a chance – go for it!'

He sensed that Bert was still there, making sounds of protest. He heard the crowd gasp, but took no heed. Your advice was aye good, dad – so play this one for me. If I'm to win, let it be a real victory, no a snatched win by a single stroke.

The club whirled, the ball went off with the speed of a rifle bullet. It fought its way on into the wind, on, on, till it cleared the dreaded water trap, to land safe, and race on to the green, close to the flag.

The crowd's applause rose like waves on shingle, but Davie made no move toward the green. Now it was all over he turned and spoke, 'Oh, Bert, my dad's away.'

He saw the stunned shock, the wish to disbelieve, in Bert's look. 'But – it canna be – how did you know, Davie?'

'At the tenth, I saw the doctors leavin'. I saw my ma pulling down the blinds.'

Bert's eyes filled with tears. He fumbled as though to remove his bonnet. 'God rest him, Davie son, he was a daicent man.'

In the moment of shared sorrow, Davie knew that no man could wish for a better epitaph. He saw Bert grow bowed and old before his eyes. 'Eh, Davie, yet ye played on – ye never said a word.'

'What else could I do? You were all wantin' me to win – my dad wanted me to win. . . .'

Bert's stumpy legs sagged, he bowed his head. Davie put a hand under his arm. 'Bear up, Bert. Don't give in now, the world's watchin' us.'

'Oh Davie, Davie, yer Da – I just canna believe it!' He began walking toward the green, his steps stumbling. Davie realised how deeply shocked Bert was. This blow, coming on top of his fatigue, seemed more than he could stand.

'I've only got to get it down now, Bert,' Davie said. 'You're tired, give me the bag.'

'And whit would folk think o' that?' Bert's tone was fierce. 'I'll finish ma job, the way you've done. It's no like I'll ever have the chance of carryin' for an Open Champion again.'

Walking together, Davie felt Bert's hand fumbling for his. 'Aye, ye're a grand gowfer, Davie, and ye've been a real good lad to yer Da. He was right proud of ye!'

And the watching crowd saw the fumbling handclasp, and thought the old caddie was overcome with delight at his man's approaching victory. They cheered and cheered again.

On the last green, tense silence fell as Davie lined up his putt. Such were the vagaries of the game that had he needed to get that stroke down to win, or tie, it would have stayed out, no matter how carefully he played. But it scuttled over the velvet turf and went down . . . the crowd's yells split the sky, and on the instant, the marshals were swept aside and a yelling horde poured over the green. 'Davie – Davie – Davie!' They pulled and yanked at him, hoisting him shoulder high. Somewhere near him, he heard Bert's voice raised in good-natured, but cursing protest, and realised that he, too, was being hoisted on brawny shoulders.

He was surrounded by faces with open mouths, yelling their delight, cheering and smiling, but never the face he would have loved to see.

For the next hour he faced the questioning pressmen and gave quiet answers to their frenzied questions. Some other man had taken possession of his body, a dazed impersonal stranger who spoke like a passionless robot.

Next came the radio people, and he was taken across to say a few words in the air. Here the atmosphere was different, an air of cloistered calm prevailed. An immaculate young man cooed at the microphone with the air of a fond parent chiding a wayward child, asked him some painfully silly questions, then plucked the answers out of his mouth before he could speak, plainly regarding Davie as some strange and slightly unclean creature with whom duty had forced him into brief contact.

More lanes of people, more claps on the back. Now he was on the big platform, along with the runners-up, the organising officials and the Town Provost. More bumbling speeches – the pride in our local victory – despite its American flavour – remains a son of the town – our grand gold links – a national asset . . . but dust and ashes, they didn't know and even if they did, the death of a greenkeeper wouldn't have moved them all that much. Oh, Dad, Dad!

He took the silver trophy and the cheque, then faced a barrage of cameras – all the time longing to escape.

He came down from the platform to face an applauding, autograph hunting mob. Then, as though conscious of authority, they parted to allow Bill Van Den Berg through. But he was unusually restrained. He patted Davie gently on the back, and shook his hand. 'Great stuff, boy – I knew you could do it. Julie'll be along in a minute, she's been with some top folks, watching you all afternoon.' He made to turn away, 'Have to go, Dave – expecting a phone call from the States.'

Still shocked with grief, Davie's mind was confused. Then he noticed Bert Sproggie, his head bowed but standing guard over the clubs. 'Give me some money, Bill.'

His manager drew a few crumpled notes from his pocket. 'All I've got on me.' He seemed reluctant to part with them. 'Come along to the hotel later. I'll have to go now.'

What was wrong with the man? Was it that he didn't know how to broach the subject of his father's death? Davie went up to Bert Sproggie. 'You're dead beat, man.' He pushed the notes into the old man's hand. 'Away over to the club, buy yourself a dram.'

Bert had tears in his eyes. 'Yer Da, Davie – I can hardly believe it.'

Grief still a hard, cold lump inside him, Davie said, 'I can hardly take it in myself. Do something for me, Bert – take this trophy over to the club for safe keeping, and get one of your pals to take my clubs – you've caddied enough.'

'It was an honour.' Bert was proud. 'Every man in the club will want to gie me a dram, because I was yer caddie. Keep yer siller, Davie.'

Half a dozen hands reached out for the big bag – for the honour of saying they'd carried it even just to the clubhouse. But they knew of his loss; their backclaps and handshakes were condolences combined with congratulations for victory. Again a crowd thickened round him; thrusting autograph books, pressmen with eager questions. He signed the books, forcing stiff lips into a smile. He was a public hero now, and had to turn a happy face to the world. To the reporters, he said, 'Please, boys, not now. I'm tired. See my manager. He'll fix up a talk session for you all later on.'

Reluctantly, they parted to let him through. Get away – away from the crowd; and then, at the corner of the putting green, he came face to face with Beth.

Her bonnie eyes were tear bright. She hurried toward him,

237

caught his hand in both of hers. 'Oh Davie – your dad – I often talked to him while you were away. He was so proud of you.'

'Ah, and I was proud of him,' Davie muttered. 'I can't believe he's away.'

The tightening clasp of her hands was comforting. 'Davie, can I do anything to help you?' she asked.

Behind her, on the road, a gleaming Rolls Royce halted, the door opened, and the ever elegant figure of Julie descended. She stood, obviously looking for him.

'Beth – please, will you go and see my mother – tell her I'll be along in a few minutes.'

'Of course, Davie.' She released his hand, and walked away.

The crowds were thinning. Julie came hurrying, her glowing beauty enhanced by the delight in her face. 'Oh Davie, its wonderful! Yor're top of the heap now.' She caught his arm in both hands. 'My friends are anxious to meet you. One is Lord Glenlonie, another Sir Michael something, and they have an Indian Rajah with them.' She began pulling him toward the Rolls Royce. 'They want you to give them some tuition at Gleneagles tomorrow, then make up a foursome. You can imagine what they'll pay for your time.'

'Julie, I can't.' His voice choked. 'My father died while I was playing the last round.'

'Oh Davie, I'm sorry.' Her voice faltered. 'I understand – you can't leave your mother at a time like this.' Then she shook his arm gently. 'But you can't linger on here too long. You're the top golfer now; you've got to cash in.'

Davie freed his arm gently. 'I'm glad you understand. I'll have to stay on here for a wee while, anyway. You go off and enjoy yourself with your friends.'

Julie pouted. 'Can't you promise to join us in a day or two?' She paused, 'It's the Open Champion they want to meet.'

Davie thought; aye, Julie's champion, Crombie the golfer. Aloud, he said, 'I'm no making any promises just now.'

She looked at him sharply. 'Does that cover me as well? Get in touch when you get back to the States. Things seem to have gone haywire since we came here. Take care of yourself, Davie.' She gave him a brilliant smile, and a swift kiss on the cheek, and was gone – back to the waiting car.

Davie walked toward home. Pedestals were shaky things. He'd just been another star for Julie; for her there would always be another and brighter one.

The wind had dropped, the scudding clouds gone, leaving an evening of blue and gold. He made his way along back lanes, and thought what would be said by the lads he had known since childhood, 'A grand golfer, but no very good at pickin' his lassies.' At the level-crossing gates, he re-membered the New Year's morning, when he had walked home alone under the frosty stars after Mary Johnston had left him at the roadside. Beth, too; the anxious pleading in her voice when she had called down the stairs, 'Don't go, Davie. Don't go.' Now she had grown into a lovely young woman. He sighed, then crossed the links to the cottage with the drawn blinds. He had lost his father and Julie, now he must try to comfort his mother. Well, it made the coming ordeal a little easier to face, knowing Beth would be there.

CHAPTER SIXTEEN

I.

'IN here, Davie,' Van Den Berg said, and led him into the private sitting-room. 'I'm expecting Mr Taylor to call, and they've switched the phone through.'

Davie sat in the proffered chair. Van Den Berg stalked the room restlessly. Suddenly he crossed the room, and laid a hand on Davie's shoulder. 'I'm real sorry about your old man that's a real loss. Reckon he was the type of man your poet Burns wrote about.'

'Thanks, Bill, what was it you wanted to see me about? When the boy brought that message to the house – I just—'

'I know, Dave, I know.' Van Den Berg still paced. 'Reckon if things had been different, I'd have been throwin' the biggest party ever but—'

'All right, Bill.' Davie felt the weariness in his voice, 'I've got a neighbour in with my mother. I knew you wouldn't bring me along here for nothing.'

Van Den Berg halted in mid-stride and smacked a fist into his open palm. 'Oh hell! I should never have talked you into signing that deal. I just couldn't believe the bottom would fall out of things – I wish – why doesn't Taylor phone?'

Davie released his breath in a long, quivering sigh. 'So sales have dropped so much that the bank's getting touchy?'

A month or so ago he would have worried over such news, now, it meant little.

Van Den Berg halted and faced him. 'Davie, it's worse than that. The bank's folded. We're bust – cleaned out – broke!'

Davie looked at him then said slowly, 'Well, there's no much we can do about it, Bill.'

240

'Davie – ' the voice was pleading, 'Don't – don't be so decent about it. Bawl me out! That way I won't feel such a heel. Honest, I didn't want to worry you during the play but the bottom's been dropping out of the market this last week. I dunno what's gone wrong. I gotta get right back, maybe I can save something out of the wreck. Then at least—'

The phone shrilled. Van Den Berg picked it up. 'Yeah, speakin' – yes Mr Taylor – go ahead.'

For a minute or so, Davie watched his manager listen to the distant speaker. Occasionally Bill would interject a 'Yes, Yes, sure,' and once, 'Jeeze – bad as that?' Then he said, 'Sure I got him here.' He turned, 'Speak to Mr Taylor, Davie.'

Davie took the instrument, 'Hello, Mr Taylor.'

'Hello, David. Bill phoned me earlier, Davie. First my deepest sympathy in your great loss.'

'Thanks, Mr Taylor.'

'Now, Davie, have you any plans?'

'No, not at the moment. I cannae seem to think, Mr Taylor – even the championship means nothing to me.'

'That's natural enough, son. I believe you're pretty badly hit in this bank fold up?'

'Bill's just told me. We're cleaned out.'

'How about your immediate needs? Guess I'm gonna be trimmed for quite a bit, but I can post a cheque tonight.'

'No, honest, Mr Taylor. I'm all right. I've the prize money today, and I know Bill lodged quite a sum over here for expenses. Mr Taylor, what's gone wrong over there?'

'Honest, Davie, I only wish I knew. Reckon the States has been living beyond its means. What's caught you, Davie, is only the first rumble of the storm. I think there's worse to come yet. There's a lotta ordinary folk gonna remember 1929 for a long time.'

'And yourself, Mr Taylor, are you all right?'

'I'm getting on the boat back right now, David. Guess I'll make out all right, though I'm sure to drop quite a bit. And, son, that girl of mine—'

'Julie – ' Davie said slowly, and felt embarrassed.

'Yeah, I believe she sorta walked out on you. Tell me, son, has it hurt you bad? Be honest—'

'Honest, Mr Taylor, I just can't feel anything much just now. If – if it had been any other day but this – I'd have been downed a bit, but today I don't seem to be able to feel anything – anything but my dad – I – I think Julie began to feel different from the day we landed at Southampton.' Was that strictly true or was it himself?

'Say no more, son. Say no more. When you get around to having kids of your own, make 'em work for their dimes and nickels, bring them up to put a right value on money. Guess Julie always had too much of her own way. Now you'd better lay off for a bit, and get straightened out, then write, and let me know what you intend doing. Guess things are going to be mighty tough over there for a bit but we could always use a guy like you.'

'Thanks, Mr Taylor,' Davie said, 'I'll write you when things get settled.'

'Do that, son, any time. I'll be glad to help you out in any way I can. God be with you, son – 'bye now.' The line clicked and went dead.

He turned to find Van Den Berg laying out bundles of money on the table. 'This is the dough I lodged here against expenses, Dave. I cabled a bit extra, thinkin' you might feel like spreadin' it round a piece – it seemed a good idea at the time. When I heard about the bank fold back home, I drew the whole lot out this mornin' – I wasn't gonna take the risk of your banks here foldin' as well.'

'Banks don't fold over here, Bill, but it was thoughtful of you just the same. Now, if you're for home straight away, you'll need some of this.'

'Na, I'm all right. I got my return ticket, and I kept a bit for eating money and overheads. It's all on the sheet there.'

Davie stood thoughtful. It seemed a large sum of money spread out on the table, but now there was no more where that came from. 'Seems I'm back where I started, Bill,' he said slowly.

'I know, Davie, I know!' Van Den Berg groaned. 'And to think if I'd done it your way, you'd 'a been well heeled instead of broke!'

Davie shook his head. 'You're not to blame, Bill, for I agreed. I remember once reading that what happened to a man wasn't important, only what he did about what happened to him – looks like I'm going to find the truth of that now.'

Van Den Berg looked at him in open admiration. 'Gee, Davie, I gotta hand it to you. You sure can take it. But we can start again, Dave. You got the makings of a stake there. We can climb up again.'

Davie was doubtful. 'Looks like the Americans will have other things on their minds for a bit.'

'But you're comin' back, Davie, you're not givin' up – heck, you're top of the world now, even if we are broke.'

Davie shook his head. 'I don't know, Bill. I'll not be comin' back for a month or so, anyway, for I'll have to help my mother a bit and get her settled.'

'Dave, you gotta come back. I'll get things hummin' again. Gimme a nickel, and I'll turn it into a buck at the drop of a hat. I'll make things right for you.'

'I know you will.' Davie managed a smile, then reached up and patted his manager's shoulder. 'But, well, I cannae make any plans just now. I'll write to you.'

'Gee, I sure feel low about things. Good luck, Davie.'

They shook hands and parted.

2.

He stumped through the next few days in a dull ache of grief, trying to comfort his mother, and see to the hundred and one things that have to be done, among them, a visit to the Links Committee to obtain the pledge that his mother could continue to live in the cottage for the time being.

Then, with a quiet Bert Sproggie beside him, he sat in the first car, leading the little cortège which threaded its way over the rough track crossing the course, over the railway crossing, up the street between the Andrew Cowans works and the Tannie, up to the cemetery.

The crowd of men waiting were a reassurance of how well-liked his father had been. When it was over, they crowded round him in silence, to shake his hand, and say, 'Aye, that was a quick call yer da' got, Davie. He was a well-liked man, we'll miss him sore.'

Still grief froze his feelings. The fact that he was no longer a man of substance had not yet sunk in. He dragged out the little duties he had to do purely for the sake of keeping himself occupied.

Walking along the front next morning, on the way to see the minister, and thank him, he paused outside the premises where he used to work. It was closed and silent now; dirt grimed the windows, and had gathered in pockets at the corners. The green curtains which had screened the window display were hanging in melancholy, sun-rotted rags. Paint had peeled from the once proud sign. Now it read. 'R. . . . OHNSTON, . . . , EEK AND . . . AKER.'

As he stared at it in silence, with a sick feeling in his stomach, suddenly, without warning, the pain hit him. It was like a steel hook tearing at his guts. The world went spinning round, he clutched at the railings for support, and sweat broke on his forehead.

After an agonising minute or so, it subsided, leaving him with a sick queasy feeling, and a dread that it would return. He shook his head to clear it, then straightened up. Better see the doctor – his mother mustn't know – she had enough on her mind already.

3.

Doctor McLean had a great shock of white hair, and a face

red as an angry farmer. Now he laid down his stethoscope and sat at his desk, while Davie pulled on his shirt. 'Aye – a fine how-de-do,' he said, waving Davie to a chair. 'Our grand new Scots Open Champion with a stomach ulcer.'

'Och, it's nothing to worry about,' he said in answer to Davie's question. 'We'll have an x-ray, just to make sure, but all the symptoms are there, adding up to too many fatty meals eaten in a hurry, too many fried and greasy foods – and a lot too much tension and excitement.'

'But Doctor, how can excitement give me stomach trouble?'

'I'm only an old G.P. so I'm no prepared to answer that one. But we're finding out more and more that the mind and emotions can affect the body in all sorts of ways. The bit sorrow and trouble you're having has likely brought it to a head. But you're a fine, healthy young man. You'll get over it, but now – I'll talk serious.'

He pushed his glasses up on his forehead, and wagged a finger. 'No late hours, no rushing about, no more fried food. East fruit, fresh vegetables, eggs, poached and boiled, but not fried, and smoke only after meals. And give up competitive golf for a year or so. Play certainly, but just with your friends for the fun of it. Work – regular hours – that never harmed anyone, but take it easy, avoid nervous tension. I'll give you a diet sheet, and a bottle, come and see me again next week, and if the pains start, take one of these tablets.'

The loss of Julie – his money – they were bad enough, but now this. No more competitive golf for a year or so, but he had to earn a living and there was his mother to support. In an effort to escape his worries, he thought back to what he had been doing when the pain struck him; of course, going to thank Mr Lawson.

Walking lightly, ever in fear of a recurrence of the pain, his feet crunched the gravel to the manse door. 'Come away in, David, come away in,' was the minister's greeting when he answered the bell. 'I'm always pleased to see you. Sit here, and I'll fill my pipe. You have cigarettes?'

The minister's hair was white now, but his face serene and kindly as ever. He sat easy in his chair and talked about golf, the course and the championship. The captains and the kings had departed, the marquees and stuff packed up and carted away, but it had been a stirring time for the town, and their pride in his victory was great.

Then, easy and gently, the minister switched the talk round to his father. How well-liked he'd been by everyone, how looked-up-to and respected for the way he did his job.

'And we were never short of news about you, Davie.' Mr Lawson puffed at his pipe. 'At every meeting of the Links Committee, when your dad was reporting on this or that, he always quoted you. "My son in America tells me the latest idea in the States is . . ." or "Davie was playing on a course in Michigan a week or so back , and he tells me they were . . .".'

The minister put his pipe away and looked kindly. 'No good man ever dies. He lives forever in the hearts of his friends. Don't grieve because you weren't able to take him away to the States. If he'd passed away in a strange land, far from here, he'd have been unhappy. What better thing for a man, when his time comes, to leave from his garden, with all his friends near him. That golf course was your dad's garden, Davie – he cherished every blade of grass on it, and left it better than he found it.'

The frozen ache in Davie's heart melted, and ran in scalding tears. Mr Lawson stood beside him, and touched his shoulder comfortingly. Then Davie could never remember just how it came about, but he and the minister were saying a prayer together.

Then they sat quietly for a minute or so, and Davie was able to speak. He told about the loss of his money, and now the doctor's instructions. Mr Lawson listened right through, then gave him another encouraging pat on the back. 'Tut! you're just a young man yet, this is only a wee bit setback! You've had a wonderful career, and only a boy yet – you'll climb even higher. But you must get back into harness of some kind. You've plenty of good friends who'll help you.

'Why, it's not only the golf you were an expert at – you were a grand craftsman as well! Poor Johnston thought the world of you, you'll do fine yet!'

Mr Lawson's words burned in his mind as his feet crunched down the gravel path. He paused for a moment at the gate, and suddenly the idea rocketed up in his mind! Now what was the name of the lawyer? Never mind, the address was 87, High Street.

4.

Mr Turnbull was a string-thin beanpole of a man, with a few strands of black hair stuck across his scalp. An avid golfer himself, he was flattered and delighted when the reigning Open Champion approached him with his proposals. They talked for over two hours. He took copious notes, then telephoned the bank for an appointment the following day.

When the time came, he ushered Davie over the road with the air of an anxious hostess, worrying about how her guests will mix. 'As – I er – mentioned, I wasna given any notice that Miss Elizabeth Johnston was given proxy power for her mother, and consequently, had no chance of getting your consent or acceptance. And, though out of my jurisdiction, it might have been better if you'd had a legal adviser of your own present – I'll do my utmost for you though I'm sort of the man in the middle. Mark you, Mr Crombie, I regard your proposals as quite a reasonable basis, but as to how McNicoll of the bank will react, well, that's another matter. As principal creditor, they have the say, naturally, and having a representative of the Johnston family present is a pure piece of window-dressing.' He drew breath. 'However we'll see.'

The bank manager was so fat and healthy-looking you might well have taken him for a butcher or farmer until you saw the thin mouth and the cold grey eyes in his head.

Then Beth came in, and sat opposite Davie, beside the

bank manager. She gave him a wee smile, like she might in the kirk on Sunday, then sat silent.

He watched her intently while Turnbull expounded and explained. 'Mr Crombie offers to meet one half of the unsecured overdraft and, in addition, to deposit a sum equalling half of the remainder, but this is to be a current account, against which he will draw to meet overheads and wages. As funds become available from trading, he proposes.'

Oh, but Beth was bonnie! Davie knew a warm rush of affection for her, remembering the bright wee lass who used to tease him, yet was so free and friendly. Her gleaming black hair, cut to show the tips of her ears, and her eyes, so calm and steady. How could he ever have forgotten her! She'd helped and comforted his mother through the worst days.

But McNicoll, the bank manager was speaking. Davie jerked himself to listen. ' – Quite unable to predict the attitude of my directors to your proposal. Personally, I feel that some guarantee of the whole sum is necessary, bearing in mind the present state of trade.'

'And he's no doing much to help things,' Davie thought to himself. 'If the Yank boys had been like this, they'd never have gotten past the log-cabin stage.' Then aloud he said, 'Clubs, made by the former proprietor, enjoyed a good sale, both in this country and in the States. I have a bit reputation as a player in America, and a lot of good friends and business connections. With my winning last week, clubs with my name on them, known to be made by me, should have a good sale.'

McNicoll gave a smile, bleak as a January day. 'No doubt, Mr Crombie, in normal times, but by present trends, trade in the U.S.A. is, well, far from normal. I hardly think this is the time for such a venture, and I do not think my directors will approve.'

Davie fought down rising anger. 'America is a great country, Mr McNicoll.' He paused, wondering if he dare risk the remark trembling on his tongue. 'Maybe they are in for a bad time, but the men I know over there have faith in themselves and one another. They'll get over their troubles – quicker than we will.'

The smile grew bleaker still. 'I take it you mean to infer that I – er – we – should show more faith in you? Now really—'

'I'm no asking you to have faith in me,' Davie broke in, 'only in yourself and in tomorrow. If a farmer didna' have faith in tomorrow, he'd never plant a seed.'

'I think the point Mr Crombie is trying to make – ' Turnbull interrupted, obviously trying to turn the talk to more constructive lines, 'is that the bank should be prepared to accept some risk.'

When McNicoll continued to doubt, Mr Turnbull changed from a lawyer to an eloquent advocate.

'With respect, Mr McNicoll, I feel you're not taking any account of the invisible assets in Mr Crombie's proposal. Here is Davie Crombie, a son of the town, who has made a great name for himself as a golfer in the New World. For the next twelve months, he is the reigning king of that sport. At this moment,' Turnbull paused dramatically, 'in my office over the road, two of my lassies are dealing with a batch of correspondence from clubs in England, France, Holland and other places, offering him lucrative engagements to play exhibition games, to give demonstrations, and to talk. Unfortunately, under doctor's orders, he cannot, at the moment, accept any of these offers although he tells me, if his health improves, he intends defending his title next year.

'And despite America's financial troubles, there are men over there who would welcome him now, and be prepared to finance him in any sphere of the golf industry he cared to try. Before coming home to compete last week, Davie was a man of substance, employing staff of his own to deal with all commercial affairs. But now, when the fine products of our town start going out over the world with the name Crombie on them, they'll sell – even in the present deflated market.'

Davie found himself starting to blush at Turnbull's words,

and turned his attention to Beth again.

'And Davie is doing our town a service, by proposing to live and work here,' Turnbull went on, 'and he is providing work for the town, which is sorely needed. Not many, to begin with, but as his business starts to thrive, as I'm sure it will . . .'

This was rotten for Beth, having to listen to these men haggling over the wreck of her father's once splendid business. Like relatives arguing over the price of a coffin at a funeral.

Now, even Davie could see that the thin-mouthed banker was wavering, and Turnbull, like a sound tactician, withdrew his forces, rising, and saying that no doubt they'd be hearing from him.

Davie would have lingered outside, hoping for a private word with Beth, but he was forced by Turnbull to come back to his office, and sign the letters his lassies would have typed, to drink the coffee pressed on him, and listen to Turnbull's assurances that his offer would be accepted. 'If McNicoll hadna acted so high and mighty, poor Johnston might still be there. A good bank manager would have helped the man, advised, and warned him – ach, least said soonest mended. I'll be in touch, Davie – you don't mind me calling you that – I mind once you caddied for me, when you were just a laddie.'

5.

In less than a week, it was settled. One fine Saturday morning, Davie paid in the last of his money, save a few pounds, signed the papers, and received in exchange the keys of Johnston's premises. The burden of his grief was lightening, his mind busy on plans for the future. Now and again, tears would sting the back of his eyes when he opened a drawer or a cupboard, to find some article belonging to his father, or an evening stroll over the links for exercise brought him to some spot holding a memory.

But he could think of his father with warm pride now, and the things he had said to him as a boy came back, true and wise as the day he'd said them. 'Folk'll aye pay for their bit pleasure more willingly than they'll pay for getting their bellies filled.' And again, 'There's so much rubbish in the world that good quality stuff aye is being sought, for there's so little o' it.'

Aye, even if trade was bad, his golf clubs would sell. Already gleaming in his mind was a range of Crombie's 'Autogrip Irons' and Crombie's 'Dynamic Woods'. He would style them to suit American tastes, all marked 'Hand Made in Scotland'. If he had a sand blast, the striking surface could be finished in the dull matt grey surface the Yanks liked. How much would a small sand blast cost?

After a light meal, carefully following the doctor's diet sheet, he walked over the links, as he'd done as a boy, to the shop. Inside it was dark, stuffy smelling and dusty. He thought of his place in Neveneck, all light and airy and slick with American know-how. Ah, well! It was the work a man turned out that mattered, not the place where it was done. The vice he used to work at was still there. He picked up a rasp, and blew the dust from it. The place was dry enough, anyway, there was little sign of rust.

A shadow fell over the threshold, and he saw Bert Sproggie, puffing a little, walking with the aid of a stick. 'Davie, I've heard the bit rumours. It's true, isn't it? You're startin' up again. I wanted tae believe it. I thocht you'd have telt me.'

'Aye, it's true, Brt,' Davie smiled. 'I didn't want to say anything till it was settled.'

'Davie, son, have you a job for me? I'm gettin' on now, there's no many keen to have a smith my age, but I'll work for the price of my meat, and a bit tobacco and maybe a bit glass on a Saturday, if it'll run tae that.'

Davie put a hand on his shoulder. 'I had you in mind for your old job from the minute I first thought of taking on the

251

place.'

He saw the wild joy in Bert's eyes. 'Oh, Davie, son, it's like bein' deid, and comin' alive again. Wait till I tell thae frozen-faced buggers at the dole. I'll be fit for my job, Davie! It's only the damp weather that gets me. Wait till I get warmed up at the fire. I'll away through and kindle it now.'

'No hurry, Bert, we'll no start till Monday,' Davie said, then another voice broke in. 'Davie, is it true? I heard the talk and wondered . . .'

Wilf Day was outside, one foot on the step. 'Come in, Wilf, your old job's here, if you want it.'

'Oh Davie! honest? That's wonderful. I'm fed up labourin' in that blasted foundry.'

'You and Bert will be all I'll be able to take on for a start,' Davie said, leaning against the bench. 'Now here's what I've got in mind. All this old stuff scattered about, we'll make up, and finish cheap as we can, using the stock of hickory that's left. We'll finish these, a good job, but no spending too much and sell them off to the local lads, cheap.

'And now,' Davie warmed up to his dreams, 'new stuff, we'll design a range suited to the American market, short hosels, broad soles, and all in stainless steel.'

'D'ye no think this stainless steel business is just a fad, Davie?'

'No, I don't, Wilf. Clubs in the future will all be stainless steel – and we'll design them for the new steel shafts. I'll write away tonight for samples.'

'I dinnae reckon much to this steel shaft business,' Bert said, but did not argue. Davie was the boss now.

'Are you awful busy, Davie – I was just passing – and—'

He whirled to the voice, a warm tide rising in him. 'Beth, come in! I've been fair wanting to have a chat with you.'

Bert and Wilf were tactful. Beth had always been a favourite with them. Bert said he had wasted too much time blethering, and he would go through the forge to make sure the fire was all set to light on Monday morning. Wilf, prompted by a nudge from Bert, thought it would be a good idea if he took a look at the big buffs in case any had cracked in the winter frost – not to bother, there was a spare or two about someplace.

Davie, alone with Beth, for the first time in how many years, became tongue-tied, conscious of all the things he wanted to say, and today she was bonnier than ever.

'How is your mum, Davie?' she asked.

'Och, she's coming round, realising my dad's away.' He touched her hand. 'I don't know how I'd have got through it without you.'

'I liked your dad; we always got on well.' Then she said quickly, 'I'm glad it's you that's starting up the business again. My dad always said you were the best he'd ever had.'

Davie's tongue came free at last. 'How is your dad? Is he any better?' Immediately the words were out, he regretted saying them, for the lovely eyes filled with tears, and she turned her head away. 'I don't think he'll ever be any better – they'll never cure his weakness.'

Davie could never be quite sure how it happened. He had her in his arms, and hers were tight round his neck. 'Oh, Davie. Oh, Davie!'

'But Beth – I'm broke – or near enough.'

'What difference does that make?' She moved closer, holding him ever tighter. 'There never was anyone else but you – for me, I mean. They used to tease me about it. I used to lie in bed and have wee weeps to myself.'

'But you were just a wee lassie.'

'Stop it.' She leaned back, fists on his chest. 'You were always saying that. I couldna help it.' She smiled, tears still in her eyes. 'I'm glad your American lass is away.' Now she strained back from him, fists still on his chest. 'When I saw her in the car that day at Invergowrie, I could have killed her, killed her.' She emphasised the words with little blows of her fists on his chest.

'Could you now?' Davie smiled, enjoying the sensation of smiling down to her. 'Let's get married.'

'Any time you like, Davie – today, if you want.' She

buried her head in his chest again. 'I'm just a brazen wee besom where you're concerned.'

'The sooner the better, Beth,' he told her, then she pulled away to look into his face again. 'But, Davie, will you be happy here? After all the braw places you've seen?'

'Ach, this is as good a place as any – better than some, even if there's no so much money to be picked up,' Davie said. 'I've aye thought of it as home.'

He pulled her cheek against his. 'But when this stomach of mine is better, I'll have another go in America, if you'll come with me.'

'I'd go to Timbuktoo, if you'd take me,' she said happily.

'I like the travel, the excitement,' he chuckled low in his throat, 'and I like winning. But we'll have to make a pound or two here first.'

'You'll do that all right, and I'll do your books, at night.'

'That's my lass – you'll be a real help. Better tell Bert and Wilf to bring their cards in on Monday.'

Alone, he picked up a half-finished brassie, and squinted at it. Huh – too much draw on the face.

He fixed it in the vice, and knocked the dust from a rasp.

'Huh, would you look at oor gaffer – workin', and efter sayin' we werna startin' till Monday.' The trio were standing, smiling, Beth between the two men.

'Ach, I'm just playing' myself, but it feels good, workin' with your hands again.' He began filing. Gradually, the strokes of the tool took up the rhythm of his song, 'Swanee River'.